THE HUSHED LIBRARIAN

a Sweet Sea Cozy Mystery

Brian Daffern

BHD Publishing

*To my daughter Jenna. Her confidence is
a continual inspiration to me.*

CHAPTER ONE

The coastal town of Sweet Sea welcomed a new resident named Nick Cern, a tall and lean man in his late forties with salt-and-pepper hair and a kind smile. After retiring from his Vice President position in corporate America, he sought solace from the grief of losing his wife by starting anew in this quiet little town. A tech-savvy individual with a passion for repairing computers and smartphones, Nick decided to open a small shop to keep himself busy.

"Nick of Time Tech Repairs" was nestled between the local bakery and the post office, ideally situated to attract locals and tourists. The shop itself was small and cozy, exuding an atmosphere of familiarity that made customers feel at ease as soon as they stepped inside. As Nick stood behind the counter, he couldn't help but take in the sight of his newly established business and feel a sense of pride welling up within him.

The large window display showcased the latest gadgets and accessories, arranged meticulously to catch every passerby's eye. From trendy smartwatches to sleek Bluetooth speakers, each item beckoned potential customers, inviting them to explore the wonders of technology. Nick had also taken great care to create a warm and inviting interior, with shelves lined with tools and parts necessary for all sorts of repairs.

Nick carefully arranged his tools and equipment on the workbench next to the cash register. The precision screwdrivers, pliers, and array of soldering irons gleamed in the warm afternoon sunlight streaming through the large window display. He wiped his brow with the back of his hand, casting a critical eye over his newly established workspace. Every tool had its place, and each piece of equipment had been tested for reliability. Nick knew he couldn't afford any mistakes in this new business venture.

For a moment, he allowed himself to get lost in thought, contemplating the bittersweet nature of life. How it could deal such devastating blows yet still offer unexpected opportunities for growth and connection. As he reached for the final screwdriver to complete his set, the tinkling sound of the door chime announced the arrival of a customer. A petite woman in her early 70s entered the shop, her eyes sparkling with curiosity as she surveyed the various gadgets and gizmos on display. Nick's daydreaming prevented him from hearing her at first.

"Excuse me," said a voice, pulling him back into the present moment. He looked up to find the elderly woman standing in front of the counter, her short, curly gray hair framing a face that lit up with a warm smile.

Nick straightened up, making eye contact with an air of purpose. "Good afternoon. How can I help you?"

"Hello there," she said, extending a hand toward him. "You must be Nick Cern, the new tech guy in town! I'm Lucy Brooks, the head librarian at Sweet Sea's public library. Well...there are only two of us, but still, the title stands."

"Nice to meet you, Lucy," Nick replied, shaking her hand firmly. Her grip was surprisingly firm for someone her age, and her smile exuded warmth and kindness. "What can I do for you today?"

"Oh, I don't need anything repaired," Lucy admitted, her gaze drifting to the rows of smartphones lined up like soldiers on parade. "I just wanted to see what all the fuss was about.

Your shop has become quite the talk of the town."

"Is that so?" Nick chuckled, rubbing the back of his neck sheepishly. "Well, I'm just trying to provide a service to the community, you know? We're all so reliant on technology these days. It's important to have someone who knows how to fix things when they go wrong."

"Indeed," Lucy agreed, nodding sagely. "It's fascinating how technology has evolved, isn't it? I remember when a telephone was just a stationary appliance with a rotary dial."

"Times have certainly changed," Nick mused, his thoughts drifting briefly to his childhood memories of more straightforward, analog times.

"Speaking of change," Lucy continued, her eyes twinkling mischievously, "I hear you're quite the book lover, Nick." She noticed the confusion on his face and smiled. "Word travels fast in small towns like Sweet Sea, and it's not every day that we get a fellow bibliophile in our midst."

Nick's eyes lit up at the mention of books, his passion for literature momentarily eclipsing his focus on technology. "Yes, I've always been an avid reader. There's something magical about getting lost in a good book, don't you think?"

"Absolutely," Lucy agreed, her enthusiasm matching his own. "I imagine you've had access to some fascinating reads. Care to share any recommendations?"

"Of course," Nick replied, eager to converse about his favorite pastime. As they spoke animatedly about their shared love of books, the cozy tech shop seemed to transform into an intimate literary salon where two kindred spirits from different generations could explore the world of words together. "I love a good mystery. I think my favorite has to be Brook Queen. She has a real knack for twists and turns."

Lucy smiled as if she knew something he didn't. She had a face that seemed to radiate warmth and genuine kindness. Her eyes sparkled like sapphires as she spoke, but it was her smile—honest, inviting, and full of life—that truly lit up the room. "She's all right. If I am not mistaken, she stopped writing about ten years ago."

"That's right," Nick said, matching her smile.

"Goodness, what an impressive array of gadgets you have here!" Lucy exclaimed, her attention now fixed on the large window display showcasing the latest devices. Nick couldn't help but feel a small swell of pride at her words. He had put a great deal of thought into arranging the various devices in the most eye-catching way possible, and it seemed his efforts had paid off.

"Thank you," he replied humbly. "I try to keep up with the latest trends in technology. You never know what people might need or want."

Lucy's fingers danced lightly over the surface of a cutting-edge tablet, her gaze filled with curiosity. "I must admit, I'm not the most tech-savvy person, but I can certainly see the appeal of these gadgets. I imagine your business will be quite successful here in Sweet Sea."

"Here's hoping," Nick said with a chuckle, watching as she continued to explore the collection of smartwatches, wireless headphones, and sleek laptops. It struck him how gracefully she navigated the unfamiliar territory, her fascination evident despite her age.

"Tell me, Nick," Lucy asked as she picked up a portable e-reader. "Do you find that people still enjoy reading physical books, or are they all switching to digital formats? As a librarian, I can't help but be concerned about the future of literature."

"From my experience, there's still a strong demand for physical books," Nick reassured her. "Many people love the tactile experience of holding a book in their hands, turning the pages one by one. Of course, e-readers have their benefits, too – being able to carry an entire library in your pocket is quite convenient. I have already sold three of those just this week. I like to say that book reading hasn't changed. It just evolved to reach even more readers than before. I'm not sure if that is accurate, but I think it is an example of technology meeting people where they are in life."

"Indeed," Lucy mused, her warm smile never wavering. "It's wonderful to see how technology can bring us closer to the stories and ideas that matter most. I suppose it's all about finding a balance between the old and the new."

"Exactly," Nick agreed, moved by the genuine connection he was forming with this remarkable woman. Their shared love of literature transcended any barriers between them. And as they continued to discuss the ever-evolving landscape of books and technology, Nick couldn't help but feel grateful for the serendipity that had brought Lucy into his cozy little shop. She was the first person to make him feel welcome in the month since he arrived.

"Speaking of classics," Lucy said, her eyes twinkling with enthusiasm, "have you read any Dickens lately? I've always been fond of his work, though I know some people find it a bit too bleak."

"Ah, I haven't read Dickens in quite some time," Nick admitted, scratching behind his left ear. "But I do remember being captivated by the vivid descriptions and complex characters. His novels do have a certain timeless quality to them, don't they?"

"Certainly," Lucy agreed. "It's fascinating how literature can be enjoyed for many generations."

"Absolutely," Nick nodded, taking in the contrast between Lucy's old-world elegance and the sleek, modern devices surrounding them. "I suppose that's part of what makes books so special – their ability to connect people across time and space."

"Very true. Almost like a time machine," Lucy smiled. "Take us, for example. We come from different eras, but our love for books has brought us together. There's something quite magical about that, don't you think?"

"So true," Nick agreed, feeling a newfound sense of camaraderie with the librarian.

"On the subject of books," Lucy ventured, her eyes twinkling with curiosity. "Have you read anything else recently that has captured your attention?"

Nick leaned back against the counter, his mind sifting through the various titles he had delved into over the past few weeks. "You know, there's this mystery novel I've been reading lately called *The Cryptic Conundrum*. It's by a relatively unknown author, but it utterly captivated me."

"Ah, mysteries, my favorite genre!" Lucy exclaimed, clasping her hands together in delight. "There's nothing quite like the thrill of unraveling a perplexing puzzle and uncovering hidden secrets."

"Very true," Nick agreed, pleased to discover they shared

a common preference in literature. "In this particular story, the detective is faced with a series of seemingly unrelated events that ultimately converge in an unexpected twist. The author does an excellent job of keeping the reader guessing until the very end. I won't give it away, but I love how nature is used as a weapon."

"Sounds fascinating," Lucy said, her interest piqued. "I'll have to add it to my reading list."

"And what about you?" Nick said. "Have you come across any noteworthy reads lately?"

"Actually, I just finished a historical fiction novel called *Whispers from the Past*. It explores the life of a young woman in the 1800s who discovers a long-lost family secret that changes the course of her life forever," she said, her voice filled with enthusiasm.

"Sounds intriguing," Nick remarked, making a mental note to look for the book at the library. "I've always enjoyed stories that transport us to different times and places, offering glimpses into worlds we can only imagine."

"Then, you would like it," Lucy agreed, her eyes sparkling with excitement. "Books have the incredible ability to open our minds and expand our horizons, don't they?"

As their conversation continued, Nick found himself increasingly drawn to Lucy's passion for literature and her insightful perspective on the written word. Most of the talk was about sharing book ideas or praise for one author over another. They could have talked all day or maybe all week if given the time. It was nice to have a friend. He wished his mother could have been more like this.

"Speaking of fantastic authors," Lucy said, her eyes gleaming as she picked up a small accessory from the display. "Have you ever read Isaac Asimov? I quite enjoy his science fiction work, particularly his Foundation series."

"Ah, Asimov," Nick responded, his eyes lighting up with enthusiasm. "I have indeed. The way he wove together intricate plots and complex characters was truly masterful. And his concept of psychohistory – creating a mathematical model to predict the future of human society – was both fascinating and thought-provoking. Plus, what boy doesn't like robots."

"Exactly!" Lucy exclaimed, clearly excited that they shared another favorite author. "I also find his robot series to be incredibly engaging. The Three Laws of Robotics he introduced are now considered foundational in the field of artificial intelligence."

"I read that somewhere," Nick said, nodding in agreement. "As for other science fiction authors, I'd highly recommend Philip K. Dick. His novel *Do Androids Dream of*

Electric Sheep? – which inspired the film Blade Runner – is a must-read. He had an uncanny ability to blend futuristic technology with psychological depth and philosophical inquiry."

"Ah, yes, I've heard of him but haven't gotten around to reading his work yet," Lucy admitted, her interest piqued. "I'll make sure to add it to my list."

"Since we're on the topic of technology," Nick continued, feeling more at ease as he delved into one of his favorite subjects, "you might also enjoy some non-fiction books about the digital age. One that comes to mind is *The Innovators* by Walter Isaacson. It provides a fascinating look into the history of the computer and the Internet and how they've shaped our world."

"Thank you for the suggestion," Lucy replied with a smile. "I must confess I'm not as well-versed in tech-related literature, but I'm always eager to expand my horizons."

"Speaking of expanding horizons," Nick said, noticing the twinkle in Lucy's eye as she examined a sleek new gadget, "I recently read a historical fiction novel that I think you might enjoy. It's called *The Nightingale* by Kristin Hannah, and it tells the story of two sisters living in Nazi-occupied France during World War II. It's a beautifully written, heart-wrenching tale that offers a unique perspective on courage, love, and sacrifice.

And then a time traveler shows up from the future."

"Sounds captivating," Lucy mused, her gaze still lingering on the gadget. She finally placed the device back on the display and turned to face Nick. "It's been a delight discussing books with you. I'm so glad I stopped by your shop today."

"Likewise, Lucy," Nick replied, his heart swelling with an appreciation for this unexpected connection. "And I hope you enjoy the recommendations. Feel free to drop by anytime you'd like to chat about books – or if you need help with any of your gadgets. I would also happily show you how to use any of them."

"Thank you for the lovely chat, Nick," Lucy said eventually, glancing at her wristwatch. "I should be getting back to the library now, but I'll definitely stop by again soon."

"Please do," Nick replied, his voice warm and sincere. "It's not every day that I get to discuss my favorite books with someone as knowledgeable and enthusiastic as you."

"Take care, and good luck with your shop." With a final smile and a wave, Lucy departed, leaving Nick feeling both grateful and inspired in this cozy little corner of Sweet Sea.

The day continued to go well for his shop, and when evening came, he was filled with dread. Night time was the worst time. He would sit alone in his upstairs apartment, think of his wife, and depressingly wonder if he would be better off if he had just died.

CHAPTER TWO

Nick sat at the kitchen table, his hands trembling as he tried to steady himself. The room was filled with the soft hum of the refrigerator and the smell of freshly brewed coffee, which did little to ease his stress. Beads of sweat trickled down his forehead as his eyes darted around the room, searching for some solace.

"Dammit," he muttered under his breath, his fingers fidgeting with the worn edge of the newspaper. He knew this wasn't how he wanted to live his life, not in Sweet Sea, where he had hoped for a fresh start. His gaze fell upon the bottle of pills on the counter, an ever-present reminder of his past addiction. Nick hesitated, knowing that those tiny capsules were nothing but trouble, yet their allure was undeniable.

Just as he was about to reach for the bottle, his phone rang. Startled, he fumbled with the device before answering the video call. "Hello?"

"Dad? It's Bridget." Her voice was warm and concerned, cutting through the fog of his anxiety like a beacon of light. Her bright blue eyes and reddish blonde hair filled his screen. "I just wanted to check in on you. You sounded off earlier when we spoke, and I can't help but worry."

Bridget's caring nature was one of the many things he admired about her, even if it sometimes felt overwhelming. As much as he didn't want to burden her with his problems, he knew she wouldn't let him suffer in silence. "Thanks, honey," he said, trying to keep the tremor from his voice. "I'm just dealing with some...stress, I guess. Nothing I can't handle."

"Are you sure?" There was a pause on the line, and Nick could almost hear Bridget's gentle persistence. "You know you can talk to me about anything, right?"

Nick sighed, leaning back in his chair. He knew his daughter was right. She and her sister had always been there for him, even when he struggled to admit how much he needed her. As he stared at the bottle of pills, his resolve began to crumble. "Actually," he said hesitantly, "maybe I could use someone to talk to."

"Of course, Dad. I'm here for you." Bridget's voice was a

gentle breeze brushing against his frayed nerves.

Nick took a deep breath and slowly exhaled, the sound of crashing waves on Sweet Sea's shores echoing in the night from his open window. "I've been struggling with stress and anxiety lately," he admitted, his fingers unconsciously tracing the pattern on the armrest of his chair. "It feels like I'm constantly fighting an invisible battle, and sometimes I just... I don't know how to cope. I met a nice lady today that distracted me for a little while, but every little thing that goes wrong seems like a huge mountain at first."

He heard a soft sigh from the other end of the line, and he could see the empathetic frown on Bridget's face through the screen. "I can't imagine how difficult that must be for you," she said softly. "But you don't have to go through it alone."

There was a moment of silence before Nick found the courage to continue. "And there's something else, too," he confessed. "I miss your mom so much. I know I'm supposed to be strong for you and your sister because you lost her too. It's just so hard. As you know, it's been twenty-five months since she passed away, but it still hurts as if it happened yesterday."

"It's okay to be sad, Dad."

"Her laughter filled every room she entered, and her love for life was infectious," Nick reminisced, his throat tightening as he fought back tears. He was not going to cry in front of his daughter. If he could not hold back, he would turn off his video. "She was my rock, Bridget. My compass when I felt lost. And now that she's gone, I feel like I've lost my sense of direction. I'm trying to find meaning in my life without her, but everything feels... empty. I thought coming here with a fresh start would cure all of that, but now I am not so sure. "

"Dad, I..." Bridget paused, searching for the right words. "I can only imagine the pain you're going through. I'm going through it as well. But you're stronger than you give yourself credit for. You moved to Sweet Sea to start over, and that takes courage. Just remember, we're all here for you, and we'll help you find that meaning again."

Nick closed his eyes, allowing the warmth of Bridget's words to wrap around him like a comforting embrace. He knew she was right. He had moved to Sweet Sea for a fresh start and couldn't let his grief consume him. The love he shared with his wife would always be a part of him, but he needed to forge a new path forward.

"Thank you, Bridget," he whispered, the tension in his shoulders slowly dissipating. "Your support means the world to me. But I am the parent. I should be the one here for you and your sister. The strong one."

"Not always, Dad. You have been plenty strong for us. It's okay to lean back." Her voice resonated with unwavering loyalty. "We're family, and that's what family does."

Nick watched the moon, low in the sky, casting long shadows across the room. The edges of his world seemed to blur as the weight of his heartache threatened to pull him under. He felt a knot tighten in his chest, his breaths coming in shallow gasps.

"Dad, please," Bridget's voice broke through the haze, tender and concerned. "You don't have to go through this alone. I love you, and I'm here for you."

He listened to her, taking in the sincerity. It was a lifeline he desperately needed.

"I..." Nick hesitated, his voice tentative. "I don't know if I can do it, Bridge. I miss her so much."

"Of course you do," she said softly, her voice virtually reaching out to squeeze his hand. "But remember, grief is like an ocean – it comes in waves. And when those waves are crashing down on you, you need to let someone be your anchor."

Nick closed his eyes, feeling the gentle pressure of Bridget's voice. Her words brought forth a memory of laughter filled nights shared with his wife over their mutual love for books, of whispered conversations beneath the moonlight. It was a bittersweet reminder that life still held beauty amidst the pain.

"Thank you," he murmured, his voice thick with emotion. "I don't think I could face this without you and your sister."

"Nor should you have to," Bridget replied, a fierce protectiveness lacing her tone. "We'll weather this storm together, Dad. You're not alone."

Nick felt a spark of hope ignite within him. It was faint, flickering, but it was there – a testament to the strength of the bond he shared with his daughter. Gratitude swelled in his chest, buoying him above the raging tide of his grief.

"Your love means everything, Bridge," he whispered, his eyes shining with unshed tears. "I don't know where I'd be without you."

"Neither of us do," she smiled gently, her own eyes glistening. "But what matters is that we're here for each other, no matter what life throws our way."

Nick felt a newfound resolve take root within him. Though the journey ahead was shrouded in uncertainty, he knew he could face it – as long as he had her by his side. With renewed determination, Nick walked over to the counter, picked up the bottle of pills, and returned them to the medicine cabinet. The darkness that had threatened to swallow him whole now seemed to recede, pushed back by the strength and love of those closest to him. As he stared at his reflection in the mirror, he knew that the journey ahead wouldn't be easy, but with Bridget and the rest of his family by his side, he was ready to face whatever challenges life had in store.

"I put the pills away," he said into the phone. "Thank you."

"Why do you still have those?"

"Just in case of an episode. However, if I do, I will only take the prescribed."

"Can you please throw those away? They could kick your addiction back into gear."

"Can we talk about something else," Nick said.

"Dad!"

"Please."

"Ok. Remember that trip we all took to the mountains?" Bridget asked, breaking the stillness as she gestured toward the picture on the wall behind him. It had been taken during happier times, when her mom was still alive, and they had all gone away for a much-needed vacation. The memories were vivid, full of laughter and love.

Nick smiled wistfully and turned to look at the picture. His eyes focused on the image of his wife, her radiant smile captured forever in time. "Yeah, I do. She was so excited about learning to ski, even though she spent most of the time tumbling down the slopes," he chuckled, recalling the way her eyes had focused with determination each time she got back up and tried again.

Bridget laughed, the sound soft and melodic in the quiet room. "She was nothing if not persistent. And she adored you. You were always her rock."

A pang of grief clenched his heart, but the warmth of the memory enveloped him like a gentle embrace. "We were good together," he admitted, his voice tinged with sadness. "I miss her so much, Bridge."

"Of course you do, and that's okay," Bridget replied, her tone tender. "But she wouldn't want you to be alone. She'd want you to find happiness again. So, pick yourself up and get to living life again."

He turned to look back at the screen, his hair falling into his eyes as he did so. There was an intensity in her gaze, one that spoke volumes about the depth of their connection. "I know," he whispered, the words heavy with emotion. " I'm grateful for that every single day. Even if some of them are miserable."

"We've been through so much together, and you've always been there for me. It's only natural that I'd be here for you now when you need me most."

Their eyes locked, an electric current of understanding passing between them. It was a bond forged by shared memories, a foundation built on love, and the strength of a parental bond.

"Thank you," he murmured, his hand touching the screen. "You mean more to me than I could ever express, Bridge."

"Likewise," she replied, her fingers tapping on her screen. "We're a family – even if it's not quite the one we originally envisioned. But we'll face whatever comes our way as long as we have each other. We're here for you."

He sighed, his brain burdened beneath the weight of his thoughts. "I know," he admitted, his fingers tapping nervously against his thigh. "But sometimes, the pain becomes too much to bear. The memories, the loss... it all comes rushing back, and I just want to escape it."

"Running from your pain won't solve anything," Bridget reminded him, her eyes filled with compassion. "Instead, let's face it together. Let me help you carry some of that burden. If you start to feel that way, call me. I will always pick up."

He looked at her – really looked at her – and saw the sincerity shining within those bright blue eyes. He nodded.

"After all, since I am the favorite daughter, I have to work to keep the title."

"You think. Thank you, Bridge," he murmured, a sense of relief washing over him like a cleansing wave. "I said it before, and I will say it again. I don't know what I would do without you."

"Hopefully, you'll never have to find out," she replied, her voice tinged with both love and determination.

"Here's to our family, Bridge," he declared, his heart swelling with gratitude. "And to face whatever comes our way together."

"Cheers to that," she agreed, her eyes twinkling as they shared a tender smile. "Now, tell me about your shop and how it has been going, Mr. Small Business Owner."

CHAPTER THREE

The Sweet Sea Public Library bustled with activity, but seemed to hush in reverence as Nick Cern strode through the entrance, the gray in his hair catching the sun from the tall windows. He'd been coming here for several months now, ever since he moved to this coastal town to meet Lucy. The library had become a sanctuary for him, a place where he could escape into the pages of a good book and forget the troubles that weighed heavily on his heart. It was a world unto itself, nestled within the quaint coastal town. Its facade, reminiscent of a Victorian manor, housed a labyrinth of shelves and reading nooks that seemed to stretch on forever. The scent of old books and polished wood pervaded the air while the soft afternoon light filtered through stained-glass windows casting multicolored shadows across the floor.

He exchanged nods and smiles with fellow patrons as he made his way to his usual spot at the back of the library, where he knew Lucy Brooks would be waiting. Over time, their conversations about books had deepened into a close platonic friendship, one that Nick cherished dearly. Who knew when she first walked into his store three months ago, they would become so close. He didn't. Even more surprising, his despair lessened and he hadn't thought of suicide once in the last few months.

"Ah, there you are, Nick," Lucy called out as he approached her desk. Her petite frame was hunched over, absorbed in the task of labeling, and cataloging new arrivals. "I was beginning to wonder if you'd found some other literary haven."

"Never," Nick replied, taking a seat across from her. "You know this is my favorite corner of the world."

Lucy chuckled, pushing aside the books she'd been working on. "Well then, let's get down to business. Have you finished reading that Agatha Christie novel I recommended?"

"*Murder on the Orient Express*?" Nick grinned. "Indeed, I did. You were right; the twist at the end was brilliant. I can't believe I didn't see it coming. However, more importantly, I can't believe I hadn't read it. I seemed to have read just about everything else she put out."

"Isn't that the beauty of a great murder mystery?" Lucy was enthused. "The author lures you in, making you think you've got everything figured out, only to pull the rug out from under you at the last moment."

"Speaking of which," Nick said, his eyes lighting up with excitement, "Did you read the author I recommended, Brook Queen?"

"Brook Queen?" Lucy paused momentarily, her eyes narrowing slightly as she considered the name. "Yes, I believe I have. She's quite popular these days, isn't she?"

"Absolutely," Nick confirmed. "Her Inspector Bupin novels have me hooked. They're set in France and are full of twists and turns. The way she weaves false clues into her stories is reminiscent of how Christie did it. I just wish I knew why she stopped."

"Ah, another master of misdirection," Lucy mused, a knowing smile playing on her lips. "I'll have to refresh myself on her library."

"Please do," Nick urged. "I'd love to discuss her books with you. There's something about sharing our thoughts on murder mysteries that makes me feel even more connected to the world within the pages."

"True," Lucy agreed, her eyes softening.

With that, they delved deeper into the conversation, discussing specific titles and authors that had left lasting impressions on them. Their shared love of murder mysteries fed their connection, strengthening the bond that had grown between them over the past months. And as they sat there, surrounded by the hallowed walls of the library, it felt as though they were part of a world that only they could understand – a world where false clues and hidden secrets were waiting to be unveiled.

Nick reached for a worn copy of *Death by the Seashore* from the shelf, his fingers brushing against Lucy's as they both grasped the book simultaneously. The contact sent a static jolt through him, and he quickly withdrew his hand.

"Sorry," he muttered sheepishly, but Lucy only smiled.

"Great minds think alike," she said, her eyes gleaming with amusement. "Brook Queen really is one of the best mystery writers out there. Huh? You believe that?"

As they sat down at their usual table, Nick couldn't help but agree. He had spent countless hours lost in Brook Queen's intricate plots and clever twists, marveling at the author's ability to weave such captivating tales. Little did he know that the truth was just within his grasp.

"Did you ever wonder what it would be like to live the life of an author?" Lucy asked, her voice taking on a wistful tone.

"To create entire worlds and characters with just the stroke of a pen?"

Nick studied her face, noticing the far-off look in her eyes. "I suppose it would be thrilling," he replied. "But also, quite lonely."

"Ah, yes," Lucy chuckled, a strange glint in her eye. "I imagine it would be quite difficult to maintain any semblance of a normal life under those circumstances."

"Definitely," Nick nodded, utterly unaware of the significance of their conversation. "I've heard that she's something of a recluse, living off the royalties from her books and rarely making public appearances."

"Indeed," Lucy mused, her fingers idly tracing the embossed letters on the book's cover. "It must be nice, though, to have that level of financial freedom. A luxury few can afford."

"So true," Nick agreed, his mind wandering to his own financial struggles. "Though I'm sure it comes with its own set of problems."

"Problems that can be overcome with time and patience," Lucy said cryptically. Then, as if realizing the weight of her words, she quickly changed the subject. "Did you know the original manuscript for *Death by the Seashore* was lost in a fire? Brook Queen had to rewrite the entire novel from memory."

"Really?" Nick's eyebrows shot up in surprise. "That must have been incredibly frustrating."

"Most definitely," Lucy replied, a knowing smile playing at the corners of her mouth. "But in the end, it only made the story stronger."

A sudden realization washed over Nick like a tidal wave, leaving him breathless. Could it be? Was Lucy hinting at something more? "If you barely heard of her, how did you know that?"

"I know things." She laughed.

"Lucy Brooks." he began slowly, his heart pounding in his chest. He couldn't believe he hadn't considered it before with all the clues. "Are you... are you Brook Queen?"

For a moment, Lucy hesitated, her eyes flickering with uncertainty. Then, with a resigned sigh, she nodded. "Guilty as charged," she confessed, her voice barely a whisper. "I never intended for anyone to find out, but I suppose there's no use denying it now."

Nick stared at her, his mind reeling from the revelation. He struggled to reconcile the image of his dearest friend with that of the elusive millionaire author who had captivated him for years. How could Lucy, the humble librarian who shared his love for books and mysteries, be one and the same as Brook

Queen?

"Please don't think any differently of me," Lucy implored, her eyes filled with vulnerability. "I've come to value our friendship over the last few months, Nick, and I hope this doesn't change anything between us."

"Of course not," he reassured her, the shock gradually giving way to awe and admiration. "If anything, it only makes our connection even more special."

"Thank you," Lucy breathed, visibly relieved by his response.

"Why did you stop?"

"It was time." She pursed her lips and gave him a look not to pursue the subject further.

As they resumed their discussion of *Death by the Seashore* and other Brook Queen novels, Nick found himself seeing Lucy in a new light. She was no longer just a kindred spirit with whom he shared a love for books; she was the mastermind behind the stories that had captured his imagination for years. He knew that their friendship had grown stronger, bonded not only by their mutual love for mysteries, but also by the secret they now shared. As corny as it sounded, he had never really had a good friend who shared his interests.

"Did you know," Lucy began, pausing to sip her tea,

"when I was a little girl that I once met Dame Agatha Christie herself? It was back in the mid-60s, during one of her rare public appearances. She signed my copy of *The Mirror Crack'd from Side to Side*, and we exchanged a few words about her work."

Nick's eyebrows shot up in surprise. "You've actually met the Queen of Crime? That's incredible!"

"I did," Lucy chuckled. "It was a moment I'll never forget. In fact, meeting her is what inspired me to try writing mysteries myself. She told me, 'A good mystery should keep you guessing until the very end.' And I took those words to heart."

As Nick listened to Lucy's anecdotes about her past, he couldn't help but feel a newfound admiration for her. The more he learned about her life – from her early days as a curious young reader to her rise as a successful author and the challenges she faced along the way. the more he realized how fortunate he was to have formed such a special bond with her.

Nick couldn't help but notice that not everyone at the library was as fond of Lucy as he was. As they sat together, discussing their latest literary discoveries, he observed the cool stares and barely concealed whispers from a few of the library regulars.

First, there was Cynthia Winters, an elegant woman in

her 50s with impeccably styled hair and a permanent scowl etched on her face. She was a prominent member of the Sweet Sea Historical Society and often came to the library for research. Nick had noticed that she tended to avoid Lucy whenever possible, though Lucy made every effort to be cordial.

"Excuse me, I need to return this book," Lucy said, excusing herself to attend to her librarian duties.

As she walked away, Cynthia approached Nick, her voice dripping with disdain. "I see you've been spending quite a bit of time with Lucy."

"Is there a problem with that?" Nick asked defensively. He could feel his hackles rising at the unwarranted animosity.

"Let's just say she's not exactly who she claims to be," Cynthia replied cryptically, her gaze lingering on Lucy across the room.

Nick frowned, puzzled by her insinuation, especially after learning about Lucy's secret identity as Brook Queen. He glanced back at Cynthia, hoping for clarification, but she had already turned away, her lips pursed tightly.

On another occasion, Nick overheard a heated exchange between Lucy and Harold Finch, the library's grumpy maintenance man. Harold was a stout man in his late 60s, with thinning gray hair that covered his head in stripes and he seemed to have a perpetual frown. He had worked at the library for decades and seemed to resent Lucy's presence.

"Your fancy titles don't impress me, Miss Brooks," Harold grumbled one day as he begrudgingly replaced a flickering light bulb under Lucy's supervision. "You may have fooled everyone else, but I know better."

"Harold, I've told you before – I'm just here to help," Lucy responded patiently, her voice tinged with weariness. "I don't want any trouble."

"Ha! Trouble seems to follow you around like a lost puppy. Maybe if you changed your tone," Harold said before stalking off, leaving Lucy visibly upset.

Nick tried to piece together the puzzle of why these people seemed so hostile toward his friend. Was it simply jealousy over her wealth or success? Or was there something more sinister lurking beneath the surface?

He watched Lucy return from shelving the book, her face lighting up as she resumed her seat across from him. At that moment, he resolved to support her, no matter what others might say or think. They were friends, and friends stood by each other through thick and thin.

"Lucy, have you ever had any...problems with Cynthia or Harold?" Nick ventured cautiously, not wanting to pry but needing to know.

"Ah, them." Lucy sighed, her smile fading. "They've never been particularly fond of me. But let's not dwell on that. We have bigger fish to fry – like figuring out who the murderer is in this new novel!"

Nick couldn't shake the lingering unease as they dove back into their discussion. He knew that despite their shared love of murder mysteries, real-life tensions were simmering just below the surface. And he couldn't help but wonder how long it would be before those tensions erupted into something far more dangerous.

Nick stared at the worn leather cover of the book in his hands, its gold lettering barely legible after years of use. "You know," he said thoughtfully, "I think *Death on the Nile* might just be my favorite Agatha Christie novel."

"Really?" Lucy leaned forward, her eyes sparkling with interest. "Why is that?"

"Something about the exotic setting and the intricate plot just draws me in." Nick tapped the book gently on the table between them. "Plus, Hercule Poirot's deduction skills are simply unparalleled. What about you? Do you have a favorite Christie novel?"

Lucy pursed her lips, deep in thought. "Oh, it's so hard to choose just one. But I suppose if I had to pick, it would be *The Murder of Roger Ackroyd*. It was the first Christie novel I read, and it changed the way I looked at mystery novels forever. Plus, I like mysteries that are not in exotic locations."

"Ah, yes – the infamous unreliable narrator! That was quite a twist," Nick agreed, appreciating the subtle nuances of their conversation. "It's not every day that an author can pull off such a bold narrative choice. Oh, and on a side note, I like the fabulous locations, especially if isolated."

"And speaking of twists, have you read any books lately that surprised you?"

"Actually, I just finished reading *The Serpent's Coil* by Brook Queen," Nick said enthusiastically. "The ending caught me completely off guard!"

"Brook Queen, you say?" A smile tugged at the corner of Lucy's mouth as she exchanged a knowing glance with Nick. "Well, I must admit, I'm rather partial to her work myself."

"Partial? " Nick teased. "But seriously, I love how you weave all those seemingly irrelevant details into the story, only to reveal their true significance at the very end."

"Thank you." Lucy nodded solemnly. " It's about understanding the depths of human nature and the capacity for both good and evil that lies within each of us. And in a way, it helps us make sense of our own lives, doesn't it? The struggles we face, the choices we make... It's all part of the bigger mystery that is life itself. I was unhappily married at the time of most of my writing. So, killing off people kept me from hurting my husband."

"Interesting perspective," Nick murmured, his thoughts drifting back to the recent tensions surrounding her. He knew that beneath the surface of their idyllic little town, darker forces were at play and he was more determined than ever to stand by his friend's side, no matter what challenges lay ahead.

Changing the subject, Nick looked around the library. "This place is huge and really is truly magical."

"Isn't it?" Lucy beamed, her gray eyes twinkling like a mischievous schoolgirl's. "I've always felt at home among these books. In fact, this very library is where my love for murder mysteries began."

"Really?" Nick inquired, his curiosity piqued. "How did that happen?"

"Ah, well," Lucy sighed wistfully, pausing beside an antique display case housing the first edition of classic mysteries. "It all started when I was just a little girl. My father used to take me here every Saturday morning, and we'd spend hours exploring the stacks together. One day, he handed me a copy of Agatha Christie's *Murder on the Orient Express* and told me it was one of his favorites when he was my age. That was after I met her and knew her works."

"Wow," Nick mused, running his fingers over the spines

of the books in the display case. "That must have been quite a read for someone so young."

"I was equal parts fascinated and terrified by the idea that a killer could be hiding in plain sight among us. From then on, I devoured every mystery novel I could get my hands on. It was very different from the first Christie novel I read."

"Did that fuel your desire to write as well?" Nick wondered aloud, recalling Lucy's revelation about her successful writing career under the pen name Brook Queen.

"Absolutely," Lucy confirmed, her voice tinged with nostalgia. "I remember sitting in the library's window seat, overlooking the sea, and dreaming up my own stories of murder and intrigue. I knew that one day, I wanted to create mysteries that would captivate readers, just as Christie had captivated me. Believe it or not, this is also where I did my first book signing ever. The whole town turned out."

"You've certainly achieved that," Nick said sincerely, impressed by her passion and dedication. "And now, here you are, still sharing your love for these stories with others. Why keep it a secret if everyone knows?"

"Ah, yes. Well, most have forgotten, and I honestly don't like the attention," Lucy replied with a wistful smile. "As much as I enjoy my quiet life here, there's no denying the thrill of creating those intricate puzzles for readers to solve. I suppose it's what keeps me coming back to the library every day – not only to share my love for books, but also to find inspiration for my own work. And don't let this go to your head. You have inspired me. I have an idea for a new book that I am going to start plotting out."

"That would be awesome. I bet it will be another Best Seller." Her smile faded, and she seemed to be lost in dread. "Lucy," he said, his voice tinged with uncertainty, "is there something you're not telling me?"

For a moment, Lucy hesitated, her eyes flickering with a hint of unease. Then, she leaned forward, her voice barely above a whisper.

"Nick, there's a reason I'm writing a new mystery. It's because I'm being haunted by one of my own."

As she spoke those words, the air around them seemed to grow colder, and the once comforting walls of the library loomed ominously overhead. Unbeknownst to them, the seeds of discord had been sown, setting the stage for a chilling tale that would test the limits of their friendship and force them to confront the darkest corners of their own souls.

Even though both Nick and Lucy felt a shared sense of belonging within their hallowed halls, they were unaware of the real-life mysteries that awaited them just beyond the library doors.

CHAPTER FOUR

The small city street seemed alive for an evening weekday as people hurried past one another, greeting, and discussing the cold weather. As Nick finished his final repair for the day, he couldn't help but feel a sense of contentment – a feeling that had been sorely missing from his life for far too long. He had found an unlikely sanctuary in his little shop and a friend who shared his passion for the written word. He was sure this town would be good for him. Little did he know that his world would soon be tested by a chilling mystery that would push him to his limit.

Nick was in the middle of a customer sale when his phone chimed with an incoming email notification. Glancing at the screen, he saw that it was from Lucy. The subject line immediately caught his attention: "Clue for my murder."

His heart skipped a beat, and he quickly opened the email. It contained only a few lines:

"Nick, *The Brown Grass.* Read it carefully. -Lucy"

"What on earth...?" Nick muttered under his breath, his brow furrowing with concern. He glanced around outside the shop's window, half-expecting to see her appear with a smile on her face.

"Everything all right?" a customer asked, noticing his sudden shift in demeanor.

"Uh, yeah," he replied distractedly, forcing a smile. He put his phone down. "Thanks for asking."

"I really appreciate you and your store. We needed this for a long time," the customer said, giving him a friendly nod before leaving.

"Thanks," Nick murmured, his mind still racing with questions. What could Lucy be trying to tell him? Was she in danger? And why had she mentioned *The Brown Grass* – a book he'd never heard of?

He decided to send her a text message, hoping for clarification. "Got your email. Are you okay? Please call me as soon as you can."

With no immediate response, Nick tried to focus on his closing tasks, but his thoughts kept returning to Lucy and her cryptic message. A sense of urgency began to build within him; he couldn't shake the feeling that something was terribly amiss. The library was closed, and he didn't know where she lived. He had to hope she would return his message.

"Read it carefully," echoed in his mind as he scanned the internet for *The Brown Grass*. He knew that Lucy wouldn't have sent such a message without good reason, and if there were even a chance that she was in danger, he would do everything in his power to help her.

Finally locating the book, he purchased it from the online store and stared at the cover – a sinister illustration of a field of withered, brown grass under a dark sky. He thought it might be the title of the new book she was working on, but the author was some Doctor he had never heard of. He opened the book and began to read, his heart pounding in his chest.

Nick switched between the book and email applications. He couldn't help but read the email repeatedly, his eyes darting between the subject line and the ominous message within. Was this some kind of sick joke? Or was Lucy truly in danger? The book was a mystery novel about deadly plants that could be used to murder. Why would she want him to read it? Was it a new mystery suggestion? He felt a cold shiver run down his spine as he picked up his phone and dialed her number with trembling fingers. "Come on, Lucy," he muttered, the ringing tone echoing in his ears. "Pick up."

But there was no answer – just the monotonous beep of her voicemail. Nick clenched his jaw and tried to keep his frustration in check, quickly sending her another text message. "Lucy, I'm really worried about you. Call me ASAP."

"Can you help me?" The voice of a middle-aged woman pulled Nick's attention back to reality. Her smartphone lay in pieces on the counter. Its screen shattered beyond recognition. "Can you fix this?"

"Uh, yeah. I was about to close up."

"Oh." The woman's eyes drooped. "Are you sure you can't help?"

"Yes, of course," Nick stammered, his mind still racing with thoughts of Lucy and her cryptic email. He forced himself to focus on the task at hand, meticulously reassembling the broken device while exchanging pleasantries with the customer.

"Your hands are shaking," she observed, concern etched into her face. "Are you all right?"

"Long day," Nick replied vaguely, not wanting to divulge any information about Lucy's mysterious situation. After fifteen minutes, he handed the now-functional phone back to the grateful customer, who paid her bill and left the shop.

"Thank you so much!" she said. She exited, oblivious to

the turmoil brewing within Nick. "I hope you get some rest."

"Sure thing," he said absently, glancing at the clock above the door. Six thirty at night, and still no word from Lucy. At that moment, Nick decided that he had to find out what was going on.

He locked up the shop and made his way to the library, his heart pounding in his chest. The city street was quiet now and seemed to blur around him as he hurried along. "Please be okay, Lucy," he whispered, his breath visible in the chilly air. "Please."

But when Nick arrived at the library, he found it locked. Its doors bolted shut. That wasn't unusual, but then he saw it. Lucy's car was still in the parking lot. Panic seized him – this was highly irregular; Lucy would never just leave her car. He pounded on the door, calling her name, but there was no response.

"Damn it!" he cursed, pulling out his phone and dialing the police. "Yes, I need to report a possible emergency at Sweet Sea Library. My friend might be in danger."

As he waited for help to arrive, Nick couldn't shake the feeling that he was running out of time. Whatever was going on with Lucy, he knew he had to uncover the truth – before it was too late.

"Why would she leave her car?" Nick paced back and

forth in front of the library while waiting for the police. His heart raced with fear for Lucy's safety, but his mind was already working to unravel the ominous message she had sent him earlier.

"Focus, Nick. Think," he coached himself, pulling out his phone once more. He frantically searched for the digital copy of *The Brown Grass* he purchased, the book mentioned in Lucy's email. Within moments, he found his purchased edition and its description made him shudder.

"Poisonous plants used to murder people," he whispered, his eyes scanning the synopsis. The novel's protagonist, an expert botanist named Dr. Greenfield, was being framed for a series of murders committed using deadly flora and covering it up with a prescription drug. The story's villain, a jilted ex-lover, sought revenge on Greenfield by destroying his career and reputation.

"Could this be connected to Lucy's past?" Nick wondered aloud, recalling her former life as a reclusive millionaire writer. It wasn't inconceivable that she had made enemies along the way – perhaps even romantic ones. But who would want to hurt her?

"Hey!" Nick called out, spotting a familiar face across the street. "Rose! Do you know anything about Lucy's friends or ex-boyfriends? "

The pretty forty-six-year-old woman turned. Her beautiful green eyes and dark brown hair were amazing to him. Nick had been building up the nerve to ask her out since he first met her. He just never got around to acting on his crush. He felt too guilty while still grieving for his wife.

"Ex-boyfriends?" Rose replied, a puzzled expression on her face. "Lucy never really talked about her personal life, but she did mention someone named Gerald a few times. She said he was a bit too possessive for her liking. I think he was her ex-husband."

"Any idea where she might live?"

"You two are always hanging out."

"I know, it just never came up."

"I think she is about a mile up that way." She pointed north. "I do know her house is pink. You can't miss it."

"Thanks, Rose."

"Nick, what's going on?" she asked, concern etched on her face.

"Lucy might be in trouble," he replied tersely. "I'm waiting for the police to show up."

"Good heavens!" Rose gasped, her hand flying to her mouth. "Please, let me know if there's anything I can do to help."

"Thanks, Rose," Nick said, nodding his appreciation.

As the police sirens began to wail in the distance, Nick felt a cold dread settle in his gut. Whoever had targeted Lucy had been incredibly clever, using a literary clue to point him toward their nefarious intentions. But was it Gerald, the possessive ex-husband? Or was there another, more sinister character lurking in the shadows?

"Lucy, where are you? Please don't be messing with me," he whispered, his voice barely audible above the din of the city. As the police arrived and began their investigation, Nick knew he couldn't simply stand by and wait for answers. He vowed to delve into Lucy's past and follow the trail of *The Brown Grass* – no matter where it led him or what dangers lurked around each corner.

"Whatever it takes," he promised, clenching his fists. "I'll find out where you are, Lucy."

As Nick stood outside the library, his mind raced with possibilities. He glanced down at his phone again, re-reading the ominous email Lucy had sent him just hours earlier. The words 'Read it carefully' echoed in his thoughts. He knew he needed to dive deeper into book and take matters into his own hands if he was going to find out what happened to his dear friend.

The police has been at the library for an hour and not a minute longer. After taking a brief statement, they asked him to wait. He had been on the sidewalk across the street since then and he was tired of waiting.

"Excuse me," a passerby said, bumping into him as they hurried along the crowded street. Nick barely noticed the young teen, lost in thought about poisonous plants and shadowy figures from Lucy's past.

"Mr. Cern!" Sheriff Joan Kent called out, striding towards him with her short blonde hair pulled back into a tiny ponytail. She looked grim, and Nick's heart sank.

"Sheriff," he greeted, forcing a smile. "Any news on Lucy?"

The sheriff hesitated, then sighed. "Not yet, but we're working on it. We've managed to get inside the library, but there was no sign of her. I understand you have some information for us about a book?"

"Right, *The Brown Grass*," Nick confirmed, handing over a printout of the cover of the digital copy he'd found online. "It's about murder by poisoning. Lucy sent me an urgent email telling me to read it."

"Interesting," the sheriff mused, scanning the page. "This could be vital evidence. We'll look into it immediately. In the meantime, I need you to stay out of our way. Let us do our job. Got it?"

"Of course," Nick agreed, though he knew deep down

that he couldn't just sit idly by while Lucy was in danger. As Sheriff Kent walked away, he decided to take action. He would investigate the people in the town, starting with Gerald if he lived nearby.

"Nick, wait!" Rose called out, catching up to him. "I overheard you talking to the sheriff. What are you planning on doing?"

"Finding Lucy," Nick replied, determination in his voice. "I can't just stand by while her life is in danger."

"Then let me help," Rose insisted, her eyes pleading. "We both care about her."

"All right," Nick agreed reluctantly. "But we need to be careful. Would you be okay locating and talking with Gerald to see if he may know where she is."

Together, they turned and walked back to his shop. Halfway there, they heard a phone ringing. Nick looked at his phone, saw it wasn't him, and looked at Rose.

"Not me," she said.

The ringing continued. He patted his jacket and pants pockets down and pulled a phone from his jacket pocket. "How did that get there?"

"That's Lucy's phone," Rose said. "How come you have it?"

"No idea." He thought for a moment. "Some teenager

bumped into me in the street over there. They must have put it in there."

Skeptical, Rose nodded. "Well, answer it."

He looked at it. "It's text messages."

"What do they say?"

"It's from an unknown number. It says, don't get involved, or you will go missing too. And tell Rose she better stay out of it as well." Nick looked up and began scanning the streets. The police at the library had drawn a small crowd. He didn't see any teenagers, but he was starting to second guess himself. It might have just been a smaller person.

Rose looked around. "Do you see them?"

"I don't."

"Well, that's not good. We should give the phone to the police."

Nick thought for a moment. "Right now, we have a way to talk to whoever has her. I think I will wait. I might be able to figure out who the unknown caller is or get more info off the phone."

"You want to keep going? Even with the threat?"

"Rose." Nick made close contact with her. "You don't have to help. I would understand. But I need to do this."

Rose slowly nodded. "I'll help."

The phone rang as a new text arrived. Nick looked at it

and read the unknown caller's message out loud, "Be smart."

CHAPTER FIVE

Nick Cern pushed open the heavy oak door to Lucy's library, a sanctuary where they had shared countless hours discussing everything from classic literature to their favorite murder mysteries. The familiar scent of old leather mixed with crisp pages greeted him like a warm embrace. But as he stepped inside, he froze in his tracks. The police had left after searching the library and discovering nothing amiss. He was sure there was something here to help find Lucy.

"Good morning?" Susan Priser said.

Nick turned to the assistant librarian. With Lucy missing, she was the only one left to open and run the library. It seemed a bit disrespectful with his friend missing, but he understood why. Returning to normal operations was inevitable. He just didn't like it.

Forcing a smile, Nick walked over to the desk. "Hi Susan. Have you happened to hear from Lucy?"

She shook her head. "Nothing. The last time I saw her was around three when I left for the day. Then all that excitement last night was the first I heard she was missing."

"It's just not like her not to come in or at least let me know how she is doing. She had to know we would be worried."

"The police were by earlier."

"And..." Nick started tapping his right foot nervously.

"They went to her home, and she wasn't there. Based on what they found, they concluded that she hadn't been home."

"Where the hell is she?" Nick turned and dragged his hand down his face. "People just don't disappear."

"Look around. Maybe you can do better than the police or me, for that matter, in finding a clue. I can only pray that she turns up safe. Maybe she slept at a friend's or something."

"I hope so as well. I will try to be quiet as I dig around."

Susan waved her hand. "No one else is here yet, so be as loud as you want."

"Thanks." Nick stepped into the rows of shelves. He was going to walk every aisle on both floors and double check the basement, although he knew she never went down there. She tried to avoid the grumpy janitor.

He searched the two floors of the library twice. Once with his head down, studying every fiber of carpet and tile for a clue, and a second time with his head up, scanning the books and the shelves they rested on. The clock on the wall showed four hours had passed. His shop would remain closed for the day. There was no other choice. Discouraged, he entered the basement. Harold Finch was hunched over a workbench when he came down the stairs.

Harold turned on him. "What do you want?"

Nick held up both his hands in a calming motion. "Just looking for Lucy. Thought she might have come down here."

"Are you with the police now?"

"No, not at all." Nick faked a chuckle. "Just a friend trying to find a friend."

Harold grunted and turned back to his bench. Nick wasn't sure what that meant. He waited patiently for permission to look around. When it didn't come, he started to glance around. It was one of the cleanest basements he had ever been in. Everything was organized and labeled.

"You can look anywhere you want. I don't care," Harold said, never turning from the bench. "The police already did, though."

"Thank you. I will say that this is really organized."

"I believe in a tidy workspace. And before you ask, no, I haven't seen her."

"Were you here last night?"

"Yesterday was my day off. I already told the police all of this."

"Sorry, I'm just worried."

"She never came down here. I think you're wasting your time, but go where you want."

"I appreciate it."

Nick walked through the room. He opened a few closet doors, looked under the tables, and scanned a few rows of shelves. He looked everywhere for any sign of Lucy and came up with nothing. She was obviously not here. "Thanks for letting me intrude."

"For what it's worth, I didn't like her, but I hope you find her. She is good for this library and has a real knack for it." Harold turned and had an air of sadness about him.

"Thanks." Nick started up the stairs. He stopped halfway and came back down. "You wouldn't happen to have any ideas of places in the library someone might hide."

"You think she is playing hide and go seek?"

Nick offered a patient smile. "I was just wondering if she hurt herself somewhere and might need help."

Harold thought momentarily, and a look of recognition came across his face. "You know. Now that you mention it, there might be a few. We used to have storage rooms upstairs, but when Lucy came in, she didn't use them and put shelves in front of the doors. I guess she could have squeezed into one of those."

"You mind showing me?"

"I guess." He wiped his hands on a towel and started to the stairs. He waved Nick up. "Let's get moving.

Harold led him through the first floor and up the stairs to the second. The far wall, with no windows, was lined with shelves. He approached the far left and stopped. "Look."

Nick followed Harold's motion and instantly saw what he missed in his search. The carpet at the corner has been torn. The shelf has been pulled out and ripped the rug. Harold pulled it from the wall with a strong grunt. The door matched the color of the wall, which helped it hide. Nick turned the handle, and the door opened in.

Harold reached in and flipped on a wall switch. There, slumped in a fancy leather armchair, was Lucy Brooks, motionless and unresponsive.

"Lucy?" he called out tentatively, his voice cracking with disbelief. "Lucy, can you hear me?"

Nick rushed toward her side, his heart pounding a

frantic rhythm against his chest. His hands trembled as he reached for her wrist, hoping beyond hope that he could find some sign of life. But there was no pulse, no gentle rise and fall of her chest, nothing but the eerie stillness that goes with death.

"Lucy... no, this can't be happening," Nick murmured, tears welling up in his eyes. He fumbled for his phone, dialing 911 and blurting out the situation, his voice heavy with grief as he desperately tried to revive her. "Please, Lucy, wake up! Stay with me!"

As he pressed his shaking hands against her chest, attempting CPR despite the sinking feeling in his gut, Nick couldn't help but think about how wrong this scene felt. Lucy, the vibrant, passionate book woman who had quickly become a dear friend since his arrival in Sweet Sea, couldn't possibly be gone forever. It was an idea he simply couldn't accept. First, his wife, and now her.

"Come on, Lucy!" he urged, his mind racing through memories of their late-night conversations and shared laughter over worn-out copies of their favorite books. "You've got more stories to tell, more mysteries to solve. Don't leave me now!"

But in spite of his desperate pleas and frantic attempts at resuscitation, Lucy's body remained limp and unresponsive.

As Nick finally slumped back in defeat, his mind raced with questions and suspicions.

"Who could have done this to you?" he whispered, his eyes scanning the room for any signs of foul play. "And why?"

Harold stood motionless. He didn't have an answer or idea.

As the sirens drew closer, signaling the imminent arrival of the authorities, Nick's resolve hardened. He would not let Lucy's death go unexplained. No matter what it took, he would uncover the truth behind her untimely demise – even if it meant challenging those who would dismiss his concerns as mere grief-stricken paranoia.

"I'll go get the sheriff when they get here," Harold said and left from the room.

"Lucy," Nick vowed softly, fingers brushing against her cold hand one last time, "I promise, I won't rest until I find out what happened to you. Your story doesn't end here."

And with that solemn oath, Nick braced himself for the storm about to descend upon Sweet Sea.

Nick stepped out of the hidden room. He wasn't sure if it was shock, but he couldn't focus. Once a sanctuary, the library now stretched out around him like a cavernous tomb. Its towering bookshelves seemed to close in on him, each volume a silent witness to the tragedy unfolding within its walls. Swallowing hard, he attempted to steady himself, taking in the sound of faint footsteps echoing from below.

"Focus," Nick whispered to himself. He stepped back into the room, trying to channel his inner detective as he surveyed the scene before him. "Damn it. Show me what I'm missing. Give me a clue, a sign...anything," he muttered under his breath, frustration mounting as he studied everything in the room again. He needed answers, and he needed them fast - before the authorities arrived and whisked Lucy's body away, leaving nothing but cold silence in her wake.

His eyes darted back and forth, scanning the shelves and boxes for any anomaly that might provide a hint of foul play. But try as he might, he found no trace of an intruder, no evidence of struggle or malice. Nick's heart pounded in his ears - a cacophonous rhythm that drowned out the silence of the library. His thoughts raced as he knelt by her side, searching for any clue that might reveal the truth behind her untimely demise. The sound of footsteps approaching sent a jolt through his body, stirring him from his reverie.

"Step back, sir," a firm voice commanded. Turning his gaze to the entrance, Nick watched as the sheriff and another officer strode into the room, their eyes sharp and alert. He hesitated momentarily, then reluctantly stepped away from Lucy's lifeless form.

"Deputy Reynolds," The sheriff nodded curtly toward her partner. "Secure the scene while I examine the body." A flurry of activity ensued as the police set about their tasks, efficiently taping off the perimeter and scanning the room for clues.

"Did you find her like this?" the sheriff asked, turning to Nick. Her tone was authoritative but not unkind, betraying a hint of empathy beneath the professional veneer. "Y-yes," Nick stammered, his voice still shaky from the shock. "I was looking for her, and Harold helped me discover a hidden room, and we found her...like this."

"Was she alone when you arrived?" she pressed.

"Yes," Nick replied, feeling an icy chill creep up his spine. "There wasn't a soul in sight."

"Understood," the Sherriff nodded, making a note in her notepad. "Please wait outside while we conduct our investigation. We'll come to get you if we have further questions."

Nick hesitated, torn between his desire to stay and his obligation to cooperate. Finally, he acquiesced, stepping out of the hidden room and into the cold embrace of the hallway beyond.

The library seemed to shrink as the officers examined Lucy's body. The once-cozy space now transformed into a cold and clinical crime scene. Nick's skin prickled with unease as he watched them work, their fingers deftly collecting samples of hair, skin, and fibers from her clothing.

"Her nails," Deputy Reynolds muttered, peering closely at Lucy's hands. "There are traces of something beneath them. Bag it up for analysis."

"Right," the sheriff agreed, carefully scraping the substance onto a glass slide, and then dropping that into an evidence bag. "It could be nothing, but we can't rule anything out at this stage."

As they continued their investigation, Nick couldn't help but feel an unsettling sense of intrusion, as though the officers' very presence was violating the sanctity of the library itself. Despite this, he knew that their expertise was crucial if he were to uncover the truth about Lucy's death and so, with a heavy heart, he waited in silence as they scrutinized every inch of the room. And yet, he knew that he wouldn't – couldn't – simply stand by and wait for someone else to uncover the truth.

"Sheriff," he called out, unable to contain his curiosity any longer. "Have you found anything?"

"Nothing conclusive," she replied, her expression grave. "But we'll need to run some tests before we can say for sure."

"Tests," Nick echoed, the word settling like lead in his

stomach. In his mind's eye, he saw the countless hours of testing and analysis stretched out before him, each one a barrier between him and the answers he so desperately sought. "Thank you," he said, his voice barely audible. "Please...let me know if you find anything."

"If we can," the sheriff assured him, offering a small, reassuring smile. "We'll get to the bottom of this, I promise."

Yet as he stood there in the dimly lit hallway, surrounded by the ghosts of stories untold, Nick couldn't shake the gnawing suspicion that Lucy's demise was no ordinary tragedy - and that somewhere within the library's hallowed walls, a secret lay hidden, waiting to be uncovered.

Nick ventured, "Do you have any working theories regarding Ms. Brooks' cause of death?"

Sheriff Joan Kent paused, rubbing a hand over her chin thoughtfully. "Well, Mr. Cern, from what we can see thus far, there's nothing obviously suspicious. It's quite possible she suffered a heart attack or stroke."

"Her complexion is rather pale, which could suggest some sort of cardiovascular event," Deputy Reynolds added, his tone clinical but not unkind.

Nick couldn't help but furrow his brow at their words, feeling an innate sense of disquiet. He knew Lucy had been cautious in her later years, but he also couldn't shake the feeling that something just wasn't right. "I don't know," he muttered, more to himself than to the officers. "Something just feels... off."

"Mr. Cern, I assure you, our team and the state police labs will do everything in our power to determine the true nature of Ms. Brooks' passing," the sheriff said, her voice firm yet compassionate. "However, it's important not to jump to conclusions until we have all the facts."

"Of course, I understand," Nick replied, nodding in agreement even as doubt continued to swirl in his thoughts. "I just... I want to make sure we don't overlook anything."

"Rest assured, we may be a small town in California, but we'll be thorough in our investigation," Deputy Reynolds chimed in, his gaze steady and reassuring. "But for now, the most likely explanation is a natural cause of death."

As Nick listened to the officers discuss their initial theories, he couldn't help but feel a growing sense of unease. The library, once a haven filled with a comforting scent and the soft whispers of turning pages, now felt tainted by the specter of death. And despite the officers' assurances, he couldn't quell the nagging suspicion that there was more to Lucy's demise than met the eye.

"Thank you, both," he said quietly, his voice barely audible as the weight of uncertainty pressed down upon him.

"I appreciate your diligence."

"You're welcome, Mr. Cern," the sheriff replied, her eyes reflecting a glimmer of understanding. "We'll do our best to find the answers you seek."

"May I have a private word with you?" Nick asked, his voice trembling ever so slightly.

"We are busy here."

"Please. It might be crucial."

"Sure, Mr. Cern," she replied, glancing at her deputy before stepping away from Lucy's chair to join Nick near the imposing mahogany desk that dominated the center of the library. The soft creaking of the floorboards beneath their feet punctuated the eerie silence that had settled over the room like a shroud.

"Lucy was in her early 70's," Nick began, swallowing hard as the words caught in his throat. "She had been struggling with high blood pressure for some time now and took medication for it. She had a few other medicines but was in great health. Walked a few miles a day. She was a fighter – always determined to overcome her ailments and live life to the fullest."

The sheriff nodded, her eyes narrowing in thought. "That certainly adds another layer to this puzzle. Did she have any other medical issues we should be aware of?"

"No, not that I'm aware of," Nick admitted, a heavy sigh escaping his lips. "And apart from her health concerns, she led a rather active existence. A librarian, Lucy lived alone, surrounded by her beloved books. She had a few friends, aside from myself and the occasional book lover."

"Thank you for sharing that information, Mr. Cern," the sheriff responded, mentally noting the details. "Every little bit helps in cases like these."

"Could it have been something more sinister than a natural death?" Nick asked quietly, his voice barely more than a whisper.

Sheriff Kent regarded him solemnly, the weight of her own experience evident in her eyes. "At this stage, Mr. Cern, we must consider all possibilities. And rest assured, we will leave no stone unturned in our quest for answers. But I really need to get back to this."

"Yes, of course."

The sheriff made eye contact with Nick. "I would like to reiterate my previous statement. Leave the investigation to us."

"Thank you," Nick replied, his voice laced with steely determination. As the shadows deepened within the library, so too did his resolve to unravel the mystery surrounding Lucy's death – whatever the cost.

The library, now bathed in the soft glow of sunset, seemed to take on a darker, more somber tone as the officers methodically moved through the room. Their experienced eyes scanned every inch of the space, searching for any clues that might suggest foul play had been involved in Lucy's untimely demise. He could tell they were rapping up.

Nick found himself pacing the length of the ornate wooden desk that dominated the center of the second floor, his hands gripping its polished surface as if seeking solace in its familiar solidity. He couldn't help but feel a gnawing sense of helplessness.

"Mr. Cern," the sheriff said, approaching Nick with a solemn expression, "We've completed our search, and it appears there are no signs of trauma to the body or wounds from a struggle. It seems likely that Lucy passed away due to natural causes, most likely a heart attack. But as I said, we will wait for the toxicology and other reports."

"Is that so?" Nick asked, his voice tight with restrained emotion. "Well, I suppose that's a relief, in one sense." He paused, his gaze drifting towards Lucy's lifeless form in the armchair. "But it still doesn't sit right with me," he murmured, almost to himself.

"Understandably," she replied, her tone gentle yet firm. "But we must follow the evidence, Mr. Cern. Our next steps will be to notify Lucy's family and arrange for her body to be transported to the morgue for further examination."

"I get it," Nick replied, nodding stiffly. "I understand that you must do your job, and I appreciate your thoroughness." As the officers moved to finish their investigation, Nick's mind raced with thoughts of Lucy.

"Sheriff Kent," Nick said suddenly, his voice filled with determination. "You may not find any evidence of foul play here, but I can't shake the feeling that there's more to Lucy's death than meets the eye. No matter where it leads me, I intend to uncover the truth."

"Mr. Cern," the sheriff replied, her eyes reflecting a mixture of empathy and resolve. "We'll do our best to bring closure to this case. But sometimes, life is full of mysteries that have no easy answers. I have already told you to stay out of this. Be smart."

"What did you say?" Nick asked. His mind reeled from the last statement.

"Be smart?"

"Did you send the message?"

The sheriff seemed confused and annoyed at the same time. He had just about used up the last of her patience. He was becoming a distraction and nuisance, and he knew it. "What message?"

"Nothing," Nick said, his gaze fixed on the half-empty glass of water still beside Lucy's open book. "But if there's one thing I've learned from my time with Lucy, it's that every story has an ending, and I won't rest until I've found hers."

"Do you have any other evidence?" the sheriff asked. "I don't need you impeding this investigation. You may have been a friend, but you are not a member of this police force and need to stay out of it. Is that clear?"

He shook his head.

"I need a verbal confirmation out of you."

"I understand. I'm sorry. You have been very patient with me. I will leave."

As Nick watched the sheriff go back to work, his mind raced with a torrent of thoughts and emotions. Grief, confusion, and an unshakable sense of unease churned within him like a maelstrom. He couldn't shake the feeling that there was more to Lucy's death than a simple heart attack or stroke – that some hidden truth lay buried beneath the surface, waiting to be uncovered.

CHAPTER SIX

Nick sat alone in his dimly lit bedroom, the shadows on the walls flickering as cars randomly passed by outside the drapes. His hands shook with an uncontrollable tremor, a physical manifestation of the storm brewing inside him. He thought he was past this, but with Lucy's death, the weight of his grief seemed to grow heavier, pressing down on him like a boulder threatening to crush him beneath its unforgiving mass. He tried desperately to distract himself, fidgeting with the frayed edge of his shirt cuff and picking at the worn material of his bed spread.

"Damn it," he whispered under his breath, his voice barely audible above the deafening roar of his own thoughts.

His eyes darted around the room, finally resting on

the bottle of pills that lay tauntingly on the mahogany side table, a reminder of a dark past he'd sworn never to revisit. The temptation gnawed at the edges of his resolve, like a rat hungrily chewing through a rope.

"Maybe just one," Nick mumbled, reaching for the bottle. "Just one to take the edge off."

As his fingers brushed against the cool glass of water next to the bottle, memories of his wife's last days flooded his mind, washing over him like a tidal wave. He saw her pale, gaunt face, her once luscious locks reduced to thin wisps of hair clinging stubbornly to her scalp. He remembered the way she'd managed a weak smile as he'd entered the sterile hospital room, her hand trembling in his as they'd prepared to say their final goodbyes.

"Nick, promise me you'll be strong," she had said, her voice barely more than a whisper. "Don't let this break you."

He'd nodded, tears streaming down his face, unable to speak as the lump in his throat threatened to choke him. Her eyes, once bright and full of life, had dulled like the embers of a dying fire as the cancer consumed her, merciless and unyielding.

"Promise me," she'd repeated, her grip on his hand tightening for a fleeting moment before falling limp. And just like that, she was gone.

"Damn it," Nick said again, his knuckles turning white as he clenched his fists in frustration. The memory of his wife's last moments lingered in the air around him like a phantom, a silent witness to his anguish.

"I promised you," he said softly, his voice cracking with emotion. "I promised I'd be strong and I screwed that up. I'm so sorry. The drug addiction, the drinking, and more importantly forcing our daughters to deal with this grief without their dad there to hold them. I promised you."

He stared at the bottle of pills, now feeling more like a venomous snake coiled and ready to strike than the temporary relief he'd sought. They were a relic of darker days, when grief had left him grasping for any means of escape, no matter how temporary. He felt the familiar urge to reach for them, to dull the pain that still clawed at his heart. With a sudden surge of anger, he snatched the bottle from the table and hurled it across the room, watching as it bounced against the wall popping off the lid, scattering its contents like so many broken dreams.

"I don't need you anymore," he declared, his voice strong and resolute. "I am stronger than you."

Nick closed his eyes.

"Never again," he vowed, his eyes shining with a fierce determination that had been absent for far too long. "For you, my love, I will be strong."

He picked up the picture sitting on the bed next to him. He stared at the framed photo of his wife that occupied a place of honor on his bed side table. Her infectious smile seemed to leap from the glass, radiating warmth and love even after her untimely passing. As he traced the curve of her cheek with his finger, memories of their life together flooded his mind.

"Remember the time we got lost during our hike in the mountains?" Nick said to himself, as if speaking to his departed wife. "We ended up stumbling upon that breathtaking waterfall, and you insisted on skinny dipping. God, you were fearless."

A soft chuckle escaped his lips as he recalled her laughter ringing through the air, the sun casting a golden halo around her as she frolicked in the water. It was moments like these that had made their life together so rich, so magical.

"Or that time when we went to that godawful murder mystery dinner party," he continued, his eyes crinkling at the corners as he smiled at the memory. "You figured out who the 'killer' was within the first ten minutes, and then spent the rest of the night dropping increasingly absurd hints to the other guests, just to watch them squirm."

It wasn't lost on him that he now found himself embroiled in a real-life mystery, one that threatened to consume him if he didn't uncover the truth about Lucy's death. The irony was a bitter pill to swallow.

But then he thought of Lucy, sweet, enigmatic Lucy, who had gently but persistently coaxed him from the depths of despair with her love for literature and her unwavering faith in his ability to heal. The countless hours they'd spent together in the library, sharing stories and laughter, had gradually mended the gaping wound left by his wife's death.

"Lucy," he whispered fiercely, gripping the bottle tightly. "You helped me find my way back to the land of the living. And now it's my turn to help you."

He knew, without a shadow of a doubt, that the months of friendship with Lucy had forever altered the course of his life. She had given him the strength to face his demons head-on and emerge victorious, and for that, he would be eternally grateful.

As he gazed at the wreckage of pills strewn across the floor, Nick felt something within him shift, an awakening, a renewed sense of purpose. He was no longer a man paralyzed by grief and addiction. He was a survivor, a fighter, and he would stop at nothing to bring Lucy home safely.

His eyes closed and without control, fell back on the bed.

◆ ◆ ◆

The cold, damp earth clung to Nick's shoes as he stood beneath the overcast sky, the relentless drizzle coating his suit and mingling with the tears that streamed down his cheeks. He could still feel the comforting weight of Bridget and Kaley's hands on each of his shoulders, their shared grief a bittersweet reminder of the love that held them together even in the darkest of times.

"Thank you all for coming," he said, his voice just audible enough to be heard above the somber melody of the raindrops striking the canopy of umbrellas that surrounded him. "My wife... she was an extraordinary woman, full of life and laughter, and I know she would have been touched by your presence here today."

"Here, Dad," Bridget murmured, handing him a tissue as Kaley squeezed his arm reassuringly. "It's okay. We're here for you."

"Thank you, sweetheart." Nick dabbed at his eyes, struggling to maintain his composure as the funeral director signaled for the proceedings to begin. With heavy hearts, they watched as the casket was lowered into the ground, the finality of the moment hitting them like a physical blow.

"Rest in peace, my love," Nick whispered, before turning to his daughters, their faces a mirror image of his own grief-stricken expression. They embraced, seeking solace in one another as the dozens of mourners dispersed, leaving them to their private agony.

As they walked away from the gravesite, Nick couldn't help but think of life without her. What was he going to do? He would never love again. Maybe everyone would be better if he was dead as well. He could do it quite easily. Get a gun, a rope, or hell, even some chemicals from under the sink might do. He looked left, then right. His daughters faces, streaming with tears and makeup, looked up at him. He couldn't leave them without any parents.

◆ ◆ ◆

Suddenly, Nick was awake. The vivid memories of those final moments still lingering from the dream. He sat up on the bed, not remembering falling asleep. Exhaustion must have overtaken him. Lucy Brooks stood in front of him. Her warm smile like a beacon of hope amidst the storm of his despair. She had been there for him in a way that few others had, providing comfort and consolation through their shared love for books and literature.

Nick blinked repeatedly, not believing his eyes, and said, "Lucy."

She was gone. His imagination taking over momentarily. The thought of her sudden death gnawed at him like a ravenous beast, threatening to consume what little peace he'd managed to find since his wife's passing.

"Who would kill her?" he wondered aloud, his voice tinged with a mixture of anger and fear. "Why Lucy, of all people?"

Nick stood and walked into the hallway. He stared at his reflection in the hallway mirror. The lines on his face seemed to have softened, as if the weight of the world had been lifted from his weary shoulders. "I won't stop until I uncover the truth about what happened to you."

He turned away from the mirror and strode down the hallway, each step imbued with newfound determination. As he walked, memories of Lucy played like a highlight reel in his mind—her laughter echoing through the library's vast expanse, the glint of mischief in her eyes as she recounted tales of her mysterious past.

CHAPTER SEVEN

Nick Cern stood in the silence of the Sweet Sea Library, his fingertips brushing against the spines of books Lucy had once cared for with such tenderness. A cool draft whispered through the empty aisles, carrying with it the faint scent of ink and age. The dim overhead lights did little to dispel the shadows that clung to every corner, creating a somber atmosphere that weighed heavily on Nick's heart. It had been three days since he discovered Lucy's body, and he had spent that time reading the book she listed in her email. It took place near the town, but beyond that, it seemed a poorly written murder mystery.

"Lucy," he murmured, his voice barely audible. His hair hung over his furrowed brow as he struggled to reconcile the senseless loss of his dear friend. Grief threatened to consume him, but the spark of determination in his chest kept him from drowning – the unshakeable belief that there was more to Lucy's death than met the eye.

As he wandered further into the library, Nick's eyes fell upon his watch. He had twenty minutes before he had to open up the shop. It would be plenty of time. He knew exactly what he was looking for.

Approaching Lucy's desk, he was happy no one was around, especially Susan. It would be tough to explain to the assistant librarian why he was at the desk. He knelt down behind it and tried the bottom right drawer. As expected, it was locked. He brought a tool in anticipation of this. Nick pulled out a thin metal rod that was about the length of a new pencil. Sliding it between the drawer and the cubby it was in, he jiggled it around until he felt the satisfying click of the lock disengaging.

The only thing in the drawer was a small, worn leather notebook tucked between two dusty books. He recognized it as Lucy's personal journal, a treasure trove of her thoughts and musings. He hesitated momentarily, torn between respecting her privacy and the nagging suspicion that clawed at his conscience.

"Forgive me, Lucy," he whispered, retrieving the journal,

and flipping through its delicate pages. The words seemed to dance across the paper, revealing a side of the enigmatic librarian he'd never known. There were hints of a rough past, something she'd been trying to leave behind, and the ideas comprising her new novel. The story was about a former addict solving a small town murder. Was it based on him?

Nick's thoughts raced with the fervor of his former addiction. It was a familiar sensation, one he'd fought hard to keep at bay. Yet now, it served as a driving force urging him to dig deeper, to question everything he thought he knew about Lucy Brooks.

"Mr. Cern?" a deputy called out, startling Nick. He hastily closed the journal and slipped it into his jacket pocket. "What are you doing back there?"

"Deputy, how are you?"

"I asked you a question."

"What do you mean? I'm just sitting here."

"Come on. Spill it."

"I don't believe Lucy's death was an accident," Nick confessed, his words tumbling out in a torrent of emotion. "There's something amiss here, and I need to find out what happened."

"Sir, I understand your grief, but the case was just closed. We have the tests back, and the Medical Examiner's office

known Lucy well enough to shed light on her final days. He knew that solving this case meant more than just fulfilling a promise to a dear friend; it could prevent another tragedy from occurring if there was a murderer on the loose. But as he considered the potential consequences of getting involved, the danger he could be putting himself in, the scrutiny he might face from law enforcement, and the risk of dredging up memories of his own demons. Nick steeled himself, knowing that justice for Lucy was worth any price. He hadn't known her for very long, but the connection was deep and hard to articulate. She had become his best friend.

"Pardon me," Nick approached an elderly man with a bushy white mustache, "do you have a moment?"

"Of course, young man," the man replied, looking at Nick curiously.

"Could you tell me if you knew Lucy Brooks? She was the head librarian at the town library."

"Ah, yes, sweet Lucy," the man sighed. "I used to see her every Saturday at the farmer's market. Terrible what happened to her. So unexpected."

"Did you ever notice anything unusual about her behavior or anyone she associated with?" Nick asked, trying to sound casual despite his racing heart.

"Can't say I did. She was always so friendly, but quiet.

Kept to herself mostly." The man hesitated.

"Was there something?" Nick asked.

"Not a person. I was just thinking. Sometimes her tone can be a bit rough. It wasn't what she said but how she said it. I guess that could have upset some people."

"Yeah. I have heard that. Thank you for your time," Nick said, shaking hands with the man before moving on to the next person.

His persistence led him to speak to dozens of townspeople, each conversation slowly building a picture of Lucy's life in Sweet Sea. He learned of her love for gardening, her penchant for baking cookies to share with patrons of the library, and her mysterious aura that captivated everyone who met her. Several mentioned her tone, but no anger about it. Yet no one seemed to know anything about her potential enemies, leaving Nick frustrated but undeterred.

He sat on a bench beneath a towering oak tree, its leaves dripping with rainwater, and let out a ragged breath. He knew the road to justice would be long and winding, but he was determined to follow it to the end. His eyes stared into the distance as if willing a clue to appear.

"Excuse me," a voice interrupted his thoughts, causing Nick to look up in surprise. The woman before him looked to be in her early fifties, her hair swept back into a messy bun and her eyes filled with concern. "You're the man asking about Lucy, right?"

"Y-Yes," Nick stuttered, taken aback by her sudden appearance. Growing up and living his life in a big city, he was still amazed at how fast news traveled in a small town. He fought the urge to ask how she heard and, instead, focused on gathering any new details. "Do you have any information that could help me?"

"Maybe," she hesitated. "But first, tell me why you're so invested in finding out what happened to her. I heard it was natural causes."

"Lucy was my friend," Nick replied solemnly. "I believe she was murdered, and I won't rest until her killer is brought to justice." He stared at the woman, his gaze unwavering.

The woman nodded slowly, understanding flickering in her eyes. "I saw her a few days before she died. She seemed nervous like she was being watched. I don't know who or what she was scared of, but maybe it's worth looking into."

"Thank you," Nick said gratefully, his heart pounding with renewed hope. "This might be just the lead I need."

The woman left, and Nick stepped into his store to help a customer. When he returned to the sidewalk, an old man sat on a bench. However, he didn't notice him at first. Instead, his deep thought made him oblivious to all around him.

"Hey there," a raspy voice said, drawing Nick's attention back to his surroundings. An elderly man, his face weathered and lined like an old map, stood up before him. "I couldn't help but overhear your conversation before you popped into the shop. I might have some information about Lucy if you're interested."

"Please," Nick urged, his eyes bright with curiosity. "Tell me everything you know. Don't leave out any detail."

"Lucy was afraid of someone," the man whispered, his gaze darting around the street nervously. "I'd see her looking over her shoulder when she walked to her car at night. She confided in me once that she had a secret, something she believed someone would kill to keep hidden. She was going to the police, but wanted to give the guy a little time to do the right thing."

"Did she say who?" Nick asked, his voice tense with anticipation.

"No," the man replied, shaking his head. "She said that she had argued with him a few times over in the café. Maybe somewhere there might know. But one thing's for sure, whoever it is, they're dangerous. You need to be careful, son. Chasing shadows can get you killed."

"Thank you," Nick said, his determination unwavering. "I'll be cautious. But I owe it to Lucy to find out what happened to her."

"Good luck," the man murmured as he shuffled away, leaving Nick to contemplate his next move.

Nick's determination grew stronger with each conversation, every scrap of evidence gathered, and the whispers of a secret that haunted Lucy. His time was limited as he kept stepping into his store to help people, but he would leave no stone unturned.

CHAPTER EIGHT

Nick hunched over his notes in the dimly lit corner of his apartment, his brow furrowed as he struggled to piece together the puzzle. The steam from his coffee cup rose before him like wisps of fog, obscuring his vision momentarily. Frustration gnawed at him, and he could feel the weight of it pressing down upon his shoulders.

"Damn it," he muttered under his breath, rubbing his temples. Just when he thought he had a promising lead, another obstacle would rear its ugly head. Some people refused to talk, while others gave conflicting accounts that only served to muddy the waters further. There were two groups of people in town, those that liked Lucy and those that did not. There was no in-between.

A sudden chime from his laptop jolted Nick from his musings. Recognizing the sound of an incoming video call, he quickly crossed the room and opened the laptop. Bridget and Kaley's smiling faces filled the screen, their youthful exuberance a stark contrast to the somber atmosphere that had enveloped him in recent days.

"Hey, Dad." Nick glanced up to see Bridget's face on his phone screen, her smile warm and reassuring. "How's the investigation going?"

"Slowly," he admitted, trying to hide the weariness in his voice. "I'm running into a lot of dead ends."

"Remember, we're here for you," Kaley chimed in, her image appearing next to Bridget's on the screen. Her blond hair, blue eyes, and facial structure made her almost a twin to her mother. "If you need to vent or just want someone to bounce ideas off, we're only a call away."

"Thanks, girls," Nick said, his heart swelling with appreciation. "Your support means everything to me."

"Promise us you'll take care of yourself, though," Bridget added, her eyes filled with concern. "You can't help Lucy if you're not taking care of your own well-being."

Nick nodded. "I promise."

"How are you doing with the other challenges," Kaley asked. She twirled her hair around one of her fingers, and her eyes darted left to right. "You look tired."

"I'm doing okay, honey," Nick replied. "This investigation has given me little time to think about anything else."

"Of course," Bridget agreed, exchanging a knowing glance with her sister. "But you have to remember to take care of yourself too, Dad. We worry about you. And when you say, okay to that question, it's sort of too vague."

Nick let out a deep breath. "I often still see your mom in my dreams, but I have not been driven to stress reduction with substances. Just my anti-depressants as prescribed."

Both girls smiled and, in unison, said, "That's great. Promise us you'll take a break tonight."

"All right, girls," Nick conceded, touched by their unwavering support. "I promise."

"Good," Bridget said firmly, a look of relief crossing her face. "And remember, we're always here for you, no matter what."

"Thank you," Nick said, his heart swelling with love and gratitude for his daughters. "Well, I'd better get back to it."

"Wait, Dad, before you go," Bridget interjected, her eyes glinting playfully. "You didn't think we'd forget your birthday, did you?"

"Ah," Nick said, momentarily caught off guard by the

mention of his own birthday. Amid the investigation, he had lost track of the date. "I suppose I did."

"Happy birthday, Dad!" Kaley chimed in, her voice vibrating with warmth.

"Thank you, girls," Nick replied, a smile unfurling across his face as he soaked in their love and concern. He felt an unexpected spark of joy in the midst of his emotional turmoil.

"Look what we sent you!" Bridget added, holding up a picture of a vibrantly wrapped package to the screen. "It should arrive tomorrow."

"Really? You shouldn't have," Nick insisted, but his curiosity was piqued.

"It's no big deal, Dad," Kaley assured him, her lips curling into a knowing grin. "Just something to help take your mind off things when you need it most."

"Thank you," Nick said again, inwardly touched by their thoughtfulness. They truly were his rock, even from afar.

"All right," Bridget said, lowering the gift from view. "We'll let you get back to it now. But remember our promise, okay?"

"Of course," Nick agreed. "I'll take that break tonight, I promise."

"Love you, Dad," Kaley whispered, her eyes glimmering affectionately.

"Love you too," Bridget added, matching her sister's sentiment.

"Love you both so very much," Nick responded, emotion thickening his voice.

As the call ended and their faces disappeared from the screen, he stared at the now dark screen, feeling both grateful for his daughters' unwavering support and burdened by the knowledge that he must succeed, not just for Lucy but for the sake of his own family. The weight of the investigation bore down on him even more, but Nick refused to let it break him. He would face every obstacle head-on, fortified by the love and support of his daughters. He couldn't let her death cause a relapse in him. The girls did not deserve it. They had encouraged him to move to Sweet Sea, believing that a fresh start would help him heal from the loss of their mother. Instead, it seemed as though he had only traded one heartache for another.

Nick stood and walked to the window, rubbing his temples as he stared out at the darkening sky. The rain had moved on, and the clear sky was full of stars. The investigation had consumed him to the point where his once lean physique looked gaunter, and the circles under his eyes deepened with each passing day.

"Damn it," Nick muttered under his breath, the

frustration simmering just beneath the surface. Despite countless interviews and late nights pouring over evidence, he was no closer to finding Lucy's killer. He couldn't shake the feeling that he was missing something crucial—something that would break this case wide open. The idea of her death being natural and the medical examiner being correct started seeping through the cracks between his thoughts. His obsession with this death was starting to scare himself. What the hell was wrong with him, he thought. He took in a deep and relaxed breath.

"Happy birthday, Nick," he whispered to himself, feeling the weight of his daughters' support propelling him forward. With the support of his daughters buoying him, Nick dove back into the investigation, his resolve as unyielding as the crashing waves outside his window. "Let's crack this case wide open."

CHAPTER NINE

A ticking clock echoed through the dimly lit kitchen, casting long, eerie shadows randomly on the walls. Nick Cern sat slumped at the worn oak table, his hair disheveled from repeatedly running his hands through it. The weight of grief and frustration had settled in the lines on his face, which were etched even deeper now as he frowned at the journal before him. He had been at it all night and was surprised to see the sun rising.

"Lucy, what have you gotten yourself into?" he said to himself, his voice barely audible above the ticking. His gaze lingered on one page of her diary. He wondered if he should share the book with the sheriff, but knew it would probably not do much good. The police refused to take her death more seriously and seemed uninterested in anything beyond their cursory investigation. Plus, they already said there was no foul play involved. It wasn't enough for Nick; he needed answers.

He rifled through the diary again, quickly scanning for anything that could help. His fingers lingered on a page. It stood out among the rest. A few paragraphs told him she had updated her will, dated just a few weeks before her death. As he read the contents, his eyebrows shot up in surprise. The page went on to say that the will stated that Lucy had left everything to the town's historical society – an inexplicable move for someone who had previously intended to distribute her wealth among various charities and organizations.

"Odd," he said aloud, rereading the document to make sure he hadn't misinterpreted the words. But there it was, in black and white – all her worldly possessions would go to the historical society. It didn't make sense to him. She had never mentioned any particular fondness for the group or any reason to drastically change her will. "Lucy," he said softly. "Why did you send me that email? What were you trying to tell me? Does it have to do with your will?"

He sat there for a moment, the gears turning in his head as he tried to piece together a possible explanation. He knew Lucy well enough to know that she must have had a reason for such an abrupt change, but was it connected to her untimely death? He stood and paced the kitchen floor, the worn linoleum creaking beneath his feet as he muttered to himself. He did his best thinking on his feet.

"Lucy wouldn't have changed her will for no reason," he said out loud, his voice echoing off the yellowed tiles. "And why give everything to the historical society?"

He stopped pacing and stared at the diary, taking a deep breath. If the police wouldn't help, he'd have to take matters into his own hands. He remembered her mentioning a nephew nearby. Maybe talking to him would help bring some clarity. Somebody had to draw up the will. They could help as well.

Nick sat back down at the table, grabbing a pen and a legal pad. He began scribbling names and contact information, starting with finding Lucy's lawyer. It was probably Mr. Denton, the only lawyer in town. Surely, he'd have some idea why she had made such a drastic change to her will.

"Next, the historical society members," he mused, tapping the pen against his chin. He recalled meeting a few of them at town events, but he didn't know them well enough to gauge their potential motives. "I'll need to pay them a visit too."

His pen flew across the page as he jotted down names, capturing every possible person to talk with. Nick's thoughts turned inward, reflecting on his bond with Lucy. She had been more than just a friend to him; she had been his confidante, inspiration, and guiding light through the darkest time in his life. She helped him ease out of this grief.

Satisfied with his cryptic list, Nick jumped in the shower and got ready for work. The rising sun told him he had no more than two hours before he had to open. Once at the shop, he would continue to brainstorm between customers.

◆ ◆ ◆

The day had not yielded any new clues. Plus, the steady flow of customers prevented him from venturing to talk to the people he had listed. The sun was now setting, casting long shadows across the shop floor and bathing Nick's workspace in a warm, golden glow. He could hear the distant sound of the ocean waves crashing against the shore, a soothing backdrop to his racing thoughts. As he prepared to wrap up the day, the door chime jingled, announcing the arrival of a customer.

"Good evening," Nick said, keeping his voice steady as he looked up from his notepad. "How can I help you?"

"Hi there," the customer replied, a middle-aged woman with a look of desperation etched across her face. "I dropped my phone, and now it won't turn on. I have all my important data on there – photos, contacts, everything. Can you help me get it back?"

"Of course," Nick assured her, momentarily pushing aside his investigation to focus on the task at hand. "Let me take a look."

He took the cracked phone from the woman and began assessing the damage, expertly unscrewing the back panel as he engaged her in conversation.

"Have you had any issues with your phone before this?" he asked, glancing up at her briefly before returning his attention to the device.

"No, not really," she hesitated. "The battery life has been getting worse lately, but I think that's normal for an older phone like mine."

"Probably," Nick agreed, mentally noting the correlation between Lucy's sudden change of will and her tragic demise. He wondered if there were any connections he had yet to uncover. He carefully removed parts with practiced hands and replaced them with spares from his stock. He replaced the screen and turned it on. It came to life.

"Your phone should be good to go now. Although it looks like you may have lost some data," he announced, handing it back to the grateful woman. "Do you happen to back it up?"

"I don't," she said sheepishly.

"Well, for the data, I'll need to connect it to my system and see if I can recover anything."

"Thank you so much," she said, relief washing over her features. "I can't tell you how important those files are to me."

As Nick connected the phone to his computer and began the data recovery process, he couldn't help but consider his own situation. Like this woman's precious files, the answers he looked for were locked away in the minds of the townsfolk – hidden behind smiles and small talk.

"My name is Nick," he said, making small talk while the system did what it could for the phone's data.

"I'm Eunice Edwards," she said. "I own the antique store a few doors down."

"I have been meaning to go in there. Just never seemed to find the time."

"Really. Anything you looking for?"

"Nah, just to browse. You never know what gems can be found in the stuff of yesterday."

She smiled. "I'm going to steal that line if it's okay.

"Sure, have at it."

"Thanks. The Historical Society needs a catchy slogan."

"Do you work with them?" Nick asked.

"I do. I'm the treasurer."

Nick fought back the excitement. He took a deep breath and asked, "Do you mind if I ask you a few questions?"

"Sure."

"Did you know Lucy Brooks?"

"Oh yes." She shook her head knowingly. "Very kind, but an opinionated woman. She is a great friend to the society."

"Was," Nick corrected.

Both her hands shot to her mouth. "Yes, of course. I guess I blocked it out. She will be missed."

"Did she work with the society?"

"She was an esteemed member of the society. She did some work, but mostly she donated things and money. We didn't always see eye to eye, but in the end, it was all about preserving history, and that we could agree on."

"Did you happen to see her in the last week or so?"

"She was at one of the open community meetings. Asked a few questions."

"Anything you can share?"

"Mostly, she was concerned about the society's decision a while back to borrow money against some of the historical buildings we had to fund restorations for. It did not go well."

"Did something happen?"

"Tourist season was down with the pandemic, and we defaulted on a loan, and the bank was going to foreclose on the property. We had to sell a few things to preserve it, and that was not okay with her."

"I don't blame her."

"It isn't ideal," Eunice said. "But who could have predicted a pandemic in 2020? We are close to defaulting on another loan, which got her angry. She just didn't understand that all of the society members were looking for ways to get money to help pay the debt. She expressed her opinion and then...."

The computer chimed.

"Then what?" Nick asked.

"Then she quieted down."

"Anything else?"

Eunice looked down at her phone. "Did you get my data back?"

Nick was going to ask the question again, but "Data recovery complete," chimed from the computer, snapping Nick back to the present. He glanced at the smiling woman beside him and handed her the phone, now brimming with recovered memories.

Nick started to ask the question again but could see the woman was anxious. He looked at the computer. "Looks like it recovered everything."

"Thank you! You've saved me!" she exclaimed, her gratitude evident in the crinkling of her eyes. "I'll be sure to recommend your services to everyone I know. I need to be going. Talk later."

"Much appreciated. Have a great day," Nick replied, his trademark kind smile returning as he watched her leave the shop. The door jingled shut behind her, leaving him alone once more with his thoughts.

He gazed at the now vacant workspace, the lingering scent of solder and burnt wires mingling with the faintest hint of the woman's lavender perfume.   Eunice had helped his investigation, whether she knew it or not. He felt talking to the Historical Society would be a good next step.

"Enough," he said under his breath, halting his pacing, and staring unblinkingly at the list of names before him. "Speculation won't get me anywhere. It's time for action." With that, he reached for his coat draped over the chair, the fabric whispering softly as he slipped it on.

"Lucy's lawyer first," he decided, his voice steady and determined. "Then the historical society members."

As Nick turned the doorknob and stepped into the crisp sea air, he could almost feel Lucy's presence at his side, urging him forward. He knew the journey ahead would be fraught with obstacles, some of which might dredge up memories of his troubled past. He locked the door to his shop and headed out to investigate.

CHAPTER TEN

The law office of Jed Denton was actually not an office at all. It was an old Spanish Colonial House that appeared to have the front section turned into his business. Nick hesitated at the entrance to the office, apprehensive about whether he should knock or just go in. He was never sure when someone's house doubled as their place of business. The door was an enormous slab of dark wood, adorned with a tarnished brass knocker that had seen better days. He decided and gave it three firm raps, releasing a dull echo down the dimly lit hallway behind it.

"Come in!" barked a gruff voice from within.

Nick entered, finding himself in a small, cluttered office. Dusty books lined sagging shelves, and a massive oak desk dominated the room, its surface buried beneath mountains of papers. Behind the desk sat Jed Denton, an elderly gentleman with a furrowed brow and a pair of half-moon spectacles perched on his hawkish nose. His eyes held a certain warmth, however, when they fell upon Nick.

"What do you need?"

"Good afternoon, I was wondering if I could ask you a few questions about a client of yours. A Mrs. Lucy Brooks."

"Ah, Mr. Cern," he said, extending a hand gnarled by age. "Lucy's friend, I presume? She spoke highly of you."

"Thank you, Mr. Denton," replied Nick, shaking the lawyer's hand. "I wish we were meeting under better circumstances."

"Agreed," sighed Denton, leaning back in his chair. "I'm still reeling from the news myself. Lucy was a fine woman and one of my easiest clients."

"Actually, that's why I'm here," began Nick, growing serious. "I was wondering if you had any idea as to why she changed her will so suddenly."

"Ah, yes," said Denton. He stroked his chin thoughtfully, then reached for a manila folder on his desk. "It did strike me as odd, but Lucy seemed determined."

"Did she say anything that might give us a clue?" asked Nick, his curiosity piqued.

"Truth be told, she was rather tight-lipped about the matter. I can't really say much more than that. I hope you can understand, but I have a duty to keep her legal affairs private," admitted Denton, adjusting his spectacles. "But I can tell you this, she seemed to like you a great deal. Perhaps she saw something in you that reminded her of herself."

"Really?" Nick was taken aback, flattered, and puzzled by the revelation. "I never would have guessed."

"Lucy was a complex woman," said Denton, his eyes glazing over with memories. "A remarkable intellect, matched only by her compassion. And fiercely private, too. But she had a knack for recognizing kindred spirits."

"Very true," agreed Nick, recalling their shared love of literature and their late-night discussions on the classics. "And there is nothing you can tell me?"

"Afraid, not. Nevertheless," continued Denton, snapping back to the present. "I can't say for certain why she changed her will. She was always full of surprises, that one."

"Thank you, Mr. Denton," said Nick. "I appreciate your help."

"Of course," nodded the old lawyer. "If you find anything that might shed light on the matter, don't hesitate to let me know."

Nick shifted in his seat, the worn leather chair creaking

beneath him as he considered his next question. The air in the office was heavy with the scent of aged carpet and stale cigar smoke, which seemed to cling to the mahogany bookcases that lined the walls. Jed Denton's gaze remained locked on him, a challenge lurking behind the foggy lenses of his spectacles.

"Mr. Denton," Nick began, his voice steady despite the uneasiness that gnawed at his insides. "I'm curious about your opinion on Doctor Victors. He seems to be quite a respected figure in this town."

"Ha!" The old lawyer barked out a laugh, his jowls quivering with amusement. "Doctor Victors? More like Doctor Quacktors if you ask me! The man may have a bunch of fancy diplomas on his wall, but I've seen better medical knowledge in a children's picture book."

"Really?" Nick raised an eyebrow, intrigued by the unexpected candor from the grumpy man. He could sense that there was something about the doctor that ruffled Mr. Denton's feathers – and he intended to find out what it was.

"Mark my words," Denton continued, leaning forward, and lowering his voice conspiratorially. "That man has more secrets than the bloody Vatican. Keeps them locked up in that hair thinning bald head of his. He might have fooled the rest of this town, but he'll never fool me. And everyone just kisses up to him. Do you know that he had a beard for about a year? It was filled with gray, patchy, but long. That idiot shaved it off just a couple of days ago or was it a week? It doesn't matter. Anyway, everyone kept telling him how young he looked and then some crap about whether he was using some secret medical procedure to look younger. Uhg. If anything, I would believe he was more of a vampire. That seems more plausible. Ha."

"Yeah, I'm not a fan," Nick said, tucking away this new piece of information for further investigation. He knew that unraveling the mysteries of Sweet Sea would require sifting through layers of half-truths and hidden agendas, and Doctor Victors was just another enigma to decode.

"Speaking of the town," Jed said, his tone extremely serious. The energy shifted in the room. "You'd best keep your wits about you, young man. Sweet Sea might be a picturesque little haven, but it's also teeming with oddballs and eccentrics. They might seem pleasant enough on the surface, but there's no telling what sort of madness lurks beneath."

"Thank you for the warning, Mr. Denton," Nick replied, his mind already racing with possibilities. As he stood to leave, he couldn't help but think that perhaps it was precisely this motley assortment of characters that would provide the key to solving the riddle that had brought him to Sweet Sea in the first place.

"Take care now," Jed called after him, his voice tinged with genuine concern. "And remember, it's not just about finding the answers you seek, it's about surviving it."

"Will do," replied Nick

"Actually," Mr. Denton added, seeming to recall something important. "When Lucy came in to change her will, she appeared to be in quite a good mood. There was no pressure, nothing out of the ordinary. It was a pleasant visit."

"Interesting," said Nick. He stopped and turned back to the lawyer, his brow furrowing as he contemplated this new information. He had expected some sign of coercion or distress, but it seemed that whatever led to the changes in Lucy's will had been her own decision.

"Ah, and speaking of family," the lawyer interjected, leaning back in his chair with a creak, "I have a daughter about your age. She's a talented artist and loves the church. She could spend hours at her easel, lost in her work."

Nick couldn't put a finger on it, but something about the lawyers switching from subject to subject seemed off. Probably a sign of age, but he hoped the nice man didn't have anything too serious going on. He hated to think of him having to rely on Doctor Victors.

"Really?" replied Nick, feeling a warmth bubble up inside him as he thought about his own daughters. He cherished those moments when they shared their passions and interests. "I have two daughters myself. Bridget, my eldest, is a fashion designer; she has an incredible eye for detail and creativity. Kaley, my younger one, is currently studying law." Nick couldn't help but feel a swell of pride as he spoke of them.

"Ah, a well worth it career, but I'm slightly bias," Mr. Denton said with a knowing smile, his eyes twinkling behind his spectacles. "It's always heartening to witness the next generation carry on our legacies, isn't it?"

"It is nice to see for sure," agreed Nick, his thoughts momentarily drifting to the last conversation he'd had with his daughters before moving to Sweet Sea. Their concern for his well-being still lingered in his mind, but he knew they were supportive of his decision to start anew. And yet, he still found himself thinking of their mother even with a fresh start.

"Thank you again for sharing what you know, Mr. Denton," Nick said, offering a genuine smile. "I appreciate your candor."

"Of course," the lawyer replied, his gruff exterior softening for a moment. "And if there's anything more I can do to help, please don't hesitate to reach out."

As Nick took his leave, he couldn't help but feel a mixture of gratitude and concern. He was grateful for the connections he'd made in Sweet Sea thus far and determined to honor Lucy's memory by uncovering the truth behind her final actions. He couldn't shake the feeling that there was more to uncover, not just about the will, but about the town itself and the relationships he would form within it.

CHAPTER ELEVEN

The air in the library was warm with a comforting heaviness, perfumed by the scent of old leather and yellowing pages. A muted hum of conversation permeated through the stacks, punctuated occasionally by the whisper of a turning page or the quiet rustle of a book being slid back into its place on the shelf.

Rose stood among the towering shelves, and her eyes narrowed as she scanned the labels on the spines of the books, searching for *The Brown Grass*. She had been asked earlier to find the book if she could. Even though she wanted to help more with the clues, Nick insisted that Rose was helping in the best way possible by doing this. The book was at the center of the investigation. Determination coursed through her veins. She wanted to help solve the possible murder, but more importantly, she liked Nick and was hoping this would be a way to get to know him better.

Having no luck, she searched until she found the librarian. "Excuse me," she said to the Susan Priser. "I'm looking for a book called *The Brown Grass*. Do you know where I can find it?"

The librarian paused for a moment, her finger tapping against her chin before she replied, "Ah, yes. That should be in the mystery section—aisle 12, about halfway down."

"Thank you," Rose said with a nod, making her way to the aisle she'd indicated.

Aisle 12 proved to be a challenge. Books were haphazardly placed, some missing from their designated spots, others crammed together without regard for order. It was as if someone had tried to sabotage Lucy's carefully maintained system. But Rose refused to let this deter her. She knew all too well the importance of resilience in times of adversity.

"Looking for something in particular?" a voice asked from behind her.

Rose turned to see an elderly gentleman in overalls, his glasses perched precariously on the tip of his nose. Harold Finch was fixing a shelf with a screwdriver and was slightly hidden behind a bookcase.

"Yes," she replied, "*The Brown Grass*. I was told it should be here."

The man nodded, and said, "As you can see, our shelves have become rather disorganized lately. I had to move some stuff around to fix this bookcase. I will get organized later today. Until then, it's just a mess."

"Tell me about it," Rose muttered under her breath. She continued scanning the shelves, frustration mounting at every gap and misplaced title. Each second that ticked by felt like an opportunity slipping through her fingers.

Her fingers brushed against the spines of countless books, their colorful jackets casting a vibrant spectrum upon the drab silver shelves. The library was silent, save for the rhythmic ticking of the grandfather clock in the corner and the hushed turn of pages. Her eyes darted over the rows, meticulously searching for the elusive title.

"Can't find what you're looking for?" asked a voice behind her, causing Rose to startle. She turned to see the young woman with auburn curls and a curious gaze she had met earlier. Her nametag read "Susan" in bold black letters.

"Uh, yes. I'm still looking for *The Brown Grass*. It's supposed to be right here, but it's not." Rose's voice quivered slightly, betraying her frustration.

Susan frowned, surveying the shelves. "That's strange. Maybe someone misplaced it. Or worse, borrowed it without checking it out. I'm sure it's here somewhere. Nobody would steal a library book."

"I'll put it all back in order when I am done," Harold said. "You can look tomorrow."

"Right," Rose sighed, feeling the weight of defeat settle on her shoulders. The book could hold vital clues to Lucy's murder, but it had vanished like a ghost in the night.

"If you would like to leave your number, I can call if I locate it," Susan said. "I'm sure it's here."

"Thank you." As Rose turned, she remembered something Nick mentioned on the phone. "Say, didn't Lucy have a nephew?" Rose asked suddenly, an idea forming in her mind. She wasn't good at it, but decided to lie. "Lucy mentioned he loved the book."

"Lucy's nephew? Yeah, she did mention him a few times. His name is Michael. I haven't met him personally, but I can find his contact information for you if you'd like." Susan offered.

"Please," Rose replied, grateful for the lifeline. If she couldn't find the book, perhaps Lucy's nephew could provide some insight into her life or even point Nick and her toward other potential suspects in her murder.

"Give me a moment," Susan said. She disappeared behind the front desk. Rose pondered over the connection between missing book and Lucy's death as she waited. Was it merely coincidence, or did it hold darker secrets? Could her nephew be involved in any way? She shook off his doubts and steeled herself for the upcoming interview. There was only one way to find out, and that was by asking questions – lots of them.

"Here you go." Susan returned, handing Rose a small slip of paper with Michael's contact information neatly written on it.

"Thank you," Rose said earnestly, pocketing the paper. "You've been a great help."

"Of course," she replied, offering a small smile. "I hope you find what you're looking for. Would you like to leave your number in case the book shows up?"

"Yes, please." Rose took paper and pen from Susan, jotted down her number, and handed it back.

"Have a good day." Susan went back to her desk.

"You too," Rose murmured as she exited the library, excited to share the information with Nick.

CHAPTER TWELVE

Nick stood on the doorstep of a quaint, ivy-covered cottage, the slip of paper with Michael's address clutched in his hand. He had met up with Rose for lunch, and she relayed the information about the lost book and the contact info for Lucy's nephew. She was eager to interview, but Nick wasn't free until after the workday, and she had promised to volunteer at the church. For the sake of time, they had agreed he would go, and they could catch up later.

He took a deep breath, inhaling the sweet scent of gardenias that surrounded the property, and knocked on the door. As he waited, his thoughts raced with anticipation and anxiety; he hoped to find answers, but feared what those answers might reveal.

The door creaked open, revealing a tall, lanky man in his thirties. His dark hair hung over his forehead, and his eyes were bloodshot as though he hadn't slept in days. Nick took note of the faint tremor in the nephew's hands and the slight hunch in his posture – signs of distress or, perhaps, guilt.

"Michael Brooks?" Nick asked, extending his hand for a shake.

"Yes," Michael replied hesitantly, shaking Nick's hand with a weak grip. "What can I do for you?"

"Nick Cern," he introduced himself, his gaze never leaving Michael's face. "I was a friend of your Aunt Lucy's. If you have some time, I was hoping we could discuss her recent passing."

"I talked to the sheriff already. They said it was a heart attack."

"I know, and I don't doubt it. But they think it was caused naturally, and I think it was induced by something. I know it is a tough time, but any information you might have could be really helpful. Would it be all right if we talked for just a little bit?"

"Of course," Michael murmured, stepping aside to let Nick in. "Go ahead and come on in."

As they entered the living room, Nick analyzed every detail, searching for any indication of foul play. The room was cluttered, with stacks of books and newspapers piled on every available surface. A scent of stale coffee permeated the air, mingling with the faint odor of cigarette smoke.

"Please, have a seat," Michael gestured to an armchair, clearing off a stack of papers before sitting down across from Nick. The younger man's right hand was shaking violently, and Nick instantly recognized it as a lingering symptom of withdrawal. He had had it himself in rehab and months after.

"Thank you," Nick said, settling into the chair. "I'm sorry for intruding at such a difficult time, but I've been trying to understand what happened to Lucy. She was a dear friend."

"Of course," Michael replied, his eyes downcast. "I understand. She was... she was a great woman."

"Can you tell me about your relationship with her?" Nick asked, watching Michael's response closely. "How involved were you in her life?"

Michael hesitated, rubbing his hands together anxiously. "We were close when I was younger, but as I grew up and moved away, we didn't see each other as often. I'd visit her at the library sometimes, though. She always loved that place."

"Did she ever mention anything unusual to you? Any concerns or fears?"

"No, not really," Michael said, shifting uncomfortably in his seat. "She mostly talked about her work and the books she enjoyed reading. She never mentioned any problems or worries."

"Lucy has left behind quite a legacy in Sweet Sea," Nick continued, observing Michael's body language. "Were you aware of her past as a reclusive writer?"

"Reclusive?" Michael echoed, his brow furrowing. "I knew she was successful, but I didn't know she was a... recluse. She just didn't talk about the writing part. That's all."

"Gotcha," Nick nodded. "Her love for literature was unparalleled. Did she ever share any secrets with you about her life or her work?"

"Secrets?" Michael shook his head, an edge of desperation creeping into his voice. "No, I don't think so. Like I said, we mostly talked about books. She never mentioned anything about her life beyond Uncle Gerald, her ex-husband."

"Interesting. I know families have rumors. Anything there?" Nick asked.

"Nope," Michael quickly answered without a thought.

This was an opportune moment for Nick to delve deeper into Michael's life. "May I ask you a personal question?" Nick ventured.

"Uh, sure," Michael replied hesitantly, rubbing his hands together as if trying to wash away the unease that clung to him.

"Your aunt had considerable wealth from her novels," Nick began, watching Michael's eyes widen in surprise. "Did she ever provide you with any sort of financial support?"

"Financial support?" Michael stammered, his cheeks flushing crimson. An involuntary tic flickered beneath his right eye. "I mean, she helped me out from time to time when I was between jobs or short on rent, but that was years ago before I got clean. What the hell does that have to do with anything?"

"Is it possible," Nick continued, his gaze unwavering, "that you might have needed her help again recently? Perhaps even felt entitled to some of her fortune?"

Michael's face contorted, a mixture of indignation and hurt battling for dominance. "No!" he exclaimed, raising his voice defensively. "I would never expect anything from Aunt Lucy! She was always so kind to me, and I... I just miss her."

"Forgive me if I'm being too forward," Nick said, his tone softening. He knew he had struck a nerve, but he couldn't ignore the mounting evidence against the man. "But I can't help but notice the state of your home. It appears to be in disrepair. Are you struggling financially?"

"Who the hell are you? You know what, never mind. Look, it's no secret that I haven't had the best luck with jobs," Michael admitted, his voice barely a whisper. "But I've been managing. Barely. Just ask the town of busybodies. In case you hadn't noticed, they know everything about everyone."

"Thank you for your honesty." Nick's thoughts raced, connecting the dots as he tried to piece together the puzzle of Lucy's murder. "I understand this is difficult, but it's crucial that I uncover any possible motives."

"Even if it means accusing me?" Michael asked, his voice cracking. A single tear slid down his cheek, leaving a glistening trail of vulnerability in its wake. "Especially since it is said to be natural causes."

"Michael, I'm not accusing you," Nick assured him, reaching out to place a hand on his shoulder. "I'm just trying to understand the circumstances surrounding her death."

"Fine," Michael whispered, wiping away more tears with visible agitation. "Go ahead and investigate my life if you want. You won't find anything because I didn't kill her. But please, hurry up and find out if someone did. We deserve to know, and if it was murder, they need to pay for it."

"Thank you." Nick removed his hand, sitting back. The weight of suspicion hung heavily in the air between them, an unspoken burden that threatened to suffocate their conversation. "Where were you the night she passed?"

Michael's eyes darted around the room like a caged animal searching for an escape route. He took a deep breath, his chest puffing out before deflating in resignation. "All right, Mr. Cern, if it helps clear my name, I'll tell you exactly where I was when my Aunt Lucy died." His voice wavered, but he maintained eye contact with Nick.

"Please do," Nick said, folding his arms across his chest. The air in the room seemed to grow heavy with tension.

"I was at the Historical Society fundraiser," Michael began, his voice strained. "You know, the one that Lucy organized to raise money for the city debt. I spent most of the evening there, helping set up and then mingling with the guests."

Nick was taken aback. In all the conversations he had, this never came up. "I wasn't aware there was an event. Was Lucy there?"

"At the beginning, then she went outside with Doc. She came back in upset, grabbed her keys, and left. I guess she went back to the library."

Nick pondered that information. This was maybe another clue. He would have to talk to the doctor. First, he would have to finish this detail. "Are you sure she went there?"

"No, I was at the event."

"Can anyone confirm your presence?" Nick asked, watching Michael's face carefully for any signs of deceit.

"Of course! There were dozens of people there, including

the mayor and several town council members. They can all vouch for me."

Nick nodded, committing this information to memory. As he did so, he couldn't help but notice a tiny bead of sweat forming at Michael's temple, betraying his nervousness despite his attempt at confidence.

"Is there anything else you'd like to share? Any other details about that night?" Nick pressed, maintaining a steady gaze on Michael.

"The next day they kicked me out of the society."

"Why?"

"I'll just say we disagreed on fund raising. Look, I've told you everything I can remember," Michael said, his voice cracking under the weight of desperation. "My aunt's death has devastated me, and I'm doing everything possible to cooperate. But every time I talk about this, I feel more and more like I'm being accused of something I didn't do."

"I understand how difficult this must be for you," Nick said gently, his own heart aching for the younger man before him. "But in order to find the person responsible for Lucy's murder, we need to explore every possible angle."

Michael's eyes welled up with tears, and he clutched his hands together so tightly that his knuckles turned white. "I loved my aunt more than anything," he whispered, his voice choked with emotion. "I would never hurt her."

"Of course," Nick said softly, taking a moment to let Michael compose himself. As he watched him struggle to maintain control, he couldn't help but notice the trembling of Michael's hands, betraying the turmoil within.

Despite the alibi Michael provided, Nick couldn't shake the feeling that there was more to the story than met the eye. It seemed too coincidental that he would be kicked out of the society right when she disappeared. The desperation in his voice, as well as the inconsistencies in his behavior, only served to deepen Nick's suspicions. He knew that it was entirely possible that grief could manifest itself in strange ways, but something about the situation felt... off.

As Nick continued to piece together the information he had gathered, his mind raced with potential motives and scenarios. He considered the possibility that the nephew could have slipped away from the fundraiser, unseen by others, to commit the crime. He also thought about the financial strain Michael was under, which might have driven him to act out of desperation to inherit Lucy's wealth.

"Thank you, Michael," Nick said finally, his voice firm but gentle. "I appreciate your cooperation. Rest assured, if it was not natural, I won't stop until I find who did this to your aunt."

"Please do, Mr. Cern," Michael replied, his voice barely

above a whisper, his eyes pleading for understanding. "Just remember that I loved her too."

Making a mental note of Michael's reaction, Nick stood. "Well, thank you for speaking with me, Michael. You've been very helpful."

"Of course," Michael said, standing up and walking Nick to the door. "Please let me know if there's anything else I can do to help."

Just as Nick was about to leave, Michael's cell phone rang with a shrill urgency that seemed to pierce the somber atmosphere. Michael glanced at the caller ID and fumbled to silence it. Nick couldn't help but notice the name displayed on the screen: "Clarence" – a name he hadn't yet encountered in his investigation.

"Is everything all right?" Nick asked, observing Michael's flustered state.

"Uh, yes, Mr. Cern," Michael stammered, forcing a smile. "Just an old friend who has been calling non-stop. He can be quite persistent."

"May I ask who Clarence is?" Nick pressed, his curiosity piqued. He had not expected to be so bold with the nephew, but he figured why not.

"Wow, you do have some balls. Clarence? Oh, just a... business associate of sorts," Michael replied, his voice wavering. "He's not important."

"Forgive me, Michael," Nick said, his tone measured but firm.

Michael hesitated, avoiding Nick's gaze. The tension in the room grew thick. Finally, he sighed, resignation etched in his features. "All right. It would be best if you didn't think it had anything to do with my aunt's death. Clarence is someone Aunt Lucy introduced me to last year. She thought he could help me with my finances. But honestly, I hardly know him. And neither did she."

Nick nodded, filing away this information for further investigation. As he stood up to leave, his keen eye caught a glimpse of a paper sticking out from under a stack of mail on Michael's coffee table. The bold, red letters on the crumpled page screamed "Final Notice" - another piece of evidence that hinted at Michael's dire financial situation.

Nick had definitely worn out his welcome, and he knew it. He was ready to leave. Stopping at the door, Nick turned back to Michael and nodded towards his hands. "Congrats on getting clean. If you need a lifeline or someone to talk to, reach out to me. I own the tech store down on the city water block. I know what addiction is like."

"I'm fine," Michael said. He quickly ushered Nick out.

As he stepped outside, Nick couldn't shake the nagging

feeling that Michael was hiding something. Was it guilt over Lucy's death? Fear of being discovered? Or simply grief? A faint scent of lavender hung in the air as Nick stood on the porch, considering his next move. The crumbling brickwork, weathered by time and neglect, seemed to mirror Michael's own frayed demeanor. A sudden gust of wind rustled through the overgrown garden, scattering dry leaves like whispers of forgotten secrets.

Though nothing concrete pointed to Michael's guilt, Nick couldn't ignore the nagging suspicion that festered within him. He knew that if he were to find the truth behind Lucy's murder, he would have to dig deeper, scrutinizing every detail and leaving no stone unturned.

Nick left the house, his mind abuzz with fresh details and suspicions. The phone call from Clarence, the possible anger at the doctor, an event he had not heard about, the mysterious business associate, the final notice on an unpaid debt – these were pieces of a puzzle that, when combined with Michael's inconsistent behavior and financial desperation, painted a disquieting picture. However, nothing bothered him as much as the email. If she knew she was going to be murdered, why didn't she just say who did it?

As he walked back towards his car, Nick couldn't shake the feeling that he was getting closer to the truth. There was no time to waste; he needed to gather more evidence and pursue this lead with relentless fervor.

CHAPTER THIRTEEN

Nick stood outside, locking his shop up for the day, his tall and lean figure huddled beneath an umbrella, shoulders raised against the chill of the stormy night. The rain pelted the ground and cascaded down from the eaves, turning the streets into rivers. The salt-and-pepper hair he usually kept so tidy was dampened at the edges, but he paid it no mind. His determination drove him. He walked up the street towards the library. He hoped that something new or missed would present itself while he walked. The library was dark as it was a few hours past its closing time.

The sky above cracked open with lightning, illuminating the scene in stark contrasts of light and shadow.

A rumble of thunder followed, shaking the very ground under his feet. The tension and unease were palpable.

"Nick!" came a voice, barely audible over the storm's cacophony. "What on earth are you doing out here?"

He turned to see Susan hurrying towards him. She was clutching her own umbrella, her cheeks flushed from the cold wind.

"Susan," Nick stammered, his heart racing. "I still can't shake the feeling that something's not right about Lucy's death. I thought a walk might help me clear my thoughts."

"Nick, dear, we all miss her, but sometimes things just happen," Susan said, her voice strained. "You should be inside, away from this dreadful weather."

"Perhaps," he conceded, still unable to tear his gaze away from the library's dark windows. "But there's a part of me that just can't let it go. I can't help but feel there's something hidden here."

"Hidden?" Susan's eyes widened in concern. "You don't think there's any foul play involved, do you?"

"Maybe," Nick replied, his voice barely above a whisper. "I won't rest until I find out for sure."

"Promise you'll be careful," Susan pleaded, her hands gripping the handle of her umbrella tightly.

"Why does everyone keep telling me to be careful? I'm

just asking questions."

"I don't want to lose another person in this town."

"I promise," he assured her, the weight of the situation pressing down on him like the raindrops on his umbrella. "But I have to see this through, for Lucy's sake and for my own."

Nick watched the lightning dance across the sky as the storm continued to rage around them, casting eerie shadows over the library.

"Goodnight, Susan," Nick said, nodding to her as she turned to leave. "And thank you."

"Good luck," she called back, disappearing into the night.

With a deep breath, he looked back towards the library, his determination unwavering. As the wind howled and rain pelted down, Nick's eyes were drawn to a mysterious figure lurking around the side of the library. Clad in a dark hoodie and carrying a backpack, the figure's presence sent shivers down his spine and heightened the suspense of this stormy night.

"Who is that?" he whispered under his breath, straining his eyes to make out the person's features or discern any clue about their identity.

The figure was medium height, nearly as tall as himself, with a lean frame that suggested agility and grace. Their movements were fluid, almost catlike, as they crept along the side of the building. Despite the storm, their steps seemed eerily quiet, as if they were treading on air rather than the wet ground. Unnerved by the stranger's stealth, Nick's curiosity intensified.

He clutched his umbrella tighter, forcing himself to remain still and watch the figure from a safe distance. He longed to confront them and demand answers, but something held him back – perhaps his own fear of what he might find or the nagging doubt that he was overreacting to an innocent passerby. It wasn't against the law to walk around the library.

"Maybe I should call the sheriff," he thought, weighing his options. "But if it turns out to be nothing, she'll never take me seriously again."

As the figure approached the library door, they paused, casting a furtive glance around before producing a key and unlocking the entrance. The sight of the key sparked a fire within Nick – after all, only a select few had access to the library at such hours. Could they have Lucy's key?

The figure slipped inside, the door closing softly behind them. Nick hesitated for a moment, torn between his desire for answers and the fear of what he might uncover. But as the rain continued to pour down, soaking him to the bone, his determination solidified.

He took a deep breath and crossed the street, leaving the safety of his umbrella behind as he ventured into the heart of the storm – and the unknown.

Through the rain-streaked window, Nick squinted as he studied the figure. The downpour distorted his view like a watery veil, but his curiosity refused to be dampened. Leaning closer, he placed one hand on the slick glass, his breath fogging up the pane. The figure had a flashlight and was using it to walk quickly. The speed of the person told him they were there for a specific reason and knew what they were looking for. A sudden flash of lightning illuminated the library's interior, casting eerie shadows across the library's facade. For a split second, Nick thought he had caught a glimpse of the figure's pale face, but it vanished as quickly as it had appeared, swallowed by the darkness once more.

"Damn it," he cursed under his breath, frustration gnawing at his resolve. He turned the door handle and slipped into the library.

The sound of footsteps echoed through the night, each footfall punctuating the steady rhythm of the rain. They were cautious, deliberate, as though the figure knew they were being watched. It only served to fuel Nick's suspicions further; there was something undeniably sinister about their presence. He tried to shake off the tendrils of doubt that threatened to ensnare him. He needed to focus, to gather every clue he could find.

Nick stepped out of the doorway and crouched down behind a bookcase. It occurred to him that the figure would have to come back his way to the exit. There was no need to go deeper into the darkness. So, he waited. Minutes passed, but the figure did not come back. He took a deep breath and stayed patient.

"What are you doing here?" a deep voice said from an adjourning aisle.

Nick spun around and found himself face-to-face with Harold. The heavy older man had scared the hell out of him. He couldn't respond. His mind overlayed the figure's silhouette over the janitor, and instantly realizing it was not him, he followed in.

"Did you hear me?" Harold raised his voice.

"Shhh," Nick said, holding his finger to his lips.

"Don't shush me. You don't belong here."

"Please, whisper." Nick held up his hands. "I followed someone in here. They had a key. They are in a hoody and look to be up to something."

"No one has a key except Susan, me, and…". He stopped himself.

"And Lucy."

"Well…yes."

"I saw Susan leave, and you are here. That made me

think the person who came in here might have stolen the key or killed Lucy."

"Lucy died of natural causes," Harold said, confused.

"Yes. Everyone keeps telling me that. I just need to know for sure."

"You got too much time on your hands. Just leave and stop chasing shadows."

"I'm not going anywhere until I find the person."

"Get...now." Harold pushed him to the door.

Nick stumbled, but managed to stay on his feet. "What the hell, man?"

"Hey, you," Harold yelled, looking over Nick's shoulder. The mysterious figure bolted past them and out the door.

"Dammit," Nick said.

"Ah, just let them go. They're out. That's what matters."

Nick ignored him and rushed out the door after the figure, his senses sharpened by the adrenaline coursing through his veins. Gripping the handle of his umbrella, he threw open the door and plunged into the torrential downpour. The rain lashed against his face, his clothes quickly becoming sodden as they clung to his lean form.

"Whoever you are," he muttered to himself, picking up speed, "I won't let you get away."

As he jogged through the deluge, he kept one eye on

the shadowy figure ahead, now partially obscured by the curtain of rain. The scent of damp earth and wet grass filled his nostrils while the slap of his shoes against puddles accompanied the rhythmic drumming of the rain.

His heart pounded in his chest as he glanced over his shoulder, ensuring no one else was following him. He felt exposed, vulnerable, but there was no turning back. The burning need for answers pushed him onward, driving him deeper into the stormy night.

"Hey!" he called out, raising his voice above the cacophony of thunder and rain. "Stop right there!"

The figure hesitated for a moment before quickening their pace, the movements fluid and purposeful. Nick cursed under his breath, his resolve growing stronger with each step, the thrill of the chase igniting something within him he hadn't felt in years.

"Come on, Nick," he encouraged himself, his breaths coming in ragged gasps. "You can do this."

He followed the figure around the corner of the library, his eyes scanning the darkness for any sign of movement. The rain continued to pour down, its relentless onslaught threatening to obscure his vision entirely, each droplet a reminder of the storm brewing both within and without.

"Where are you?" he growled, frustration mounting as

he lost sight of the figure. "Don't think you can escape me that easily."

His thoughts raced, a torrent of questions and fears swirling within him like the storm raging outside. What if this person held the key to Lucy's murder? What if they had been watching her all along? Would the police even believe him, or would they dismiss his concerns as mere paranoia? Nick continued his pursuit.

Rain splattered. Boots squelched. Nick's heart hammered.

The figure darted behind a tree, peering around its rain-soaked bark. The figure vanished momentarily before reemerging near the edge of the woods. The woods were looming closer. If the figure entered there, Nick would have to stop. He hadn't been in the woods yet and knew it wouldn't take much for him to get lost.

"Wait!" cried a voice in his mind, but it was too late. The figure entered the forest, and Nick went after them. He could no longer see the figure in its entirety. At best, he would spot glimpses of movement in the darkness. Focusing on keeping some view of the figure, he stumbled forward as his foot caught on a hidden root, falling headlong into the undergrowth.

"Ugh," he groaned, attempting to disentangle himself

from the thorny embrace of the bushes. He was pretty sure he was bleeding from the rock he hit on the way down.

He spotted a glimpse of movement in the darkness and, with one final effort, pulled himself free with a grimace. But as he lunged forward, the figure disappeared into the wooden shadows. Defeated and disappointed, he thought about a drink at the bar. He brushed himself off and scanned the trees one more time. The figure was gone.

"Damn it!" Nick kicked a rock, frustration and disappointment boiling within. He said under his breath, "So close, yet so far." The figure vanished into the woods, leaving Nick with questions and rain-soaked clothes.

There wasn't much more he could do out here. He at least had another witness of the figure and would feel better telling the police. They could find the answers.

Nick limped back towards the library. The pain in his leg was real. It felt like it was swelling. The sheriff's car was parked out front. The lights on the roof were spinning. He guessed Harold must have called them. He entered the library and saw the sheriff talking with Harold.

"Sheriff Kent, I need to report something," Nick said, stepping into the dimly lit library, water dripping from his coat.

"Ah, Mr. Cern," she replied lazily, chewing gum, "What's

got you out and about on a night like this?"

"She just got here," Harold explained. "I was about to tell her."

As Nick came closer, their eyes widened. He had cuts across his face and arms, torn pants, and a bloody knee.

"What the hell happened to you?" Sheriff Kent asked. She was instantly serious. "Do you need an ambulance?"

"I'll be fine. Someone with a black hoody was lurking around the library," Nick explained, urgency lacing his words. "I tried to follow them, but they disappeared into the woods."

"Sounds like the same teens that vandalized the place before," Sheriff Kent dismissed, yawning. "They'll tire of it soon enough."

"Something's not right," Nick insisted, recalling the mysterious figure's movements. "This isn't just some teenage prank. They had a key. I saw them unlock the library. And the only key unaccounted for is Lucy's. It's got to be connected to her murder."

"Mr. Cern." The sheriff sighed, dragging her hand down her face, "We have had this conversation. I understand you're grieving, but trust us to handle this. We're professionals."

"Professionals?" Nick scoffed, anger surging through him. "If you were professionals, we'd have answers already! Instead, you're sitting here, doing nothing!"

"Watch your tone," Sheriff Kent warned, her eyes narrowing. "We can't chase after every shadow you see. We have procedures to follow. "

"Procedures?" Nick's mind raced. "What about justice? What about finding the truth?"

"Mr. Cern," she said sternly, stepping within a foot of him, "I suggest you leave this to us and go home. If there's anything worth investigating, we will handle it. Plus, look at yourself. I said you would get hurt if you kept looking into this. Now, do you believe me?"

"I'm okay."

"That's debatable. I know you're new here, but the doctor is one of the best. If he said she died of natural causes, then she did."

"You mean the medical examiner."

"No, I mean the doctor. We don't have the budget for a separate medical examiner. Doctor Victors pulls double duty."

Nick's eyes widened. One of the suspects he had on his list was the one that pronounced her cause of death. It could be a coincidence, but what if? He started to say something but stopped himself. He would not gain any ground for accusing the doctor or throwing out a conspiracy theory. The sheriff already thought he was a little unhinged.

"Please just go home," the sherriff said.

"Fine," Nick snapped, defeated but far from finished. He stormed out of the library, each step echoing his desire to seek answers elsewhere. He was going to find out what teens vandalized the library and go have a chat with the delinquents.

CHAPTER FOURTEEN

The Sweet Sea Diner, with its checkered linoleum floor and cracked red-vinyl booths, seemed to be trapped in a time warp. The air was thick with the scent of bacon grease and burnt coffee, a smell that hung heavy in Nick's nose as he pushed open the door. He glanced around, trying not to feel too conspicuous in his black turtleneck and jeans. He caught sight of Rose sitting at a booth by the window, her eyes scanning the local newspaper.

"Rose," he said, sliding into the seat across from her. "Thanks for meeting me."

"Of course. Anything to help. Plus, you're buying right?" She folded the newspaper neatly and tucked it in her purse sitting next to her in the booth. Her green eyes hinted at concern, but she masked it well behind her usual stoicism.

"Sure," he said with a smile.

"Seriously though, glad to help."

"Any news on those vandals?" Nick asked, eager to get straight to business. He leaned forward, resting his elbows on the worn tabletop, his silver-streaked hair falling across his brow.

"Actually, yes." Rose reached into her purse and pulled out a small notebook. She flipped through the pages, pulled one out, then handed it to him. "I got their names from an administrator I know at the sheriff's office. We go to the same church."

Nick raised an eyebrow, impressed. "You're quite resourceful, Rose."

"Sometimes it helps to know people. Growing up in a small town and all." She offered a wry smile, sipping her coffee. "The address is there too."

"Much obliged," Nick replied, tucking the note into his pants pocket. The thought of confronting the vandals filled him with a sense of purpose, something he'd been missing since this all started. Solving this case might just be the key to finding a new chapter in his life.

"Be careful, Nick," Rose said, her voice soft and measured. "We don't know what we're dealing with here."

"Trust me, I know the importance of caution." He met her gaze, trying to convey his gratitude. "But I'm not going to let them destroy Lucy's legacy in that library."

"Neither am I," she agreed, her eyes narrowing. "I won't rest until we find out who's behind this and hold them accountable."

As Nick studied Rose's face, he couldn't help but notice the subtle lines around her eyes, a testament to her own resilience. She was a formidable ally, and together, they would get to the bottom of this mystery.

The waitress came by the table, and they ordered food and coffee. She seemed pleasant enough, but it was easy to see she would rather be anywhere but in the diner. Nick didn't mind because this diner made one of the best burgers he had ever eaten. Attitude aside, they also were really quick. In less than five minutes, they had their drinks.

Nick slid his now-empty coffee cup back and forth between his hands, the rhythmic motion underscoring the weight of their conversation. "You know, there was something that happened last night at the library," he began, his voice low and tinged with a hint of urgency. "I was closing up shop and stepping out to get something to eat. I saw someone unlock the library and go in. Susan had already left. I followed them in, and I heard footsteps in the stacks."

"Footsteps?" Rose asked, her eyes widening in concern. "What did you do?"

"I went to investigate, of course." Nick's brow furrowed as he recalled the events. "I found someone near the rare books section. Ran into Harold, the person ran. "

"Did you catch them?" Rose leaned forward, her attention riveted on Nick's story.

"Almost." He shook his head, frustration creeping into his voice. "I chased them to the woods and got tangled up in some roots and fell. They slipped away before I could get a good look at them. But it just made me more determined than ever to figure out what's going on."

"The forest is dangerous. All kinds of vines and odd plants. As a kid, we were told never to go in there. We still went, lol. Lots of overgrowth in there. Some old horticulturists use to plant weird stuff all in there," Rose said, worry etched across her face. "Promise me you'll be careful, Nick."

"Of course," he reassured her, touched by her concern. As if to emphasize her point, Rose reached across the table and placed a gentle hand on his arm, the warmth of her touch lingering long after she withdrew it. Part of him wished she would have left it there. The electricity through his body was soothing and exciting at the same time. "Nothing a little ice couldn't fix," he reassured her, though he couldn't help but revel in her worry for him. "The important thing is that we now know someone's feeling the heat."

"Good," Rose murmured, her gaze unwavering. "Because I don't want anything to happen to you, especially not when you're trying to help Lucy. Were you hurt when you fell?"

"My leg was a little sore, but it didn't last long. Nothing will happen to me," Nick promised, his resolve bolstered by her faith in him. "We'll solve this together, Rose. I won't let you down. I just need to figure out how to get the sheriff on board."

"She is okay enough. Maybe a little misguided, but she is a good sheriff."

"I've encountered some... resistance from local law enforcement."

"Resistance?" she queried, her brow furrowing in confusion. "What do you mean?"

"Well," he sighed, setting down his spoon with a clatter that seemed to reverberate through the hushed diner, "I spoke with Sheriff Kent yesterday."

"Go on," Rose prompted, her interest piqued.

"Sheriff Kent is a peculiar woman," Nick continued, recalling their terse conversation. "She seemed more interested in dismissing my concerns than actually pursuing any leads. In fact, when I mentioned that someone appeared to have a key to the library, she almost laughed at me."

"Laughed?" Rose echoed incredulously. "But that's a serious breach of security!"

"Exactly," Nick agreed, frustration seeping into his voice. "But she brushed it off like it was nothing, claiming that the vandal must've picked the lock or something. She didn't even bother to ask for a description of the person I saw. And Harold didn't seem bothered enough to help me question."

"Sounds like she isn't taking the after-hour entry seriously at all," Rose muttered, anger flashing in her eyes. "But why? What could she possibly have to gain by ignoring potential crime?"

"Your guess is as good as mine," Nick replied, his hands tightening around his coffee cup. "But one thing's for sure, we can't count on her for help."

"Clearly not," Rose agreed, her expression grim. "So, what's our next move?"

"Actually," Nick said, his eyes narrowing as he recalled another recent encounter, "I've already taken matters into my own hands."

"Really?" Rose leaned in closer, her curiosity piqued. "What did you do?"

"I confronted Harold about the library keys," Nick confessed, a hint of pride creeping into his voice.

"Harold? The janitor?" Rose's eyes widened in surprise. "Why him?"

"Call it intuition," Nick replied, shrugging off the risk he'd taken. "But there was something about the way he reacted when I mentioned the break-in that made me suspicious."

"Wow, confrontations and intuition," Rose mused, clearly impressed by Nick's daring. "You're turning into quite the amateur detective, aren't you?"

"Maybe," he admitted, a wry smile tugging at his lips. "But Harold wasn't too pleased with my line of questioning. In fact, he got downright hostile."

"Hostile? What happened?" Rose asked, her concern evident.

"Let's just say pushed me," Nick chuckled. "Luckily, I managed to stay on my feet."

"I never did like him."

"Back to the sheriff." Nick began as their meals were delivered. He took a bite of his burger and smiled with joy.

Rose smiled. "Ah, Joan. Yeah, she is a tough cookie. Both her and her husband grew up in this town. She is nice enough, but very fact and process driven. Facts are facts and everything else is a distraction."

"You never cease to amaze me with who you know. I really appreciate you helping on this."

"Thank you. That means a lot to me." The vulnerability in her eyes spoke volumes, and Nick felt a pang of gratitude for their newfound partnership in this tangled web of mystery.

"Let's get to work, then," he said, his voice firm with determination. "We've got vandals to apprehend and a killer to catch."

Nick took a sip of his coffee after the waitress refilled it, the bitter taste grounding him in the present moment. He looked over at Rose and said, "I had a chance to talk to Michael, Lucy's nephew."

"Really?" Rose leaned forward, her interest piqued. "How did that go?"

"Surprisingly well," Nick replied, recalling the guarded young man who had eventually opened up to him. "He admitted that he knew about the change in Lucy's will, but he seemed genuinely happy with it. I believe him."

"That's interesting," Rose said, her brow furrowing as she processed this new information. "It's good to know that not everyone in this town is out for themselves."

"I was surprised." Nick paused, taking another sip of his coffee. "Michael appeared determined to turn his life around. Underneath that rough exterior, there's a sensitive soul just waiting to be understood."

"Let's hope that understanding comes before it's too late

for him," Rose added softly, her eyes reflecting her empathy for the troubled young man.

"Agreed," Nick nodded, feeling the weight of responsibility settle on his shoulders once more. "He also seemed to genuinely miss her and be distraught. However, there was something off."

"Like what?"

"Well first, as I mentioned he wasn't bothered about the will, but I noticed past due bills in his house. If it was me, I would be a little annoyed if I was in financial trouble. It just didn't make any sense to me. Also, he got a call as I was leaving, and I asked about it. Apparently, it was for help managing his finances. He seemed really irritated with me. Not sure if it is grief or a lie, but he was just off."

"Do you think he was involved?"

"My gut says no, but he has the motive and the opportunity no matter what he says. He is clean, but still going through some withdrawal symptoms."

"How do you know that?" Rose looked confused.

"Just some past experiences. We will keep him on the list, but let's focus on some of the other details."

As they sat there, united in their quest for answers and their determination to see justice served, Nick felt a strange sense of comfort and camaraderie. Despite the challenges that lay ahead, he knew that he and Rose were stronger together and that, come what may, they would face it head-on, side by side.

Nick glanced around, taking in the faded wallpaper and chipped Formica countertop, feeling the weight of his investigation tugging at his thoughts.

Rose flipped through her notebook. "Let me catch you up on my interview with her ex-husband, Gerald. I was able to track him down and get some of his time."

"Really?" Nick's eyes widened in surprise. "What did he have to say?"

"Quite a lot, actually," Rose replied, her voice hushed and filled with emotion. "He expressed deep remorse over how their relationship ended. It was clear that he still cared for Lucy, even after all these years."

"Wow," Nick breathed, taken aback by this unexpected revelation. "That must have been difficult for him to admit."

"Very," Rose agreed, her gaze meeting Nick's with an intensity that spoke volumes. "But I think it was also cathartic for him. In a way, it seemed as if he was finally letting go of some long-held pain."

"Sometimes," Nick mused, his thoughts drifting to his own past struggles, "the most difficult conversations are the ones we need to have the most."

"True," Rose concurred, her eyes softening with understanding. "But those conversations can also lead to the deepest connections and the most profound healing."

"You're not wrong," Nick nodded, locking eyes with Rose as they shared a moment of silent connection.

"Speaking of difficult conversations," Rose continued, her fingers tracing the edge of her coffee cup as she recalled her interview with Gerald. "He shared something quite personal with me about a car accident he was in several years ago."

Nick leaned in, his dark brows furrowing in curiosity. "A car accident? How is that relevant?"

"Well," Rose explained, her eyes reflecting the weight of her words, "it seems that the accident was a sort of catalyst for him. It changed his outlook on life, made him realize how fragile and fleeting our time here can be." She paused, realizing what she had just said. She wanted to apologize, but instead took a deep breath before continuing. "Gerald told me that, if he could go back in time, he would have been a better husband to Lucy, more attentive and supportive."

"Regret can be such a powerful emotion," Nick said, his thoughts once again drifting to his own past experiences. He imagined the weight that must have settled on Gerald's shoulders after the accident, the crushing realization that he had wasted precious time and opportunities.

"One of the most powerful, I think," Rose agreed, her voice tinged with wistfulness. "But it's also a testament to human resilience, don't you think? That we can learn from our mistakes and grow stronger because of them?"

"You're always so positive. But right," Nick responded, his gaze locking with hers, the intensity of their shared understanding igniting a flame of determination within him. They were not only seeking justice for Lucy, but also unraveling the tangled threads of regret, love, and missed chances that connected her with those who had once been part of her life.

"Anything else from him?"

"He's permanently in a wheelchair. If he poisoned Lucy, he would have to have someone else collect the plants. But my gut says he didn't do it."

"Rose," he said softly, reaching across the table to place a hand on her arm, feeling the warmth of her skin beneath his fingertips. "Thank you for sharing this with me. It's important that we consider every angle, every aspect of these people's lives, in order to solve this case. More importantly, thank you for being you."

"Of course," Rose replied, her cheeks flushing pink beneath the diner's neon lights.

They finished their meal with idle chit chat and came up

with a plan for next steps. After they were finished, Nick paid, as promised.

They stood and Rose put her hand on Nick's forearm. "We're in this together, right?"

"Right," he affirmed, a feeling of gratitude and camaraderie swelling within him. As they prepared to leave the diner, Nick hesitated for a moment, then opened his arms in an offer of embrace.

Rose stepped into the hug, her body stiff with surprise at first but then relaxing into the warmth of their connection. They stood there, wrapped in each other's arms, as the world around them continued to bustle and buzz – two souls united in their quest for truth, justice, and healing. He wanted to kiss her. He just couldn't. Not right now.

As they pulled apart, their eyes met, and Nick knew that it was in their shared strength that they would find their way through the labyrinthine mystery that had brought them together.

"Let's go," Nick said softly, his words a promise and a vow. "We have work to do."

Nick and Rose stepped out of the diner, the evening air cooler than they had anticipated. The moon cast long shadows on the pavement as they walked, the glow from streetlights illuminating their path. Nick could feel the weight of the case pressing down on him, as if it were a physical burden upon his shoulders.

"Rose," he said, choosing his words carefully, "we must tread cautiously in our investigation. Lucy's death is like an intricate web, with each strand leading to another unknown."

"I will," she replied, her voice earnest and steeled with determination. "But we've made headway, haven't we? Like the information about the vandals and the address I got from my friend at the sheriff's office."

"Yes," Nick nodded, grateful for her tenacity. "But with each new revelation comes further complexity. I can't help but feel there are forces working against us, perhaps even within the very institutions we're trying to navigate."

A gust of wind whipped around them, causing Rose to shiver and wrap her arms around herself. She glanced at Nick, her eyes filled with uncertainty. "Do you really think that's possible?" she asked quietly.

"Having dealt with corporate politics for years, I've learned that one should never underestimate the lengths people will go to protect their interests or conceal their misdeeds. Even the sheriff is a suspect."

As they continued walking, Nick pondered the myriad obstacles they had encountered so far: the unhelpful police officer, the mysterious figure at the library who seemed to possess a key, and Harold's evasiveness. He knew their progress hinged on their ability to surmount these challenges – and on forging a strong partnership with Rose.

He returned her smile and felt a renewed sense of purpose surging through him. Despite the dark corners and hidden threats, Nick knew that he and Rose would persevere – guided by their shared passion for justice and a growing bond that transcended the shadows.

CHAPTER FIFTEEN

The dank hallway reeked of stale cigarette smoke as Nick approached the shabby door, its peeling paint barely clinging to the warped wood. He hesitated momentarily, wondering what secrets hid behind it, and took a deep breath before knocking firmly. The investigation into Lucy's death led him to this grimy corner of Sweet Sea, where he hoped to find answers. A group of teens, known for their mischievous antics, were said to have been involved in the vandalism of the library. And now, it fell upon Nick to uncover the truth.

"Who is it?" a surly voice demanded from within.

"Nick Cern," he replied, trying to keep his tone steady and authoritative. "I'd like to ask you some questions."

The door creaked open, revealing a group of unkempt teenagers with sullen expressions, their defensive postures seemingly at odds with their disheveled appearances. Immediately, he noticed they all wore dark hoodies like the one on the person from the night before. They stared at Nick with a mixture of suspicion and hostility as if daring him to challenge them.

"All right," the tallest of the group muttered, crossing his arms. "What do you want?"

"Can I come inside?" Nick asked, hoping to set up a less tense atmosphere for the interview.

"Talk here," the teen replied curtly, not budging from his position against the doorframe. Behind him, another teen's eyes widened, and he pulled the hood of his jacket further across his face.

Nick sighed inwardly but decided to press on. "I'm investigating the murder of Lucy Brooks, the librarian," he began, observing their faces for any flicker of recognition or guilt. "I understand that you were all involved in the vandalism of the library the week before she died. Is this true?"

The teens exchanged uneasy glances, their shoulders hunching as they avoided direct eye contact. One boy, his acne-scarred face framed by unruly black hair, spoke up hesitantly. "We were just... hanging out, y'know? At the old playground.

We didn't do nothin' that can be proven."

"Who was there?" Nick asked, studying their faces for any signs of dishonesty.

"Um, all of us, I guess," another teen mumbled, her voice barely audible as she stared at her scuffed sneakers.

"Was anyone else with you? Any adults or other friends?" Nick pressed, his eyes narrowed.

"Look, old man," a tall, lanky boy with a pierced lip cut in, his tone defensive. "We already told the cops everything we know. We didn't have anything to do with the old lady's death. Just leave us alone. We're all eighteen or older. We don't need no supervision."

Nick suppressed a sigh, well aware that his questions were pushing them further away. Still, he couldn't shake the feeling that they knew more than they were letting on.

"Look, mister," one of the girls piped up, tossing her hair back defiantly but not leaving the couch. "We don't know nothin' about no murder. We just wanted to have some fun, that's all."

"Fun?" Nick echoed, his voice tinged with disbelief. "Vandalizing public property is your idea of fun? You realize that could have consequences, right?"

The teens glanced at each other, uncertainty flickering in their eyes. It was clear they were torn between the urge to share and the fear of getting in more trouble.

"Whatever," another boy grumbled, leaning against the wall, and avoiding Nick's gaze. "It ain't got nothin' to do with that old lady dyin'. The police already had the talk with us."

"Can you tell me where each of you were last night?" Nick persisted with a different tactic, determined to unearth any shred of information.

"None of your business," the tall teen snapped, visibly agitated. "We told you already; we don't know nothin' about it."

Nick pushed by the teen at the door and entered the room. The six teenagers scrambled to their feet and moved back. He didn't wait for them to object. "Which one of you did I chase last night?"

They looked worried, and almost in unison, they all denied it. All except one girl to the left. She looked irritated but also guilty. Nick decided to push her. "Was it you?"

"I'm sorry." She looked up and made eye contact.

Nick had seen her before. He wasn't sure where, but he was sure he knew her. Narrowing his eyes, he asked, "Sorry for what?"

"I knew Ms. Lucy. She was helping me to learn how to read."

"You were learning stuff," the teen at the door asked.

"Yes," she replied. "I don't want to be living like this my

whole life. I graduated from High School and can barely read. Ms. Lucy was helping me."

"To read," Nick clarified.

"Yes. She gave me a key because she knew what these asshats would say if they knew I was reading. So, I would go at night."

"That's not right," the teen at the door said. "We wouldn't judge you. You is one of us. I was just surprised."

"She was also teaching me to not talk like that moron." The corner of the girl's mouth twisted up with almost a smile. "She gave me a key to go in there and talk with her. When I heard she died, I kept going in to read. Nothing else. I swear. I really liked her."

The kid from the door put his hand on Nick's wrist. "That's enough. You need to go."

Nick turned on him. The kid was an inch taller than him and probably could hurt him significantly if the other kids in the room jumped in. "Did one of you bump into me on the street and give me this phone?" He held up Lucy's phone.

"Yeah," a teenager said from a chair by the kitchen. "Some guy paid me fifty to do it."

"Do you know what he looked like?"

The kid shook his head. "Nah. But even if I did, I ain't no snitch."

"All right," one girl finally said, her voice trembling slightly. "If it will make you leave, I will tell you. There was... there was this guy. We didn't know him, but he was hanging around the playground that night. Kind of creepy looking, y'know?"

"Can you describe him?" Nick asked, his interest piqued.

"Uh, he had, like, really thin gray hair, almost bald, and a scruffy beard. Old like you," she replied, fidgeting with her sleeves. "He just stood there, watching us. It freaked us out, so we left. But he stopped us and offered us some money to put the phone on you. He said it was a prank."

"Did you see where he went or what he did after you left?" Nick probed, trying to keep the urgency from creeping into his voice.

"No, we just got out of there as fast as we could," the lanky boy answered, shifting uncomfortably.

"Thank you," Nick said, nodding. "I appreciate your honesty."

"Will you leave now?" the boy from the door asked.

Nick's gaze flitted from one face to another, trying to discern whether these young perpetrators held any more secrets. Their disheveled appearances and evasive eyes spoke volumes, but he needed something solid.

"Listen," Nick said, trying yet another different

approach. He slowly twirled around to make sure he had all of their attention. "I understand you may be scared or worried about getting into trouble. I'm not here to accuse you of murder. But this is serious. A woman is dead, and I'm just trying to find out what happened to her. If you know something, anything, please tell me. Do you know anything about her death?"

"Whoa, hold on," the lanky boy said, raising a hand in protest. "We already told you everything we know about that night."

"Right," added another teen, her voice cracking with defiance. "We didn't have anything to do with that old lady's death."

Nick's frustration mounted as he studied their faces, searching for even the slightest hint of deception. But all he saw were nervous expressions and defensive postures. He took a deep breath, tasting the stale cigarette smoke still lingering in the air.

"Like we said, we don't know anything," a girl muttered, crossing her arms tightly over her chest. "We just did some stupid shit and left."

"Fine," Nick said, exasperated. He knew when he was fighting a losing battle. "If you remember anything later, please contact me."

"Look, we already told you, we don't know nothin'. And we wouldn't kill no one. Maybe hurt them, like we could you. But murder is a whole other thing." a girl spat from the kitchen, her eyes narrowing. "Now get outta here before we make you."

"Who even are you?" one of the boys sneered, his arms crossed defensively over his chest. "You ain't no cop. You don't scare us."

"Maybe I'm not a cop," Nick admitted, "but I am someone who cares about the truth. And if you're involved with Lucy's death, even tangentially, there will be consequences." His mind raced as he tried to gauge their reactions. Were they genuinely ignorant of what had happened to Lucy, or were they simply afraid to come clean?

"Consequences?" another boy scoffed, his voice dripping with disdain. "What are you going to do, old man? We ain't done nothing wrong."

"Vandalism isn't a small crime," Nick retorted, trying to keep his cool despite the rising tension. "And if it turns out you were involved in something more serious..." He let the implication hang in the air, hoping it would stir a sense of responsibility within them.

"Hey," the girl from before said, her eyes wide and fearful. "What if he's right? What if we really messed up?"

"Shut up," the boy at the door snapped, glaring at her. "Go read a book. Don't listen to him. He's just trying to get inside your head."

"Is that true?" Nick asked, focusing on the girl. "Am I getting inside your head, or are you starting to realize that the truth always comes out, one way or another?"

"Enough!" the boy shouted, his face flushed with anger. He stepped forward, his fists clenched at his sides. "You better back off, old man, or I swear I'll—" The threat went unfinished, but the message was clear.

"Easy," Nick said, holding up his hands in a gesture of surrender. "I don't want any trouble. But remember what I said. If you know something, it's better to come forward now."

The threat hung in the air between them, and Nick knew he had pushed as far as he could without risking his own safety. He nodded curtly, his frustration simmering beneath the surface as he turned and walked toward the door. The teens had helped with a few things, and he couldn't shake the nagging feeling that they were hiding more than they let on.

With a final nod, Nick backed away from the group of teenagers and stepped out into the dimly lit hallway. The door slammed shut behind him, echoing in the emptiness of the apartment complex like a gunshot. He sighed, feeling the weight of disappointment settle heavily on his shoulders.

"Damn," he muttered under his breath, anger and frustration mixing with the stale odor of cigarette smoke that clung to the walls. He knew it wouldn't be easy to coax information from the teens, but he had hoped for some glimmer of truth in their eyes, some hint of guilt that could lead him closer to solving Lucy's death. Instead, all he'd found was hostility and defiance, as impenetrable as a brick wall.

As he strode back down the dimly lit hallway, Nick's mind raced with possible next steps in his investigation. Maybe it was time to revisit the library, the scene of the crime, or perhaps there were other witnesses yet to be found. While the interview hadn't provided any concrete answers, it had given him a new lead to follow. "Scruffy beard and thinning hair," he said under his breath, committing the description to memory. "I'll find you."

His frustration gnawed at his insides, his mind racing with thoughts of what he could have done differently. A chill ran through him, despite the stagnant warmth of the hallway.

"Wait," a quiet voice called after him.

Nick stopped in his tracks, turning back towards the room he had just left. The girl who had earlier described the mysterious man was fidgeting with her sleeve, looking down at her feet. He noticed that now with her standing, she was almost as tall as him.

"Did you... did you maybe find something weird at the scene?" she asked hesitantly.

"Something weird?" Nick pressed, his heart pounding in his chest.

"Like, I don't know," she stammered, "maybe some kind of clue or something?"

Nick frowned, trying to make sense of her words. Was she genuinely curious, or was there something more hidden beneath her inquiry? "If you have any information that could help, now is the time to share it."

"This again," she said, her eyes flicking up to meet his for a brief moment before darting away again, "I already told you what I saw. That's it. The only thing is she wasn't feeling well."

"Did she say what didn't feel right?"

"No. Nothing else, really."

"All right," Nick replied, his voice heavy with disappointment. "Thank you for your time. And hey, keep up the reading. You can totally be whatever you want to be in life."

"Thanks. I don't need your permission."

Nick's frustration threatened to consume him as he walked away from the girl. He couldn't shake the nagging feeling that they knew more than they were letting on, but without any solid evidence, all he could do was trust their words. He descended the creaky stairs, replaying the interview in his mind, searching for any detail he might have missed, any thread he could pull to unravel the mystery.

His thoughts churned as he left the oppressive hallway and stepped into the crisp evening air, determined to uncover the truth, even if it meant digging deeper into the shadows of Sweet Sea.

He got in his car and looked in the rear-view mirror. Disheveled hair, bags under his eyes, and crow's feet for days looked back at him. Suddenly, he remembered his promise to the girls to take care of himself. He needed to eat something and sleep. If he passed out from exhaustion, he wouldn't be any good to anyone. As eager as he was to dive back into the investigation, Nick knew he needed to pause, to catch his breath and collect his thoughts. The world had been spinning ever since Lucy's death, a whirlwind of emotion and uncertainty that threatened to swallow him whole if he didn't find solid ground soon.

Nick smiled at his reflection, put the car in gear, and drove home. After cooking up a small meal in his kitchen, he took an extra-long shower, and went to bed. He slept for a little over ten hours.

CHAPTER SIXTEEN

Nick Cern leaned against the counter of Sweet Sea's coffee shop, his fingers absentmindedly drumming on the cold marble surface as he mulled over his morning encounter. He had bumped into a few members of the town's historical society outside the cafe, their hushed voices and darting glances immediately catching his attention.

"Excuse me," Nick had interjected, "I couldn't help but overhear your conversation about Lucy Brooks. She was a dear friend of mine."

The group exchanged uneasy looks before a tall man with a receding hairline stepped forward. "Nick Cern, isn't it? We're sorry for your loss, but this matter is private." His tone was curt, dismissive, leaving Nick with a nagging sense of unease. He recognized him as Doctor Victors.

"Private?" Nick raised an eyebrow. "Lucy's death has affected everyone in this town. I think we all deserve to know what happened."

"We understand your concern, Mr. Cern," a woman with horn-rimmed glasses chimed in, her voice trembling ever so slightly, "but we assure you that the police are doing everything they can, including ruling it as a natural passing. It would be best if you asked them. Now, if you'll excuse us." The group hurried away, leaving Nick with suspicion blossoming in his chest.

Now, sipping his lukewarm coffee, Nick couldn't shake the feeling that the historical society knew more than they were letting on. It was well-known around town that Lucy's nephew had been dismissed from the society for refusing to accept his aunt's money, and whispers had circulated about the organization borrowing heavily from a bank in San Diego. Nick couldn't ignore the possibility that Lucy's murder might be tied to the society's financial troubles.

Determined to investigate, Nick dug out his cell phone, brought up his note app, and began drafting a plan. If the historical society was involved in Lucy's death, they were bound to have secrets they wanted to keep hidden. Nick knew that uncovering those secrets would require persistence and cunning, but he was no stranger to challenging authority. He had come to Sweet Sea to start anew, and now he found himself with a mission – to honor Lucy's memory by exposing the truth behind her murder.

He took a long sip of his coffee, grimacing slightly at the bitter aftertaste, then began jotting down the names of the society members he remembered. As he scribbled on the pages, his resolve solidified. There was something amiss in Sweet Sea, and he was determined to get to the bottom of it, no matter how deep the roots of deception lay.

Nick spent the better part of his morning researching every detail he could find about the historical society and its members. It helped that traffic in his store was slow. The more he uncovered, the deeper his suspicions grew. Many of the long-standing members held positions of power or influence in the town, and Nick couldn't shake the nagging feeling that they were hiding something.

He took meticulous notes on his phone, adding a list of questions he intended to ask during the interviews. He jotted down names, dates, and potential motives.

Nick decided to conduct the interviews at the historical society's building, where he hoped the familiar surroundings might make the members feel more at ease – and perhaps more likely to slip up. It was easy to set up an appointment to talk with them as they had a meeting later that night. He chose a late afternoon time slot when the day's warmth had begun to dissipate, and the sun cast long, golden shadows across the quaint town of Sweet Sea. He imagined that the setting sun might provoke a sense of urgency in the members as the day's end drew near, and their secrets remained precariously close to being unearthed.

◆ ◆ ◆

The historical society's building stood tall and imposing amidst its picturesque surroundings, an old Victorian mansion with peeling white paint and ornate wooden trimmings. The house seemed to have its own set of secrets as if the walls themselves could speak of past intrigues and scandals. Nick felt a shiver run down his spine as he approached the aged structure, its creaking steps echoing his mounting unease.

"Mr. Cern," a voice greeted him as he entered the dimly lit foyer. "My name is Martha. We've been expecting you."

"Thank you," Nick replied, keeping his tone polite yet firm. He was here on a mission, and any attempts at intimidation wouldn't easily deter him. It was still surprising to him that they so readily accepted his request to interview each member of the Society. He expected a lot of pushback, but their openness to talk was a bit disarming.

"Please just have a seat. Once all the members are here, we will take you to a room, and you can interview them individually, as promised."

He smiled and said all he could, "I really appreciate it."

"No worries. The director thought it best to grant your request but knows this is not normal. You must be very lucky."

"And who is the director?"

"Doctor Victors. He took over about two years ago. Now, if you will excuse me."

Nick nodded as she returned to her desk. The doctor had come up again in his investigation. That couldn't be a coincidence, he thought.

As the members began to file into the building, Nick took a deep breath, steeled himself for the task at hand, and prepared to delve into the heart of darkness that lay hidden beneath the facade of Sweet Sea's most revered institution. Each member knew why they were there and still managed to give him a smile and greeting. He had no delusions. They didn't have to talk to him, and this was a courtesy they did not have to extend.

After about twenty minutes, the new arrivals had

stopped. The secretary stepped into a room off the entrance. Nick could hear muffled voices, and a moment later, she returned.

"Please, follow me." The secretary led him into a large, dusty room with tall bookcases and antique furniture. A heavy wooden table stood in the center, surrounded by mismatched chairs that seemed to have been collected from various eras of the town's history.

"Make yourself comfortable," she said, gesturing to a chair at the head of the table. "The members will be arriving shortly."

"Thank you," Nick replied, taking his seat and watching as the afternoon sun filtered through the stained-glass windows, casting eerie patterns on the worn wooden floorboards. The atmosphere was oppressive, and he felt the weight of the town's history bearing down upon him. In this very room, decisions had been made that shaped the lives of generations of Sweet Sea residents.

The first member to enter the interview room was an elderly woman, her silver hair braided into a tight bun. Her eyes were sharp and calculating as she took her seat across from Nick. She clasped her hands neatly on the table, observing him with the air of a predator sizing up its prey.

"Good afternoon," Nick greeted her warmly, trying to

put her at ease. "I appreciate your willingness to speak with me. My name is Nick Cern."

"I know who you are. Gertrude Simmons," she replied curtly, her voice like gravel crunching underfoot.

Nick opened his phone, his fingers drumming rhythmically against the shiny glass screen. "Mrs. Simmons, how long have you been a member of the historical society?"

"Forty-two years," Gertrude answered without hesitation, her thin lips pursing slightly. The finality in her tone suggested that this was information she believed he should have known already.

"Can you tell me about the society's recent financial troubles?" Nick ventured, deciding not to mince words.

"Financial troubles?" Gertrude scoffed, her eyes narrowing suspiciously. "Who told you that? We are managing just fine, thank you very much."

"Forgive me," Nick said, attempting to smooth over the sudden tension. "I've heard rumors of a loan taken from a bank in San Diego. I'm merely trying to understand the circumstances surrounding the matter."

"Rumors tend to be just that, Mr. Cern. Inaccurate and blown out of proportion," Gertrude retorted, her fingers tapping impatiently on the tabletop.

"My apologies," Nick conceded, sensing her growing

reluctance. "Let's move on to another topic. Were you acquainted with Lucy Brooks?"

"Of course," Gertrude replied, her demeanor softening only slightly. "She was an active member of the community, and I knew her well. She is the only reason we agreed to this farce."

"Farce?" Nick asked.

"You." She spat it out with as much venom as she could muster. "You come in here and waste our time as you play police. We are accommodating you because she was important to this society, and if there is even a less than one percent chance that her death was not natural, we would like to know. So please do not mistake our kindness for weakness. You are annoying, and we hope this one-time interview will keep you out of our hair. So, proceed, please, and let's get this over with.

Nick felt like he was smacked in the face. He wanted to say so much, but then he remembered they could pull away at any time. These interviews were acts of kindness. He pushed down his responses and continued the discussion. "Did you ever have any disagreements with her or know of anyone who might have?"

"Disagreements?" Gertrude repeated, her eyes narrowing once more. "No, nothing out of the ordinary. People in a small town like this will always have their differences, but that doesn't mean they go around killing each other."

"Of course not," Nick agreed, inwardly musing on the defensive tone her voice had taken. "I'm just trying to gather information and understand the relationships in town."

"Lucy was well-liked by most. She butted in sometimes where she shouldn't, but nothing that would be worth her dying," Gertrude said dismissively, pushing back her chair and standing up. "Now, if you'll excuse me, Mr. Cern, I have other matters to attend to. I don't have anything else to say."

"I have a few more questions."

"No, you don't. Not for me."

"Uh... Ok. Thank you for your time, Mrs. Simmons," Nick replied, watching as she briskly left the room.

Within five minutes, another society member came in. He wasn't as old as the first and looked to be in his sixties. Nick leaned forward, elbows on the table, as he fixed a steely gaze on the next member to be interviewed. The room was filled with the faint ticking of an antique clock, marking the passage of time in this tense atmosphere.

"Mr. Thompson," Nick began, his voice level but firm. "Were you close to Lucy Brooks at all?"

"Lucy and I... we shared a mutual interest in local history," Mr. Thompson replied hesitantly, fiddling with the frayed sleeve of his tweed jacket.

"Did she ever mention any conflicts or disagreements within the society?" Nick pressed, studying the man's nervous demeanor.

"Disagreements? No, no..." Thompson stammered, avoiding eye contact. "We all got along fine."

Nick tightened his jaw, feeling the frustration bubble up inside him like a boiling kettle. He knew these people were hiding something, and their evasiveness only served to strengthen his resolve.

"Let me rephrase the question," Nick said, drumming his fingers on the table. "Were there any unusual incidents leading up to the night of her death?"

"Unusual incidents?" Mr. Thompson repeated, darting a glance at the painting to his left as beads of sweat formed on his brow. "No, nothing out of the ordinary."

"Really?" Nick retorted, unable to mask the skepticism in his voice. "Because it seems odd that a well-liked woman like Lucy would be murdered without any apparent motive."

"Are you suggesting we had something to do with it, Mr. Cern?" Thompson snapped, his eyes narrowing in indignation. "We're a historical society, not a band of criminals!"

"Of course not," Nick replied calmly, though his mind raced with suspicion. "I'm simply trying to understand what could have led to her death."

"Perhaps you should focus your investigation elsewhere," Thompson suggested icily, crossing his arms defensively. "The police have recorded it as a natural death."

"Perhaps," Nick conceded, though he knew better than to back down now. "But I'll continue asking questions until I have all the facts."

"Fine," Thompson muttered, begrudgingly answering more questions with as little information as possible.

"Back to the night of her death." Nick swallowed hard for the next question. "I have been told that she was seen arguing with the doctor. In the parking lot, I believe."

"I didn't hear about that. I was in the building during that time."

"If you didn't hear about it, how do you know you were in the building at the time."

"Just an assumption. I saw Lucy leave."

"Who did she leave with?"

"I didn't see that."

It was clear to Nick that he was getting nowhere. "One last question. If Lucy's death was not an accident, who do you think would have the motive to kill her."

Mr. Thompson almost choked as he coughed. The question had disrupted him terribly. He was full-on sweating. "I have no idea," he managed to say between hacks.

As the interview concluded, Nick's frustration reached its peak. He couldn't shake the feeling that the historical society members were concealing a vital piece of the puzzle. Their collective stonewalling only fueled his determination to uncover the truth, whatever it may be.

"Thank you for your time," Nick said stiffly, watching as Mr. Thompson hurried out of the room. Discontent simmered within him like an unattended pot threatening to boil over. "You may want to get some water for that cough."

The subsequent interviews followed a similar pattern. Historical society members entered one by one, their body language tense and guarded as they answered Nick's questions with terse, evasive responses. It was as though they were hiding something - a secret they were unwilling to divulge, even under the guise of helping solve Lucy's murder.

Nick found himself growing increasingly frustrated with each unproductive conversation, his mind racing to piece together the elusive truth. As he prepared to interview the final member, the doctor, he couldn't help but feel a sense of foreboding settling over him. The shadows in the room seemed to lengthen, sharpening into sinister shapes as he considered what dark revelations might still lie hidden within the heart of Sweet Sea's historical society. He would get to the bottom of this mystery, no matter how deep the secrets were buried.

Nick scanned the room while he waited. The air was heavy with the dust. Shadows clung to the corners, dancing with each flicker of the overhead light that cast an eerie glow over the antique furnishings.

As he awaited his next interviewee, he couldn't shake the feeling that something sinister lurked beneath the surface of this seemingly innocuous group. He recalled how Lucy's nephew had been ousted from the society for refusing to accept his aunt's money – an act that seemed rather extreme given the circumstances. And now, their mounting debt to a nearby bank only heightened his suspicions.

"Doctor Victors," Nick greeted, standing up as the door creaked open to reveal the doctor's imposing figure. Dressed in a crisp white coat, which contrasted sharply against his balding head of gray hair and piercing green eyes, the doctor carried himself with an air of authority that demanded respect. However, Nick couldn't help but notice the slight tremble in the man's hands as he took a seat across from him.

"Mr. Cern," the doctor replied, his voice smooth and calculated. "I must say, I'm quite surprised to find myself being interviewed by an amateur sleuth."

"Lucy's murder has affected us all," Nick said, forcing a smile. "I just want to get to the bottom of it."

"Of course." Doctor Victors shifted in his seat, crossing his legs, and folding his hands in his lap. "But I'm not sure what kind of information I can offer you. The police ruled Lucy's death as an accident."

"You mean, you did. Correct?"

"I guess you could say that. I gave my report to the police, and they made the final statement. But yes, I did not find any signs of foul play. However, I am happy to chat if it will help a citizen and business owner of our fine town."

"Let's start with your relationship with Lucy," Nick suggested, trying to gauge any reaction from the doctor. "How well did you know her?"

"Like everyone else in Sweet Sea, I knew her as a kind, intelligent woman," the doctor replied, his words carefully measured. "And as her physician, I occasionally treated her for minor ailments. But our interactions were purely professional."

"Was the argument professional?"

"I'm not sure what you mean."

"The night she died, you were seen arguing with her." It was an exaggeration, but Nick hoped it would lead to an admission.

"You have been misinformed. She left with someone." The doctor leaned back. "Come to think of it; he looked like you."

"Well, I wasn't there. So, try again."

"No need to be hostile," Doctor Victors said. "I could be mistaken. But I do know it wasn't me."

"Did you know about her involvement with the historical society?" Nick pressed.

"Of course," Doctor Victors answered, a hint of impatience creeping into his voice. "But I fail to see how that's relevant to your fantasy investigation."

"Perhaps you could tell me more about the society's financial situation," Nick suggested, watching as the doctor's eyes narrowed ever so slightly. He was not going to take the bait. The interview would be over if he lost his temper with the doctor.

"Mr. Cern, I'm not sure how my knowledge of the society's finances would be of any use to you," Doctor Victors said with a forced smile. "Surely there are other avenues you could be exploring. Or better yet, find a new hobby."

"A woman is dead, Doctor. I would think you, of all people, would take it seriously."

"Absolutely, I do. It is tragic, but life happens. We all will go in our time, and hopefully, it will be peaceful like Lucy. Anything else you want to ask before I go back to doing real work with the rest of the society?"

"Every detail matters, Doctor. Why are you hesitant to talk about the financials? Something to hide, maybe?" Nick insisted, his mind racing with questions and speculations. He noticed the doctor's hands tremble again, betraying his otherwise calm demeanor.

"Very well," the doctor sighed, clearly uneasy. "It's no secret that the society borrowed money from a bank in San Diego, and we have been struggling to repay it."

"Is there anything else you can tell me about the circumstances surrounding the loan? Or about Lucy's role in the society?" Nick asked, leaning forward in anticipation.

"Lucy was a valued member," Doctor Victors replied, evading the question.

A subtle shift of air pressure alerted Nick to the doctor's evasive tactics as he sidestepped the question about the loan, and as he observed Doctor Victors fidgeting with the edges of his coat, an unwelcome sense of foreboding took root in the pit of his stomach. He decided he would come back to that question later.

"Doctor," Nick began, trying to maintain a civil tone, "would you mind telling me about any recent disagreements within the historical society? Perhaps something involving Lucy or her nephew?"

"Disagreements?" Doctor Victors repeated, his voice

tinged with feigned confusion. The corners of his mouth quivered as if he were attempting to suppress a smile. "Why, the society is like one big happy family, Mr. Cern. We all work together for the preservation and promotion of Sweet Sea's history."

"Really?" Nick pressed, raising an eyebrow. "A happy family that kicks out one of their own for refusing to take his aunt's money?" He watched closely as the doctor's eyes flickered with unease before settling into a steely gaze.

"I'm afraid that is a private matter, and I can't discuss it. Any other questions?"

"Back to the loan?"

"As for the loan, I believe Mr. Thompson or Ms. Haversham would be better equipped to discuss such matters."

"Neither wanted to talk about it or add any detail."

The doctor stood. "Their participation was voluntary. If they encountered hostility from you as I have, maybe they decided not to share. Either way, I need to get back."

"If I have any more questions, can I contact you?"

"I'm afraid I've already told you more than I should have. Mr. Cern. However, I will leave you with this advice. Sometimes sacrifices must be made for the greater good," Doctor Victors replied, his voice wavering slightly. "Good day." With that, the doctor turned on his heel and left the room, leaving Nick to ponder his next move.

As the door shut behind Doctor Victor's, the atmosphere in the room seemed to constrict, choking the remaining warmth from the space. Nick rubbed his temples, frustration bubbling within him like a cauldron ready to boil over. This was not how he had envisioned the interviews would go – these people were hiding something, yet they danced around the truth like performers in a twisted ballet. The members of the historical society were hiding something – something significant enough to shake even the respected Doctor Victors. The last statement felt like a threat from a desperate man. He knew he was inching closer to the heart of the mystery, despite the obstacles.

Nick stood up, the chair scraping against the hardwood floor in protest. He could not let the historical society continue to elude him. His mind raced with possibilities and connections, attempting to weave together the scattered threads of information he had gathered so far.

If Doctor Victors and the other members of the historical society thought they could keep their secrets locked away in the shadows, then Nick was prepared to drag them into the light – one unspoken truth at a time.

CHAPTER SEVENTEEN

Nick sat on the sill of his large open window, the salt-tinged breeze bringing a calm to his racing thoughts. The rhythmic sound of waves crashing against the shore echoed in the distance as he sipped his coffee, contemplating how life had changed so dramatically. Dusk had come to Sweet Sea, casting a warm golden glow over the coastal town.

Suddenly, his phone buzzed and lit up with an incoming video call. He answered it with a grin. Bridget and Kaley's faces appeared on the screen, their smiles flanked by the tiny icons of their respective cityscapes.

"Hey, Dad!" they chimed in unison, their voices tinged with concern. "How are you holding up?"

"Hi girls," Nick smiled warmly, his eyes brightening at the sight of his daughters. He stretched out his back and turned, allowing the camera to capture the setting sun behind him. "I'm doing alright, thanks for asking."

"Look at that view!" Kaley exclaimed, adjusting her glasses as she squinted at the hazy orange backdrop. "Almost makes me want to drop law school and move to a seaside cottage myself."

"Speaking of which," Bridget interjected, her fashionably tousled red hair bouncing as she tilted her head. "How are you coping with losing, Lucy? It must be hard, but we're here for you, okay?"

Nick let out a long sigh, his fingers idly tracing the rim of his coffee mug. He had raised his girls to be strong, but her directness even surprised him at times. "It hasn't been easy," he admitted, his gaze momentarily distant. "But I've been keeping busy. You know me - I can't sit still for too long."

"You're still trying to figure out if Lucy was killed?" Bridget asked.

Nick hesitated.

"Dad?" Kaley said.

"Yes. Sort of. Everyone keeps telling me there is nothing there. I just know it."

"Have you been attending those support group

meetings?" Kaley asked gently, her blue eyes full of empathy. "We know it's not your thing, but it might help with the anxiety."

"Actually," Nick said, a hint of pride in his voice, "The tinkering I do as part of the business has really kept my mind occupied. You'd be surprised how many people in town have ancient machines gathering dust or can't seem to keep their phone safe. At least once a day I have to replace a screen."

Bridget chuckled, shaking her head fondly. "Only you, Dad, would find comfort in circuit boards and hard drives."

"Hey, it's helping me heal," he replied defensively, but the twinkle in his eyes betrayed his amusement. "It's nice to feel useful and give back to the community."

The three of them shared a warm, affectionate silence as the sun slipped beneath the waves, leaving only the pinkish hues of twilight in its wake. They knew that time could never erase the pain of loss entirely, but each day spent in the embrace of loved ones was a step closer to healing.

"Enough about me," Nick said, his voice softening as he shifted the focus of the conversation to his daughters. "How are you both doing? Bridget, how are things at the fashion company?"

Bridget sighed dramatically, her eyes rolling heavenward. An impeccable strand of her hair seemed to quiver in sympathy. "Oh, Dad, you wouldn't believe the deadlines I'm juggling. I swear, each day feels like I'm waltzing through a maze of to-do lists designed by some sadistic genius."

Kaley chimed in with a chuckle, her smile bright and mischievous. "Sounds like you're living your own Agatha Christie novel, Bridge."

"Very funny, Kales," Bridget retorted, but her expression remained good-natured. "At least I have you two to keep me grounded amidst the whirlwind of taffeta and silk."

"Speaking of whirlwinds," Kaley interjected, her enthusiasm palpable even through the screen, "I've got some news. I'll be joining you Dad during the summer! I can't wait for us to be together again, especially after this intense semester at school. Bridget, you should try to come down and we can all be together."

"Really?" Nick asked, his eyes lighting up with happiness. "That's wonderful, sweetheart."

"I can try," Bridget added. "Guess we can expect some thrilling courtroom tales, eh?" Bridget teased her sister, who replied with a playful grin.

"Absolutely. Now, Dad, tell us about your visit to the historical society," Kaley prompted, eager to hear more about Nick's life in Sweet Sea.

"Ah, yes," he began, his brow furrowing slightly as he recounted the details. "Well, I went there to research some things on my mind, and it seems they are not all that pleasant. They were all quite tight-lipped, and I couldn't shake the feeling that something was amiss."

"Looking into Lucy's death?" Bridget asked.

"Sort of."

"Sounds like you've stumbled upon a conspiracy, Dad," Bridget remarked, her eyes wide with mock astonishment. "Just imagine if the FBI gets involved!"

"Or even better, the mafia!" Kaley added, their laughter filling the airwaves.

"Very funny, girls," Nick chuckled, his heart swelling with love for his daughters. They had always been his pillars of strength, their wit and vivacity acting as a balm to soothe the wounds of grief and loss. Even in the midst of such darkness, their laughter served as a beacon, guiding him back toward the light.

"Thank God I have two daughters that think they're funny."

They both mocked an exaggerated look of shock and insult.

"Anyway," he continued, still smiling, "I'll keep digging into this mystery. It's good to have something to focus on, and who knows? Maybe I'll uncover some long-lost treasure."

"Or a secret society," Bridget quipped, her eyes twinkling with mischief.

"Only time will tell," Nick replied, his voice tinged with wry amusement.

"Whatever you discover, Dad, just remember that we're here for you," Kaley said, her tone sincere. "We love you so much."

"Thank you, girls," Nick whispered, his eyes glistening with unshed tears. He knew, without a shadow of a doubt, that the bond they shared could withstand any storm. "I have some clues and people to interview. My goal is to build a case and then take it to the sheriff. I think she will be open to listening as long as I have proof."

"Sounds like you've got it all figured out, Dad," Kaley chimed in, her eyes alight with admiration. "But what about your social life? Have you been hanging out with Rose lately?"

Nick's cheeks flushed a red hue, betraying his surprise at the sudden change in topic. "Oh, uh, Rose and I have been spending some time together, yes. But we're just friends, nothing more."

"Come on, Dad, you can tell us," Bridget teased, her voice lilting and conspiratorial. "Have you taken her out to dinner, perhaps? Or maybe you've gone for romantic walks along the beach?"

"Girls, really, it's not like that," Nick insisted, his laughter tinged with a hint of exasperation. Yet, even as he denied their insinuations, he couldn't help but feel a warmth blossom within his chest at the thought of Rose – her easy smile, her quick wit, her unwavering kindness.

"Okay, okay," Kaley relented, her lips curling into a knowing smirk. "We won't press you on it. But just remember: if you ever need advice on wooing women, your lovely daughters are only a phone call away."

"Thanks, but I think I'll manage," Nick replied dryly, though the corners of his mouth twitched with amusement. He could always count on his girls to keep him grounded, even when the weight of grief threatened to pull him under. And as he mulled over their playful banter, he found himself grateful for the unexpected gift of levity.

"By the way, Dad," Bridget interjected, her voice tinged with curiosity. "Did you happen to receive our birthday present for you?"

"Ah, yes," Nick replied, his eyes lighting up. He moved the camera to reveal the sleek screen picture frame resting on a polished mahogany side table. The frame cycled through a kaleidoscope of family memories – from sun-drenched summer vacations and cozy Christmases to joyful birthdays and quiet moments spent reading together. Each image seemed to capture a fragment of time that Nick could hold onto forever.

"Your mother would have loved this," he said, unable to keep the emotion from his voice. His throat tightened as he watched the images flicker past, each one a testament to the love that had once made his world whole. He dabbed the corner of his eye threatening to release a tear or two.

"We thought you could use a little reminder of the good times, especially now," Kaley said softly, her eyes shimmering with unshed tears. "We wanted you to know that no matter where you are, we're always with you."

"Thank you, girls. I really do love it," Nick choked out, his heart swelling with gratitude. "It's truly one of the most thoughtful gifts I've ever received." As he spoke, a photograph of his lovely wife appeared on the screen, her radiant smile seeming to fill the room with warmth. For a fleeting moment, Nick felt as though she was there with him, her presence an undeniable force that transcended the boundaries of time and space.

"You can add new photos too. Maybe you and Rose," Bridget implored, her voice filled with enthusiasm. "We can see all the pictures as well and even add some remotely."

Nick nodded, his eyes never leaving the screen as it

continued to cycle through the images of his life. "I will add pictures," he whispered, the weight of their love and concern settling around him like a comforting embrace. He knew that their support would serve as a beacon of hope in even the darkest moments, guiding him through the challenges if he started spiraling down again.

"Good," Kaley said firmly, her expression softening into a gentle smile. "Don't forget that we love you, Dad."

"Alright, Dad," Bridget said, flashing him a warm, affectionate smile. "We'll let you off the hook – for now. But keep us posted on your progress with both the mystery and Rose, alright?"

"Of course," Nick promised, his voice steady and sincere. "I'll call you both as soon as I have any updates."

"Promise us you'll take care of yourself, okay?" Bridget implored, her voice thick with emotion. "We love you, Dad."

"Always," Nick assured them, his heart swelling with gratitude for his daughters' unwavering support. "I promise."

"I will email you the information again on the grief counseling group. It's only a thirty minute drive outside of your town and it's completely anonymous."

"Is anything anonymous in a small town?" Nick said.

"I think it is far enough out that you should be okay. So go," Kaley said, her eyes widening to show how serious she was.

"Okay, okay. I get it."

"Take care of yourself, Dad," Kaley added softly, her concern evident in the furrow of her brow. "We love you."

"Love you too, girls," Nick whispered, his heart swelling with devotion. And as he ended the call, he knew that no matter what challenges lay ahead – be they buried secrets or burgeoning romance – he would face them head-on, buoyed by the unwavering love and support of his family. The last remnants of daylight vanished, enveloped by the encroaching darkness. But in the quiet solitude of his seaside apartment, surrounded by memories both joyful and painful, Nick found solace and strength - and perhaps, the first glimmers of hope amidst the shadows.

CHAPTER EIGHTEEN

The quaint electronic repair shop, nestled within a row of small businesses on Main Street, was flooded with the warm glow of the afternoon sun. Doctor Victors paused momentarily at the doorway, taking in the comforting scent of coffee mingling with the faint aroma of solder and electronics. The walls were lined with shelves filled with an assortment of gadgets and cables, while a high counter separated the work area from the customers.

"Ah, Mr. Cern's establishment," Doctor Victors mused to himself as he stepped inside, his polished shoes clicking softly against the wooden floorboards. He stood tall and poised, hands clasped behind his back, betraying no hint of anxiety or urgency. Anyone looking at him would see the picture of a distinguished gentleman, one who held the respect of the Sweet Sea community in the palm of his hand.

The door chime announced his arrival, and Doctor Victors waited patiently near the counter, observing the various knick-knacks that adorned the space. A small smile played on his lips as he spotted the numerous tech-themed coffee mugs, each sporting a witty slogan. In this quiet corner of the world, life seemed unabated, untouched by the shadows that lurked just out of reach.

"Curious," he thought, his eyes narrowing ever so slightly. "How even the smallest of actions can ripple through the lives of others, causing waves that cannot be undone."

As he waited, Doctor Victors let his gaze wander to the framed photos hanging above the counter, taking note of the smiling faces that stared back at him. The joy captured in those images was palpable, and yet, he could not help but feel a twinge of unease deep within him. The past had a way of catching up with people, even in a place as seemingly idyllic as Sweet Sea. And for some, the truth would prove to be a bitter pill to swallow.

"Mr. Cern certainly has made a new life for himself here," he thought, his calm demeanor belying the storm of thoughts brewing within. "But I wonder, how long can one truly escape their past?"

Nick stepped out from the back, and his eyes widened. The doctor was the last person in the world that he expected to see. After the interviews, he figured the Doctor would never actively speak to him. Be that as it may, he was a customer, and he was in his shop. He put on a fake smile and walked to the counter.

"Ah, Doctor Victors! What can I help you with today?" Nick Cern's voice was warm and welcoming. It was fake, but the doctor didn't need to know that. "Is your computer giving you trouble?"

"Indeed, Mr. Cern," Doctor Victors replied, his voice smooth and measured. "I seem to have forgotten my password. A minor inconvenience, but one I would appreciate your assistance with."

"Of course, let's have a look." Nick motioned for the doctor to hand him the laptop and settled into his worn leather chair behind the counter upon receiving it. With practiced ease, he began tapping away at the keys, with each click, a staccato beat in the quiet rhythm of the shop. "Any ideas on what it could be?"

The doctor rattled off a few choices, and each failed. The screen said he had made too many attempts and would have to wait five minutes to try again. Convinced this would not work, Nick grabbed a portable rescue reboot device and plugged it into the USB port on the side. As Nick worked, his thoughts drifted towards more questions for the doctor. However, this was neither the time nor the place.

"Do you know about how long this will take?" The doctor looked at his watch.

"I am going to need to recover your password. It won't be long. Maybe ten minutes, probably less."

Nick tried to make small talk. "So, how long have you lived in town?"

"All my life," the doctor responded curtly.

"With still being fairly new, I haven't had a chance to check out the area much. Any recommendations for good places to eat?"

"Not really."

"How about fun stuff to do? I have two daughters. One is out of school and the other is still in college. When they come to visit, I would love to have things to do beyond go to the beach."

"I don't really do much fun stuff. Check with the tourism office."

Nick ran out of questions and just focused on the work. The doctor waited patiently. He wandered among the devices and had no interest in speaking with Nick. The completion of the program could not come soon enough. Luckily, it ended up being less than ten minutes.

"All right, Doctor Victors, I've reset your password," Nick announced, his fingers dancing across the keyboard with practiced ease. "Do you want me to write it down for you?"

"Thank you, but no need," the doctor replied, his voice calm and measured. He leaned closer, eyes scanning the screen as if ensuring everything was in order.

As Nick typed in the new password one last time to confirm the change, he said, "The password is 1-d-1-d-1-t!!!."

The doctor committed it to memory and smiled. "I did it with three exclamation marks," he confirmed.

"Yes, just replace the I's with 1's."

"Should be easy enough to remember." The doctor smiled. "Of course, I said that about the other ones too."

Nick's fingers danced across the keyboard, deftly navigating the pathways of the computer's inner workings. In a matter of minutes, the final step of the new password had been reset, and the screen sprang to life, bathing Nick's face in an eerie glow. The WEB browser was up. The latest search had been for poisonous plants. It was hard for him to hide his surprise and shock.

"Poisonous plants local to me" – the words burned into Nick's mind like a brand, searing his curiosity. He couldn't help but lean in closer to the computer screen as he glimpsed the search results displayed before him.

"Aconitum napellus, Atropa belladonna, Cicuta maculata..." he read to himself, his voice barely more than a whisper. The Latin names of the plants danced across the page, each one a carefully crafted symphony of letters and syllables, hiding their true nature beneath a veil of poetic beauty.

"Is there something interesting on my screen, Mr. Cern?" Doctor Victors asked, his voice calm and even. Nick could feel the weight of his gaze upon him, an almost tangible force that threatened to crush the breath from his lungs.

"Ah, no, just... I was wondering about these plants you were looking up. Are they dangerous?" Nick stammered, trying to seem casual despite the hammering of his heart.

"Indeed, some of them can be," the doctor replied, his eyes never leaving Nick's face. "In fact, many of these plants are quite toxic."

Nick's fingers hovered above the keyboard, itching to click on one of the search results for further investigation. But just as he was about to give in to his urge, Doctor Victor's hand shot out like a striking snake, closing the laptops lid with a swift, practiced motion.

"Thank you for your assistance, Mr. Cern," he said tersely, his lips curling into a tight-lipped smile. "I appreciate your discretion in this matter."

"Of course, Doctor Victors," Nick replied, feigning innocence while his mind raced like a thousand galloping horses. What was the doctor hiding? Why was he so interested in poisonous plants? Was there a connection to Lucy's death? The questions tumbled through his thoughts, each one a jagged shard of ice that threatened to pierce the fragile fabric of his composure.

He swallowed deeply and forced a pretty good fake smile. "That should do it, Doctor."

"Thank you, Mr. Cern," Doctor Victors said, his face unreadable as he observed the technician's skilled ministrations. "Your expertise is always appreciated. How much do I owe you?"

"On the house after you extended the courtesy of the interviews. Happy to help," Nick replied, a nagging curiosity tugged at the edges of his mind like a stubborn weed refusing to be uprooted. He couldn't quite put his finger on it, but something about the doctor's visit felt... off.

"Think nothing of it. Hopefully, you find peace."

"Have a great day, Doctor," Nick said, trying to shake the feeling as he watched the older man turn to leave.

"Likewise, Mr. Cern." With a curt nod and a cryptic smile, Doctor Victors disappeared out the door, leaving Nick alone in the shop once more. Nick noticed the laptop cradled protectively in his arms like a precious treasure.

As the echoes of the doctor's footsteps faded away, Nick stared into the void of the now vacant store, the silence settling around him like a heavy cloak. He was alone with the ghosts of his doubts and suspicions. His thoughts swirled like eddies in a murky river, questions spinning and colliding with one another, each demanding answer that remained elusive. Or was the doctor just messing with him? The physician had to have known that a screen would have come up.

"Poisonous plants," Nick said aloud, the phrase lingering in the air like the scent of something long since decayed. "What could you possibly want with those, Doctor Victors?"

Nick's thoughts trailed off as he pondered the implications of his discovery. He knew he should let it go, leave well enough alone, but something inside him – an insatiable hunger for the truth, perhaps, or simply an innate stubbornness borne of years spent battling against the world – refused to be silenced.

Nick grabbed his personal laptop from beneath the counter. He sat there, bathed in the cold glow of the computer screen. He knew he could no longer ignore the gnawing suspicion that had taken root in his heart. He had to find answers – for Lucy, for himself, and for the sleepy little town of Sweet Sea that now seemed to be harboring a deadly secret beneath its tranquil surface.

"All right, let's see what you were looking for, Doctor Victors," he said, fingers flying across the keyboard as he searched for information on poisonous plants native to Sweet Sea. The results filled the screen, and Nick leaned in closer, eyes scanning each entry with fervent intensity.

As he delved deeper into the botanical world of toxins and deadly beauty, the pieces of a puzzle began to form. A puzzle that whispered secrets and hinted at a darkness hidden beneath the surface of their quaint coastal town.

"Curiouser and curiouser," he breathed, his heart pounding in tune with the relentless march of his thoughts.

A residual chill lingered in the air as Nick, still bemused by Doctor Victor's peculiar search query, silently promised himself to keep searching the internet for the enigma of poisonous plants native to Sweet Sea. The computer before him hummed softly, and its screencast a pale glow upon his creased face. His fingers drummed against the tabletop, their rhythm both absentminded and eager - an embodiment of the questions swirling within him.

"Maybe he has a patient who ingested some poisonous plant," Nick reasoned, attempting to silence the nagging doubts. "Or maybe he's just screwing with me. Trying to bait me in to doing something stupid. Or, I guess it's possible that maybe he's just curious about the local flora."

But as much as he tried to rationalize, the seed of doubt continued to take root. A connection, however tenuous, formed in his mind's eye, and he knew he couldn't ignore it any longer. And so, the stage was set for a game of cat and mouse, where each player held their cards close to their chest, and the stakes were higher than anyone could have imagined.

As the day wore on and customers came and went, Nick found himself unable to shake off the unease that had settled over him. Finally, locking the door to the shop, he sank into his chair, the weight of his thoughts pulling him down. The screen before him flickered, beckoning like a lantern in a dark forest. He had read as much as he could on poisonous plants and realized there was much more to go through. His eyes were heavy, and his stomach hadn't stopped growling over the last few hours. He would give the search one more hour and then go eat.

CHAPTER NINETEEN

N ick Cern's fingers drummed on the countertop, a syncopated rhythm that echoed through the empty shop. He couldn't help the nervous habit during deep thought. He tried in the past to stop it, but never could shake it and as a result never could play poker with such an obvious tell.

The scent of soldering iron and ozone lingered in the air, a testament to the countless computer repairs performed within these walls. He glanced at the clock, noting the seconds that ticked by with maddening slowness. His thoughts returned, unbidden, to Doctor Victors and the poisonous plants that seemed to have captured the man's interest.

"Nick! Good to see you!" Lucy Brooks' voice rang out,

warm as the sun filtered through the blinds, casting a dappled pattern on the floor. She stood in the doorway, arms laden with books, her gray hair gleaming like silver.

"Lucy," he greeted her, a smile breaking through his furrowed brow. Something felt off. "What brings you here?"

"Ah, well, my computer is acting up again," she said, her eyes twinkling. "I thought I'd bring some light reading while I wait."

"Of course, let me take a look." Nick moved to help her and then stopped. Something was wrong. This wasn't real. Lucy was dead. Or was she? He looked up to say something and saw the light reading she had brought. The title read: *Deadly Flora: A Compendium of Poisonous Plants.*

"Interesting choice," he remarked, unable to keep the curiosity from his voice.

"Ah, yes," she replied, her own curiosity piqued. "I've always been fascinated by the darker side of nature. It's amazing how such small, delicate things can harbor so much danger."

"Speaking of dangerous plants," Nick began, hesitating for a moment before plunging ahead, "I helped Doctor Victors with his computer earlier, and I couldn't help but notice he had been searching for information on local poisonous plants."

"Really?" Lucy arched a delicate eyebrow, her curiosity

evolving into concern. "Did he say why?"

"No, he didn't," Nick admitted, his heart pounding like a jackhammer against his ribs. "But it got me thinking, and I did some digging myself. It turns out there are quite a few poisonous plants native to Sweet Sea."

"Such as?" Lucy prompted, leaning in.

"Angel's trumpet, poison hemlock, even deadly nightshade," he listed, watching her face for any flicker of recognition or alarm.

"Good heavens," she murmured, her eyes widening. "Those are all highly toxic."

"Exactly." He leaned closer, lowering his voice to a conspiratorial whisper. "It makes me wonder what someone like Doctor Victors would need with such knowledge."

"Perhaps it's best not to jump to conclusions," Lucy cautioned gently, her gaze steady and wise. "There could be a perfectly innocent explanation."

"Maybe you're right," he conceded, his thoughts still churning like a storm-tossed sea. "But I can't shake the feeling that something is off."

"Do you think he poisoned me? Is that what killed me?"

Nick's eyes widened. "You know you're dead?"

"Of course. I'm not stupid."

"What is this then? A dream? Are you a ghost?"

"You're asking the wrong questions."

"What would be the right ones?"

"Trust your instincts, Nick," she advised, an enigmatic smile playing on her lips. "But be careful not to get lost in the shadows."

She stood and walked to the door; the sun dipped low, casting long, ominous shadows across the floor. Nick couldn't help but feel those shadows held secrets, waiting just beyond his grasp, beckoning like a lantern in a dark forest. Suddenly, he sat up. The keyboard marked the portion of his face his head had rested on.

It was all a dream, he told himself. Exhaustion had taken him. However, it seemed so natural. It felt like she was here. His mind, reeling from the imagery, told him it was break time. He grabbed his coat from the chair and left. He needed to eat and then sleep.

Nick stepped out the door and locked it behind him. The rain had stopped, and he could see the diner was not very busy across the street. Looking both ways, he crossed.

"Hey, Nick!" a voice called from a nearby doorway, breaking through his reverie. Eunice Edwards, the proprietor of the antique store down a few doors, swept across the street like a gust of fresh air. Her eyes sparkled with curiosity as she looked at him up and down. "You seem a bit pensive today.

Everything all right?"

"Hi, Eunice," he responded, forcing a smile. The dream played over and over in his thoughts. "I'm just... thinking about something that happened earlier."

"Ah, I see," she said, nodding sagely. "I just wanted to say sorry that I missed the interviews at the Historical Society. I had an event I could not get out of."

A light bulb went off in Nick's head. Eunice was the Historical Society Treasurer. How had he not noticed she wasn't there? Especially with the question on Finances. "That's okay. Not sure if you heard, but it didn't go well."

"I hadn't heard that. I am free now if you want to ask anything?"

"Thanks, Eunice. I appreciate that." Nick couldn't help but feel a slight sense of relief. Eunice's keen intuition could be both an asset and a liability. "Would you care to join me for dinner?"

She smiled apologetically. "Sorry, I can't. I can answer any questions you have really quickly here."

He thought hard. "I really only have three questions for you."

"Shoot."

"Is it true that the society defaulted on a loan and is having financial issues?"

"Sort of. We did not default, but we were late and did have financial issues. We decided on some ways to raise money and ended up selling off a property to make it work. We are going to do some fundraising soon to help make up the difference in another loan."

"So, you never asked Lucy or anyone to contribute their money?"

"Never. We are members of the society, but we would never ask people to put in their personal money."

"I am confused. If that is not the case, do you know why Michael Brooks was removed from the society?"

She nodded. "I do. When we were discussing fundraising, he was not helpful and started negatively calling out members for the situation. We asked him to contribute or be quiet. He got really angry. One member, I can't remember which one, asked if he was on drugs. Michael flipped out and punched him."

"Wow. I did not hear that."

"We try to keep things like that quiet. We all decided to not talk about the incident."

"I appreciate it. I promise not to say anything."

"Thank you. You said three questions. What is the other one."

He nodded. "Yeah. What do you think of Doctor

Victors?"

"He's an ass." She laughed. "But he really cares about the Historical Society. He has given so much time and energy to it. He has said it is the most important thing in his life."

"That's a little odd."

"It is, but his dad and grandfather had both been on the board. I think it is a pride and legacy issue."

"Do you think he could have killed Lucy?"

Eunice's head snapped back. "Don't be direct or anything."

"Sorry."

She thought deeply. "I hate to think anyone, especially a doctor, would kill anyone. But they did not get along. So, I guess it is possible. He just doesn't come across as a killer to me."

"Did you see either Lucy or him on the night of her death at the Historical Society event?"

"I did."

"Did you see anything between the two?"

She looked up and nodded her head. "Come to think of it. They left around the same time. I think they were talking. Beyond that, not much."

"Hey, Nick."

Nick turned towards the sound of the voice. Rose stood

at the diner entrance, holding the door open. "Would you two like to join me for dinner? We can talk through stuff."

Nick held up his index finger and turned back to Eunice. "Sure, you don't want to join us?"

"Sorry, I can't."

"Ok. I'm starving. If I think of anything else, do you mind if I stop by?"

"Please do. You still have to see my shop."

"Certainly."

Nick headed to the diner as Eunice walked off.

"Is she not joining us?" Rose asked.

"She has another engagement. It's okay. I have a lot to catch you up on."

"Great." She gave him a peck on the cheek and a hug. "Good to see you. Let's eat."

Later that evening, after a good meal and comparing notes with Rose, Nick sat hunched over his computer, poring over articles about poisonous plants indigenous to their region. His mind raced with questions. Rose wasn't sure the doctor's search on the plants was a clue, but she was excited to hear about the interviews with both the teenagers and the Historical Society. She didn't really have any new information from her side of the investigation but was a great sounding board. He laid out everything he heard, saw, and thought. In the end, she offered to go out and collect samples of the plants. She tended the gardens at the church and was very familiar with each plant.

Nick's mind had a new question after dinner. Was Rose's kiss on his cheek and her warm hug an indication that she liked him? Or was she just being friendly? He would add it to his list but had to stay focused on Lucy's death.

CHAPTER TWENTY

The sun streamed through the narrow slits between the tightly drawn drapes of the library, casting amber rays that danced on the dusty hardwood floor. Nick stood beside Lucy's mahogany desk, his fingertips gliding over its polished surface as he contemplated the next steps. After a good night's sleep and a slow morning at the shop, he decided to stop by the library for lunch. He walked around, hoping to find something that would speak to him. He knew it was a long shot, but he had to try.

He eventually found himself at Lucy's desk. Or, more appropriately, Susan's desk now that she was made head librarian with his friend passing. He sat down in the chair and recalled the suspects and clues he had. The two pages of names, motives, and clues to support lay in front of him after printing them the night before.

At the top of the first page, it read 'Cause of Death." Natural causes were crossed out, and below it was the word poison. Below poison was unknown means covered up by Doctor Victors. He pondered that for a moment and concluded that if the doctor was the killer, then the cause of death could be many things. For the sake of simplicity, he stayed with poison for now. It made sense with Lucy's cryptic email.

Next, he went to the suspects. Michael Brooks was the first one. As Lucy's only living relative, he stood to inherit her fortune. Except, he knew well before her death that he was getting no money. With money no longer the motivator, could he have done it out of anger for the change or perhaps a fight with her about it? Maybe he was trying to get revenge for being removed from the Historical Society. However, if that was the case, then why not kill the Doctor? Something didn't make sense there.

He went to Harold Finch next. The grumpy janitor at the library definitely had the opportunity, and if it weren't for him, Nick would not have found the hidden room with Lucy's body. Had Harold told him that because he wanted to seem helpful to throw suspicion off of him? Or was he really trying to be helpful, and it was only lucky they found her? Nick pondered it but could not come up with a reason to kill her. The janitor could have snapped or gone crazy, but it just didn't make sense that he would use poison. He was more of a blunt object kind of guy, Nick thought.

Nick moved on to the next name, Doctor Victors. He was in his late 60s and was a well-respected figure in the community. However, he was an ass as Eunice had so elegantly put it. Everything he said to Nick seemed condescending, and even though he gave the illusion of helping, he hadn't really done anything to move him further. The main point Nick had underlined on the paper was that he had access, knowledge, and even a clue that he was looking up poisonous plants. He definitely could have done it. He also may have been arguing with Lucy right before her death. However, he could not confirm. The feeling that the doctor was involved somehow ate away at Nick. He also did the cause of death report. He could have faked it. But why? Was it about the money?

Nick drew a line through the next two names listed. The sheriff had kept telling him to stop and insisted it was natural causes. Originally, he thought she was blocking him because she had something to hide, but now he couldn't confirm her involvement if the doctor claimed natural death. She was off his list. The second crossed out line was for the vandals. The teenagers were idiots and had the opportunity with the key. He just couldn't come up with a reason. Maybe robbery, but they were barely educated, and it was a stretch to think they could know about the poisonous plants and use them. If they killed anything, it was their brain cells. His gut said to ignore them. And if the dream he had of Lucy was any indication, he should follow his gut.

The next name was a new addition, but it seemed like a stretch. Eunice Edwards. She was the antique store owner and treasurer of the Historical Society. She hadn't even been on his radar until last night. It wasn't because she didn't want to have dinner with them, but more about how helpful she was. Nick knew it was contradictory, but something about her being the only helpful person in the society and so eager to fill in the gaps seemed too convenient. Was she trying to throw him off the track? Something in his gut told him she was hiding something. He just wasn't sure it was murder. The other Historical Society members were just elusive, but he didn't really think any of them would have done it. They just didn't seem to care enough.

The remaining people were possible but seemed highly unlikely. He couldn't cross them off the list yet. Susan Priser got a promotion to Head Librarian after Lucy's death. He was unsure if it came with more money, but people had been killed for less. Motive was thin, so he kept her on the list.

Gerald, Lucy's ex-husband, had an alibi and lived a few hours away. He and Lucy didn't appear to have any issues. But he was the ex-husband. If all the mystery books had taught him anything, it was that the ex seemed to be involved more often than not. Rose had interviewed him and was certain he was not involved. Plus, he was in a wheelchair and it would have been difficult for him to traverse the forest floor to retrieve the plants.

Nick sat back and closed his eyes. The next best step for him was to narrow the list. His top three were Michael, Doctor Victors, and Harold. His bottom three were Eunice, Susan, and Gerald. The top three were going to get the rest of his time for now. At dinner last night, Rose said she was going to focus on finding out anything new on the bottom three.

"Nick," Rose called from the doorway, jolting him from his reverie. "I figured you would be here when you weren't at the shop. I found something you might want to see."

"Show me," he urged, his heart pounding in anticipation.

Rose laid a thick file on the desk, spilling forth documents with red ink and numbers circled in urgent strokes. Nick's eyes scanned the pages, growing wider with each line. The papers revealed the dire financial straits the Sweet Sea Historical Society had fallen into. He noticed that the Society had shown immense interest in Lucy's wealth, requesting significant donations multiple times. This was an angle he had considered before; perhaps the Society's desperation could be linked to Lucy's untimely demise. But Eunice had been clear that this was not the case. She lied to him.

"According to these records," Rose explained, "the Society's debts have been mounting for years. They're on the verge of bankruptcy."

As Nick absorbed this new information, he pieced together a potential motive. Could it be possible that someone within the historical society had taken matters into their own hands, killing Lucy to secure her fortune? He knew Lucy was passionate about literature and deeply involved with the Society, so it was not a stretch to think that they saw her as their last hope for survival. Eunice was moving up on his list.

"Rose, were you able to figure out if Lucy ever responded to these requests?" he inquired, his voice edged with concern.

"From what I can tell, she declined most of them," Rose replied, her expression somber. "She believed in preserving history but thought the Society needed to find more sustainable sources of income."

"Interesting...," Nick mused, rubbing his chin thoughtfully. A nagging sensation gnawed at the back of his mind, urging him to dig deeper into the Society's affairs. He knew the truth would not reveal itself through mere conjecture alone; he needed concrete evidence. "These look like internal documents. How did you get these?"

"Their admin, Martha, is a close friend of mine. She gathered these for me."

"Great. At least we don't need to search the Society's records," he declared, hope glinting in his eyes.

"Let's dive in," Rose agreed, pulling a chair up to the desk.

As they sifted through the tangle of documents and financial records, Nick couldn't help but feel a sense of unease. The Society's mounting debts, coupled with their dogged pursuit of Lucy's wealth, painted an ominous picture. It was impossible to ignore the fact that, in their desperation, someone might have decided to kill Lucy, hoping to gain control of her fortune and save the organization from ruin.

"Look at this," Rose whispered, holding up a letter addressed to Lucy. Nick and Rose, with furrowed brows, glanced at each other. Their faces betrayed the weight of the revelations from the document.

The words seemed to leap off the page, confirming their suspicions: "Your generous donation could be the lifeline our Society desperately needs to survive."

"Could one of them have gone so far as to commit murder?" Nick said, his stomach churning at the thought.

"We can't rule anything out until we find the killer," Rose

trailed off as the door swung open, revealing a visibly distressed Michael. He took the stairs two at a time until he was before the second floor desk.

"Please, listen," Michael pleaded, his face flushed with urgency. "I know I might not be the most trustworthy person, given my past, but I swear I didn't kill Aunt Lucy."

"I told you before, I wasn't accusing you," Nick said. It was a lie of omission. He had wanted to accuse him. "But you…"

Michael held up his hand, stopping him. "I thought about what you said and think she may have been killed. I've got reason to believe someone else is involved."

"Who?" asked Nick, his gaze fixed on the young man's trembling form.

"Members of the Historical Society."

"Michael." Nick rubbed the bridge of his nose. "We know about you being kicked out."

"That isn't it."

"There was an incident about fundraising where you behaved poorly and were removed again."

"Behaved poorly? I'm not sure what you heard, but I defended this town."

"How so?" Rose asked.

"As you may know, the members have a lot of clout in

this town. They were suggesting ways to siphon off tax money to fix the debt and even passing new local tax laws. I was adamant that I would not vote for that. The people should not pay to fix their problems. When one of the members attacked me, I pushed him back. They used it as a way to kick me out. I did nothing wrong. Those people are all crooks. Not a single one took my side."

Nick pondered the response. "That's a little different than the way we heard it. I appreciate your perspective. Anyone else?"

"Doctor Victors was my aunt's physician," Peter stammered. "He had access to Aunt Lucy's medication, and they knew about her heart condition. I overheard them talking about replacing her meds with something else. I didn't think much of it at the time, but now..."

"Are you suggesting that the doctor switched her to a medicine that poisoned her?" Rose asked, her voice colored with disbelief.

"Look, I don't know for sure, but it's worth looking into," Michael insisted, his hands clenched tightly together. "I can't shake the feeling that they had something to do with it. Aunt Lucy also complained about her getting shorted pills in her prescriptions or some that even went missing."

"Did she think it was you?"

"Not at all. I would never steal from her."

"Very well," Nick said slowly, his eyes never leaving Michael's face. "We'll look into it. But we're doing this for the sake of finding the truth, not merely to clear your name."

"Thank you," Michael replied, relief evident in his features. He turned and left the library, leaving behind a lingering sense of unease.

"Nick," Rose spoke up, her tone cautious. "Do you think there's any merit to his claims?"

"Who knows?" Nick murmured, a heavy sigh escaping his lips. "That guy needs a sponsor. Also, one thing is certain; the doctor is looking more and more guilty."

"Wouldn't he be too obvious? What if someone was framing him? He is an easy mark with his attitude."

"Good point. We will have to see." Nick stood up and stretched. It was about time to head back to his shop. "You mentioned there was more on the medication before Michael rushed in here."

"Oh, yeah. Thanks for the reminder. I found a medical article about heart medicine. In some cases, its chemical compound makes it hard to detect poison in the body."

He put his hand on Rose's. "Are you saying she could have been poisoned, but the medicine could cover it up?"

"That is what the article said. It wasn't specifically about poising someone. It was more geared towards the impact of long-term heart medicine. But it did jump out at me," Rose replied.

Nick sighed.

"I thought you would be glad to hear it," Rose said, confused.

"Oh, I am. Thank you. It just adds a complication. Maybe the doctor is not hiding her death or his incompetence. This could have legitimately been missed. Which would lower him on the list?"

"Sorry."

"It's okay. I have to go through it. Take care, and talk to you later tonight."

"Sure. Okay. Bye."

Nick left the library in dismay. He thought for sure the doctor was the mastermind behind Lucy's death, but now he had to consider he wasn't. The guy was a jerk, that was for sure. But that didn't make him a murderer.

Nick returned to his shop, where he spent the next few hours on the internet, poring over old newspapers and documents in-between helping customers. He found an article that detailed a heated argument between Lucy and Doctor Victors during a town hall meeting six months prior. The issue was allocating funds for resources at the library versus new medical equipment for the doctor's practice. Witnesses reported that both parties were unusually passionate in their arguments, with raised voices and accusatory statements.

"Interesting," Nick murmured to himself, saving the link to the article. "I suppose that could have given the good doctor reason to hold a grudge against Lucy."

He continued his search, eventually uncovering evidence of Michael's past involvement with the historical society. Apparently, Michael had been an active member during his teenage years, organizing fundraisers and events. However, he was kicked out after he was caught stealing money from the society's cash box to fund his drug habit. His expulsion had caused quite the scandal within the community, further straining his relationship with his Aunt Lucy.

"Ah, there it is," Nick mused, tracing his finger over the damning article. "Michael's connection to the historical society from the past. Eunice didn't mention this one. He has been kicked out of the society a few times."

As he pondered over these new revelations, the sheriff entered the shop, her brow furrowed. "Good afternoon, Mr. Cern."

Momentarily shocked, Nick fumbled to close the laptop lid. "How can I help you sheriff."

"I've just spoken with a member of the community. They seemed quite...distressed."

"Distressed?" Nick asked, intrigued. "What did they have to say?"

"Apparently, they're facing severe harassment," she replied, wringing her hands. "They fear that if the situation doesn't improve, they may have to file a restraining order."

"Really?" Nick said, his eyes narrowing. "Not sure how I can help with that?"

"You can very much help. You're the cause of it."

"Me," Nick faked a shocked reaction. He knew this was bound to happen. "What's going on?"

"Don't play stupid with me. You have been going all over town asking questions about Lucy's passing. I told you not to, but you had to push on."

"It isn't against the law, is it?"

The sheriff smiled. "Listen. I get it. You miss your friend. But you are not helping her or yourself by going through town and harassing people with accusations of murder. It further alienates you and makes my department look bad."

"I can't be responsible for your department. I'm just

asking people questions. I've not accused anyone of anything. I have been very careful about this. Who complained?"

"That is not important. You are ruffling a lot of feathers."

"Like who?"

"Just stop." Sheriff Joan Kent glared at him. "I happened to like Lucy. We talked a few times. I get why you would want to help her. But she is gone, and you must move on. You seem like a nice guy. Please do yourself a favor and leave it alone. It will only get you in trouble."

"Is that an order?"

"It's a request and advice. The complainer is an ass anyway. The is nothing worse than an ass with a legitimate complaint."

Nick instantly knew who had complained. He thought about defending himself, but deep down knew it wouldn't do any good. He let it go.

"I will take it into consideration. Now, if you don't need anything else, I need to get back to work."

The sheriff continued to glare. It seemed like an eternity to Nick. Eventually, she looked away. "If that's the way you want to play it. Just remember, I came here with a friendly warning. Have a good day?"

Nick held his breath until she left. With a sigh, he

marveled at how intense that was. Who could have lodged a complaint about him? It had to be the Doctor. Maybe one of those Historical Society interviews?

It was nearly time to close. His mind raced as he pondered the implications of the evidence he had uncovered. The shadows cast by the flickering lamplight on the street outside danced on the walls, their movements mirroring the shifting thoughts within his head.

"Michael's theft from the historical society and the subsequent expulsion certainly provide a motive. And then being kicked out a second time definitely did," Nick mumbled to himself, tapping his fingers on the keyboard. "But it doesn't explain the missing medicine or the doctor's suspicious behavior."

"Good evening. Is there something on your mind?" Rose asked, her gentle voice slicing through the silence like a knife. She stood in the doorway, a tray laden with steaming cups of tea held delicately in her hands. Concerned he had been in such deep thought, he nodded and blinked his eyes.

"Rose, I've been thinking about Lucy's murder and how everything seems connected," Nick replied, accepting a cup of tea from her trembling hands. "The historical society's financial troubles, Michael's drug addiction, and ousting, the doctor's potential involvement... It all feels too convenient. I can't shake the feeling that there's more to this than meets the eye."

"Perhaps you're right," she mused, slowly sipping her tea. "But where do we go from here?"

"First, we need to dig deeper into the doctor's relationship with Lucy and the missing medicine," Nick said decisively, his eyes narrowing with determination. "And secondly, we should investigate the Historical Society more and their possible connection to the tax thing. I have a feeling those three leads might help us uncover the truth."

"You seem slightly obsessed, but I get it," Rose agreed, her gaze steady and resolute. "Tomorrow, if you want to visit the doctor's office and see what more we can learn, I will talk with Martha more about the society."

"Excellent idea," Nick said, finishing his tea with a decisive gulp. His mind buzzed with the excitement of the investigation, each new piece of evidence opening up a plethora of possibilities. "And after that, we'll meet up and see if they have any further information. "

"I worry about you. Are you sure you're up for this?" Rose asked, concern etched into her features. "This investigation has taken quite a toll on you. I don't want you to push yourself too hard."

"You sound like my daughters. They have messaged me

several times about taking a break."

"I'm not suggesting that. Just that we should slow down. You need to eat and sleep. I would hate for you to make yourself sick."

" I appreciate your concern," Nick reassured her, placing a hand gently on her arm. "But I need to see this through for Lucy and for my own peace of mind. I won't rest until I've uncovered the truth. I'll sleep after."

"Very well," Rose conceded, her eyes filled with understanding and support. "Then let's leave no stone unturned in our pursuit of justice for Lucy."

CHAPTER

TWENTY-ONE

N ick took a deep breath, allowing the crisp, coastal air to fill his lungs as he stood outside Doctor Victor's office. The afternoon sun cast a golden glow on the cobblestones, illuminating the quaint charm of Sweet Sea. Nick's thoughts, however, were far from charming. He needed answers and hoped that confronting Doctor Victors might provide some. He had no plan to follow the sheriff's instructions.

"All right," Nick said under his breath, gathering his resolve. "Let's see if Michael's accusations hold any water."

He opened the door to the doctor's office, an electronic

beep announced his arrival. A receptionist, seated behind a cluttered high desk, looked up, curiosity piqued by the unexpected visitor.

"Is Doctor Victors available?" Nick asked.

The man behind the desk gave a genuine smile. "I can check, sir. Your name?"

"Nick Cern."

"I'll be back in a moment, Mr. Cern."

The nicely dressed man disappeared through a door. As promised, he returned. "He is free. Follow me."

Nick was led into a hallway. They passed exam rooms and labs to the very end. Through the last door, Nick saw Doctor Victors sitting behind a fancy desk. His diplomas and awards covered each of the walls of the corner office.

"Ah, Mr. Cern," the doctor greeted, attempting a genuine smile that didn't quite reach his eyes. "Have you changed your mind about giving me free services?"

"Doctor Victors," Nick acknowledged curtly, taking a seat across the desk, and ignoring his sarcasm. "I have a few questions about Lucy Brooks."

"This again?"

"Please, this is about her medicine. I was talking with her nephew and just wanted to get some clarity."

Doctor Victors seemed to relax a little. His fingers

tapped the edge of his desk nervously. He replied, "Of course," I'll do my best to help you with your investigation."

"Michael Brooks mentioned a recent argument between you and Lucy about her medicine," Nick began, watching the doctor closely for any signs of discomfort. "Would you care to elaborate?"

"So, it is indeed going to be more accusations."

"Not at all. I'm just curious about her medical history. I know it is private, but after getting the report of your coroner exam, we were curious. I understand if you want to decline."

"Very well. I guess that is public knowledge, and with her passing, the patient to doctor privilege isn't too big of a deal. However, it depends on the questions. Lucy and I disagreed over her choice of medication," the doctor admitted, his voice steady but his eyes betraying a hint of unease. "But it was nothing serious. It's not uncommon for patients to question their prescriptions."

"Is there any reason why Michael would think you were in the wrong?" Nick pressed, noting the beads of sweat forming on the doctor's brow.

"Michael is a troubled young man," the doctor replied, avoiding direct eye contact. "I'm afraid he's been known to make wild claims without any basis in reality."

"Speaking of Michael," Nick continued, "he mentioned

that some of Lucy's medication had gone missing and suggested that you could be responsible. A pill was missing here or there, maybe. Do you know anything about this?"

"Lucy was under my care, Mr. Cern," the doctor said dismissively. "I can assure you that her medication was always accounted for. As for my prescriptions, they are innocent in this matter."

"Dr. Victors," Nick began, struggling to maintain his composure, "before Lucy passed away, did you prescribe her any new medications?"

"Ah, yes," the doctor replied, his voice cold and clinical. "I prescribed her Ativan."

Nick blinked in surprise, an icy shiver running down his back. "Ativan? And could that have masked the effects of the poison that killed her?"

Dr. Victors narrowed his eyes, a flicker of annoyance crossing his face. "It's possible, I suppose. The drug does have sedative properties, after all. But you are assuming she was poisoned. You already know that there was no proof of that in her system."

"Can you tell me more about the dosage and how it might have affected her?" Nick asked, trying to keep his tone even as his suspicions grew stronger.

"Mr. Cern," the doctor said, his voice growing defensive,

"I am bound by patient confidentiality laws. I cannot provide you with more details."

"Please understand, Dr. Victors," - Nick's voice took an urgent note - "Lucy's death wasn't just an accident. Someone murdered her, and we need all the information we can get to find out who did it."

The doctor's lips tightened into a thin line, his face reddening with anger. "If you persist in this line of questioning, Mr. Cern, I will have no choice but to call the police. This is my final warning."

"I just want to know about the medicine, and then I will leave."

"Lucy's medication?" Dr. Victors echoed, his bushy eyebrows knitting together in a frown. "I don't see how that's any of your concern, Mr. Cern."

"Her death came as quite a shock, and I'm just trying to understand what happened," Nick explained, his fingers flexing unconsciously at his sides. His mind raced with possible reasons for Lucy being on medication, and he struggled to keep his growing unease hidden behind a mask of calm inquiry.

"Mr. Cern, while I appreciate your concern, I must remind you that I am bound by patient confidentiality laws." Dr. Victors began tidying his desk, a clear attempt to create a barrier between them both physically and emotionally.

"Of course, I understand that," Nick replied, digging deep for patience. "But surely there's something you can tell me? Anything that might help shed light on her untimely passing?" His heart pounded in his ears, drowning out the clock's incessant ticking.

Dr. Victors pursed his lips, studying Nick with an intensity that made him feel like a specimen pinned to a dissection table. Finally, he sighed and sank back into his chair, the leather protesting under his weight. "Very well," he conceded, his voice low and cautious. "I can't disclose specifics, but I will tell you this: Lucy was dealing with some personal issues, and I prescribed medication to help her cope."

"Personal issues?" Nick echoed, his mind whirring as he tried to reconcile this new information with his image of the vibrant, passionate woman who had shared her love of literature with him.

"I draw the line at that."

"Did Lucy ever mention experiencing any adverse side effects?" Nick asked, his mouth suddenly dry as a bone. "Or did she seem... different, somehow? Perhaps more vulnerable or less alert than usual? Was it a high dosage?"

"Very well, Mr. Cern," he said, his voice betraying a hint of trepidation. "The dosage I prescribed to Lucy was relatively low – just enough to help manage her symptoms. However, Ativan can cause drowsiness and disorientation, especially when taken in conjunction with alcohol or other medications. It is possible she didn't take it or took the wrong dosage. I wouldn't be able to tell you that."

Nick's heart pounded like a gavel against his chest, echoing through the courtroom of his mind. Had Lucy unwittingly ingested a lethal cocktail of substances, sealing her own fate in a tragic act of negligence? Or had someone else mixed the deadly concoction, intent on silencing the sweet, silver-haired librarian forever?

"Just to be clear, she seemed fine on the medication?"

"Lucy did mention feeling a bit drowsy at times," Dr. Victors admitted, his eyes darting away from Nick's penetrating gaze as if trying to escape an uncomfortable truth. "But she didn't seem overly concerned about it. She trusted the medication would help her."

"Did you ever consider that it might have... facilitated foul play?" Nick's words hung in the air like a storm cloud, casting a palpable shadow over the room. The doctor shifted uneasily in his seat, his eyes narrowing into thin slits of suspicion.

"Mr. Cern, I assure you, my primary concern was – and always has been – the welfare of my patients," he said, his voice strained with indignation. "I cannot predict every possible outcome, nor can I be held responsible for the actions of others."

"Doctor Victors, I understand you have a responsibility to your patients," Nick said, his voice steady and calm. "But right now, I need more information about the Ativan you prescribed Lucy. We're trying to solve her murder."

"Mr. Cern, I sympathize with your desire to find answers, but there are laws in place for a reason." The doctor's lips pressed into a thin line, his eyes cold and unyielding. "I cannot further discuss the specifics of Lucy's treatment without violating patient confidentiality."

Nick clenched his fists, feeling the blood pounding in his temples. He took a deep breath, attempting to maintain his composure in the face of the doctor's obstinacy. "I understand."

"Anxiety can be a terrible burden, Mr. Cern, as I know you well know from your medical records," Dr. Victors said cryptically, his eyes darting away from Nick's probing gaze. "I suggest you talk to a professional about your grief. That is both my personal and professional opinion. Now, if there's nothing else, I have other patients to attend to."

A peculiar chill crept its way up Nick's spine as the doctor's words hung heavy in the air like a noxious cloud. The revelation that Lucy had been prescribed Ativan was startling, to say the least, and a myriad of questions clamored for attention within him. Nick's piercing gaze never wavered from the doctor's inscrutable face; he knew he needed answers, and somehow, he felt the doctor threatened him with reference to his own past addiction.

For a moment, Nick hesitated, weighing his options. He knew pushing the doctor further might jeopardize his own standing in the community, but the gnawing desire for justice burned within him. He decided to back off for now, making a mental note to investigate Dr. Victor's prescription records later.

"Very well," Nick conceded, sensing he would get no further with the doctor. "Thank you for your time, Doctor Victors."

"Of course," the doctor replied, his relief palpable as Nick stood to leave.

As Nick exited the office, he couldn't shake the feeling that something wasn't adding up. The doctor had every right to kick him out. He didn't have to answer his questions, but he did. Could Michael be leading them to target the Doctor? There was only one way to find out. Nick had to uncover any clues to support or contradict Michael's claims.

Nick stepped out of the doctor's office, the door clicking

shut behind him. The sterile scent of antiseptic lingered in the air, clinging to his clothes as he made his way down the dimly lit corridor. The cold linoleum floor provided an unyielding surface beneath his feet, echoing the lack of compassion he had just experienced within that room.

"Damn it," he muttered under his breath, raking a hand through his hair. What good was a doctor who refused to aid in the pursuit of justice? Nick knew he had to keep a cool head, but the frustration gnawed at him like a persistent itch.

His footsteps echoed through the empty hallway as he made his way to the exit.

CHAPTER

TWENTY-TWO

Nick Cern stood outside Lucy's house with a key in hand. It was a beautiful three bedroom ranch style home just far enough from the ocean to have privacy from the town. Michael had been coming by and taking care of plants while he figured out what to do with the only thing left to him in her will. When asked, he agreed quickly to Nick visiting the place if it would help figure out what happened to his aunt.

The door clicked open, and Nick entered. The air was heavy with the scent of books and lingering memories of a woman he had come to admire and call a friend. His gaze drifted over the rows of neatly arranged novels and well-thumbed classics, each title whispering secrets to him that only they shared. In this sanctuary of words, Nick felt both close to Lucy and painfully aware of her absence. He knew she would want him to find the truth, and despite the gnawing ache in his heart, he was determined to uncover what had happened to his friend.

He surveyed the room once more, taking in every detail as though it might suddenly reveal itself to be the key to unlocking this mystery. His keen eyes fell upon Lucy's desk – a large, antique piece of furniture that seemed to possess both elegance and authority.

Nick noticed something peculiar about one of the drawers as he approached the desk. There was a subtle indentation on its surface, a tiny blemish in an otherwise perfect piece of furniture that suggested a hidden mechanism. Intrigued, Nick pressed down on the indentation, and with a soft click, the drawer popped open on the side of the desk to reveal a concealed compartment.

"Hello, what have we here?" he muttered, excitement coursing through his veins.

The hidden space was small, barely big enough to contain whatever secrets it held within its wooden embrace. His heart raced as he stared into the compartment, a feeling of accomplishment and curiosity washing over him. Nick's fingers hesitated for a moment, unsure if he should disturb the contents, but curiosity got the better of him. His fingers trembled as he reached in, brushing against something solid and rectangular. He carefully pulled out the item and found himself holding a worn copy of *The Brown Grass.*

Nick's persistence had served him well in the past, both in his professional life and during his struggle with addiction. It was a trait that had helped him to rise from the ashes, and he knew it would be crucial in solving Lucy's murder.

Studying the book more closely, he noticed it was a different version than he had found and read on the internet. This copy was older, its pages yellowed and brittle, the spine cracked from years of use. As he leafed through the fragile pages, he noticed several passages underlined and annotated in Lucy's elegant handwriting. This particular copy appeared to hold a special significance to her, though the reasons remained unclear.

He sat down at the desk, the weight of the investigation bearing down on him. With each new clue, he felt the urgency to solve the mystery. The hidden compartment, the aged book – it all seemed like pieces of a puzzle he desperately needed to complete.

Nick began to study the book methodically, comparing it

to the newer copy on his phone. He paid close attention to the sections she had underlined, trying to decipher their meaning. There was something special about this book. She would not have sent him a message about it at the time of her death.

The email was still something that stabbed at his thoughts. Why send it? Why so cryptic? Could she not say, I was killed by person x? It seems that it would have been much easier to get justice. Then, it occurred to him. What if she didn't know who the killer was? She had read enough mysteries to know about the book and poison effects. Did she feel symptoms of the poison and sent the email? Why didn't she just call? Or dial 911? So many questions. He turned back to the book.

"Was this your way of guiding me?" he questioned, a hint of melancholy creeping in. "Am I on the right path?"

The minutes ticked by as Nick delved deeper into the printed copy of *The Brown Grass*, his mind racing with theories and connections. He felt an overwhelming mix of emotions – frustration at the lingering mystery, sadness for the loss of his dear friend, and a burning desire for justice.

As the sun began to set, Nick continued his search for answers within the pages of the worn novel. With each turn of the page, he felt closer to unraveling the truth behind Lucy's murder, but also acutely aware that danger might be lurking around every corner. It occurred to him that his business would suffer by being here for so long. Every hour he was closed meant lost revenue or upset patrons. He shook that thought away, but it still nagged at him.

"Stay focused, Nick," he told himself. "You've overcome obstacles before, and you can do it again."

Nick's eyes widened as he spotted a small, crumpled note tucked between the pages towards the back of the book. He carefully unfolded it, his hands trembling with anticipation. As his eyes scanned the neat, looping script on the paper, he recognized Lucy's handwriting.

"Nick," the note began, "if you're reading this, then I'm afraid my suspicions were correct, and I'm no longer here. I have been feeling off today, and the doctor says nothing is wrong. He even had the lab do blood tests and they showed me the results. It all looked clean. After reading this book, I think I may have been poisoned. I found a message on my door last night. My life has been threatened by someone who knows about my disagreement with the Historical Society. The key to my murder lies within the pages of this book. I could not go to the police because I had no evidence." Nick squeezed the note in his left hand as he read on, his heart pounding in his ears.

"Within *The Brown Grass*, there is a hidden message— one that only you can decipher. It may not be easy, but I trust your intelligence and intuition. Remember our conversations about literature and think back to the stories we shared. Find the pattern within the pages, and you'll uncover the truth. I am sure I was poisoned like the person in this book. Don't' return it to the library. It will be your guide."

"Pattern...truth," Nick whispered, his determination flaring like a phoenix from the ashes of his grief. He spread the worn novel open on the desk before him, the tattered pages seeming to beckon him closer. His fingers traced the lines of text, searching for patterns or anomalies that might reveal a hidden message. Each word seemed to taunt him, daring him to unravel their cryptic meaning.

As the hours passed, Nick's concentration wavered, fatigue creeping into the corners of his vision. And yet, he refused to give up. He knew he was on the brink of a breakthrough, and with each page, he felt closer to the truth.

Suddenly, a specific passage caught his attention. The words seemed to leap off the page as if illuminated by an unseen light. A pattern emerged—a pattern that only Nick could have noticed. Lucy was the only one in town, except for the doctor that knew his medical history. Specifically, his addiction and recovery. He wished he hadn't shared with the doctor, but he had no reason to doubt the man when he first arrived at Sweet Sea. The passage talked about how to hide the effects of the poison plant, heart medicine. It confirmed what Rose had discovered. Plus, the killer in the book was a prominent figure in the small town. A doctor. Did that mean that Lucy thought it was Doctor Victors?

The revelation sent shivers down his spine, electrifying every nerve in his body. The note had led him to another clue. But what did it all mean?

Nick's phone rang, shattering the silence like a hammer striking glass. He stared at it, his pulse racing as if the device harbored some deadly secret. The name 'Rose' flashed insistently on the screen.

"Hello?" he answered, trying to steady his voice. The shock of the ringing had him breathing heavy and heavy heartbeats.

"Nick, are you okay?" Rose's tone was laced with concern. "You sound... off."

He hesitated, his fingers unconsciously caressing the spine of the book. "I'm fine, Rose. Just a little tired."

"Come on, Nick," she chided gently, her intuition guiding her like a beacon in the fog. "You and I are in this together. No need for you to lie to me. Something's not right."

The words hung in the air, heavy and undeniable, and Nick found himself struggling beneath their weight. He wanted desperately to confide in her—to share the burden that threatened to crush him—but doubt gnawed at his resolve.

"Okay," he admitted, his throat constricting around each syllable. "There is something I found, but I don't know if I should tell you yet. It seems weird and maybe a stretch."

"Don't stop sharing now. Whatever it is, you can trust me." Her voice was firm, reassuring, but he could hear the underlying tremor—a testament to the gravity of the situation. She sounded different. The sweetness in her voice was gone. It was strict determination and slightly demanding.

With a deep breath, he began to recount his discovery, starting with the hidden compartment in Lucy's desk, the note, and finally, the cryptic clue concealed within the pages of the book. As he spoke, he felt a strange sense of release—like a balloon slowly deflating, releasing its pent-up energy.

"Nick," Rose whispered, her usually vibrant voice subdued. "That's... incredible. And terrifying."

"I know," he replied, his heart pounding against his ribs. "We are getting closer. We just need to connect the clues. But I have to see this through."

"Of course, you do," she agreed, the steel in her voice returning. "But you don't have to go it alone. Lean on me. I'm here for you, no matter what."

"Thank you," he murmured. "I appreciate that more than you know."

"Good." She paused, as if gathering her thoughts like scattered leaves. "Now, promise me you'll be careful. This isn't some cozy mystery novel—it's real life, and there could be real danger."

"I promise," he vowed, his voice firm with conviction. "But I can't stop now, not when I'm so close."

"All right," she sighed, resigned. "Just remember, you don't have to be a hero. Sometimes, asking for help is the bravest thing you can do."

"Understood," he replied, his heart swelling with gratitude. "And... thank you."

"Anytime, Nick," she assured him, her voice warm as a summer breeze. "Promise me when you are done, you will get a good meal and some rest."

"I will try."

"Don't try. Do." The demanding voice was back. "I am going to bring you a relaxing tea later. Call me when you get home."

"That is not necessary."

"I hear you. I will wait for your call."

As they hung up, Nick's gaze returned to the book lying before him like an open wound. He knew he was walking a tightrope between truth and danger, but he couldn't look back now.

He plunged once more into the labyrinthine world of *The Brown Grass*, following the trail of breadcrumbs left behind by his murdered friend.

◆ ◆ ◆

The evening sun filtered through the curtains of his above shop apartment, casting a warm glow on the worn pages of the book he had to read carefully. What could she have wanted him to read so carefully? Surely, not the entire book. Nick could almost feel Lucy's presence in the room, guiding him like a beacon in the dark. He swallowed, his heart pounding with anticipation and uncertainty.

"Nick," Rose's voice trembled from the kitchen, her concern palpable. "I don't like the sound of this at all. If the killer poisoned her, couldn't they poison us?"

"I guess. We will just have to be careful not to accept food or drink from a suspect."

Rose entered the living room with two cups of tea. She handed one to him. "Here you go. My special blend."

The timing was not lost on Nick as he took a sip. He sat it down and stood up. "I'll be right back. I'm going to get an ice cube. You want one?"

"Sure."

Nick turned and left the room. When she was sure he was gone, Rose reached into her bra and produced a vial. She quickly poured the contents into his tea and returned the empty container to her bra. Seconds later, Nick returned. He dropped the cube in the water and took another sip.

"Wait, Rose," he said, rubbing the back of his neck. "Is this tea going to make me sleepy?"

She smiled. "Clearly, you can't sleep on your own. This will help you along," she snapped, worry sharpening her tone. "You're no good to anyone dead from exhaustion. Plus, you will think better after a good night's sleep. "

"Listen," Nick argued, pacing back and forth across the room. "I appreciate your concern, but I've got things under control. Besides, if there's any real danger, I don't want you getting caught up in it too."

"Caught up in it?" she scoffed. "This isn't some sort of solo mission. We're friends, and we help each other out. That's what friends do."

"Of course," he conceded. He wanted to be more than friends and was pretty sure she was feeling the same. "But I need to do this my way. I promise I'll let you know if I come across anything I can't handle."

"Fine," she relented, her voice softening. "But you better keep that promise, or so help me, Nick Cern."

"Scout's honor," he replied, offering a wry smile she couldn't see.

"All right then," Rose sighed. "At least drink up for me."

Grabbing the cup and taking another sip, he stared down at the cryptic note again, the words swimming before his eyes. He knew Rose meant well, but the weight of responsibility for uncovering the truth was solely on his shoulders. He couldn't risk involving anyone else, not even a trusted friend like Rose.

Rose picked up *The Brown Grass*, her fingers tracing the worn cover as if trying to coax its secrets to the surface. She opened it and scanned the pages of the book, her eyes darting back and forth as she searched for any hint. She read each word carefully, wanting to take advantage of every potential clue. Yet, despite her diligence, nothing seemed out of the ordinary. It was just a well-worn copy of an old novel.

"Damn," Nick muttered under his breath, rubbing the goosebumps from his arms. He couldn't shake the feeling that someone—or something—was watching him. He sat down. Something was not right. Pressing his fingers against his temples, he attempted to focus his racing thoughts. They each seemed to scatter in different directions. He looked down at the empty teacup and felt drowsy. "That stuff works well. What did you put in it?"

"It's okay," Rose said. "Just close your eyes for a bit."

Before he could respond, his eyelids shut, and he drifted to the side.

"Rest easy," Rose said. "I hope you can understand why I did this."

She tapped him a few times to make sure he was asleep. Once convinced, Rose stood, grabbed the book, and headed towards the door. The quiet room was suddenly interrupted by the shrill ring of Nick's cell. Startled, she nearly dropped the book onto the floor. Frantic, she rushed to the table and picked up his phone. She didn't recognize the number and silenced it. Nick was still out cold, oblivious to the call. With a smile, Rose slipped out of the apartment.

CHAPTER TWENTY-THREE

Nick Cern opened his eyes. He immediately noticed it was still dark out. He stumbled through the apartment to the bathroom. Looking in the mirror, he was surprised at the stubble on his face. He didn't look that way an hour or so ago. He looked at his smart watch and had to blink his eyes. On second look, his eyes grew even wider. According to the time, he had been asleep almost a full day. It was seven at night, but remembered talking with Rose around nine. "Rose," he yelled, exiting the bathroom.

He walked from room to room, but the place was empty. He must have fallen asleep, and she left. He sat at the kitchen table, an antique lamp casting a warm glow across the table. He reached for Lucy's book. However, it was gone. Frantic, he stood and checked the room. Even though he knew it was unlikely, he even lifted up the couches slightly damp cushions to look under. The book was gone.

Nick patted his pockets to find his phone. He immediately dialed Rose. It rang four times and went to voicemail. It was early enough that she should be awake unless she pulled a Rip Van Winkle like him. Something didn't feel right. No normal person sleeps that long on their own, and he could only assume that Rose took the book, but why? He had to find her.

He put his shoes on, grabbed his coat, and was out the door in under a minute. Her house was the first place he would start, and then go from there. It was within walking distance, but there were dark clouds in the sky, and he didn't want to get caught in it. He would drive.

Within ten minutes, he was parked outside of Rose's home. The house was dark. He was still trying to make sense of the events when he noticed the light pop on in the top left room of the small cottage. At least she was there and, hopefully, could help him understand what happened. He walked fast to her door and knocked twice.

Nick couldn't hear any movement within, so he

knocked again. "Rose."

"I haven't seen her all day."

Nick turned, jumping slightly with surprise. To his left was an older woman walking a small dog on the sidewalk. "Excuse me?"

"I said she hadn't been home all day. She drove off at some point this morning and hasn't been back." The lady's voice was scratchy like, and her posture gave the signs of a rough life. The discoloration around her lips pegged her as a lifelong smoker.

Nick stepped down to the sidewalk. "I saw the light go on and thought..."

"What light?" the old lady said.

"The one right there." Nick pointed up to the room, but the light was out. "It was just on. I saw it come on when I walked up."

"Maybe, it was one of those new motion sensor things, and her cat set it off. She has so many of those damn things."

Nick nodded. That seemed logical. It still begged the question of where she had gone. "Any idea where I might find her?"

"And you are?" She narrowed her eyes and sized him up.

"Sorry," he smiled. "I'm Nick. Nick Cern. I own the repair shop down on the water."

"Oh, yeah. I've walked by there a few times. I'm not into all the technology stuff. Seems unnecessary. You can call me Mrs. Westerby."

"Pleasure to meet you. And I get it, it's not for everyone," Nick said. "Rose and I are friends, and I wanted to chat with her. Any idea?"

The old woman seemed less suspicious. "She is probably down at the Baptist church. That is where she spends most of her time."

"Thank you, mamn." Nick walked to his car. The lady waved and continued on with her dog.

The subsequent chain of events didn't help Nick find Rose. He went to the church, but they hadn't seen her all day. She had even missed a Bible study group, which she never does. He was starting to get worried. The church gave him a few other places to look. However, each of those were empty as well. Concerned for yet another friend now, he went home to see if she had left him a note he might have missed.

His thoughts were interrupted by the loud ring of the cell phone in the quiet car. Startled, he swerved, narrowly missing a trash can on the side of the street. He had to find a different ring tone. This one always scared the crap out of him. Cautiously, he picked it up.

"Hello?" he asked hesitantly, his heart pounding in his

chest. He didn't look at the caller id, assuming it was probably Rose. But it wasn't.

"Nick, it's Eunice," came the voice on the other end, sounding unusually tense. "You need to get out of your apartment right now. There's something you need to know, and it's not safe for you to be there."

"What do you mean? What's going on?" he demanded, his grip tightening on the phone.

"Please, just trust me," she urged, her voice cracking with emotion. "Meet me at my store in fifteen minutes. I'll explain everything then."

"All right, all right," he agreed, his voice shaking with a mixture of fear and frustration. "I'll be there in more like twenty. I'm not at home."

"Good, just hurry," she said, relief evident in her tone. "And Nick? Be careful."

The line went dead, leaving him with nothing but the ominous silence of the car. Nick stared at the phone in his hand, his mind racing with questions and dread. If Eunice was right and he was in danger, who could be behind it? What did they want? And could it have anything to do with why he couldn't reach Rose?

◆ ◆ ◆

Nick hastily exited his car and dropped his phone in his jacket before making his way toward the Antique store door. As he reached for the handle, he couldn't help but glance back at the car one last time, paranoia gnawing at the edges of his consciousness. With a deep breath, Nick stepped into the dim light of the store. As the door clicked shut behind him, a figure emerged from the darkness, her eyes fixed on his retreating form, an enigmatic frown playing across her lips.

"I'm glad to see you," Eunice said, stepping in from the back.

"Jesus," Nick yelled, grabbing his chest. "You trying to kill me."

"Not me," she said. "But I think I know who?"

"What does that mean?"

"It's Rose. I was not sure whether Lucy was killed or if it was natural causes. I now agree with you. I think she was killed, and Rose did it."

Nick had never even considered Rose. She was a sweet, church going lady and didn't seem to have a violent bone in her body. He refused to believe it was her without some evidence. "I'm not sure about that. Do you have any evidence?"

"Yes," Eunice said. She looked out her the front window of the store. She was twitching, and she studied the street.

"Good, I don't see anyone. Come in back."

Hesitantly, Nick followed her through a curtain to a sitting area. The walls were draped with purple tapestries. It was definitely an odd room. She motioned to one of the chairs. "You are going to need to sit down."

"Come on, Eunice. I have things to do. What is with all this cloak and dagger stuff."

Eunice sat down opposite him and leaned forward. "Ok. I've seen you around town hanging out with Rose."

"We are investigating Lucy's death together."

"Whatever. I saw you two together, so when I saw and heard what I did today, I became concerned for your safety."

Nick waved his hand in a circle. "And..."

"I went to a Historical Society earlier, and Rose was in the lobby with our receptionist, Martha."

"Yeah. They are friends."

"They were talking. Rose mentioned something about putting something in your drink to make you sleep for a long time so you would stop investigating. I'm not sure when she plans on doing it, but to drug anyone without permission is evil."

Nick's mouth fell open.

Eunice continued, "Then she handed Martha some old book. They didn't see me at the coffee machine, so I kept listening. She mentioned it being a fiction book, but the plant details were real and nearby. Apparently, that is where she made this thing she was putting in your drink. She wanted her to help her collect some more plants or something."

Nick dragged his hand down his face and stood. "You're sure?"

"Why would I make it up? I just wanted you to be careful and not accept any food or drink from that lady."

"Too late," Nick mumbled.

"I'm sorry."

"Never mind." He sat back down. "Thank you. I really appreciate you reaching out to me. Did you hear anything else?"

"That was it. I had to get back into the meeting."

"I really appreciate the heads up. I will take the necessary steps."

"I don't think you're taking this seriously. You are in danger."

"I am taking is seriously. Trust me, more than you know."

"Just be careful," Eunice said.

"Everyone is so concerned about my safety." Nick chuckled with a negative tone. "I need to go. Thank you again."

Eunice led him to the door. After he left, Nick could

hear her click the multiple locks on her door. If he hadn't already experienced the long sleep and missing book, her real fear would have been enough to convince him she was telling the truth.

Nick was sitting at his kitchen table an hour later. He had driven around the town and neighborhoods trying to find Rose. Coming up empty, he headed home. There was something he had to confirm.

He was flipping through the electronic copy of the book, the faint sound of waves crashing against the shore in the distance providing a soothing backdrop to his reading.

"Ah, here it is," he muttered to himself, his eyes widening as they fell upon a passage describing a toxic plant known as the Tears of Medusa. The plant's leaves were described as serrated and dark green, with clusters of small, white flowers that emitted a sickly sweet scent. The author detailed how just a single drop of the plant's sap was enough to cause deep sleep and paralysis.

"Interesting," Nick mused aloud, rubbing his stubble thoughtfully. His mind raced back to the day he had helped Doctor Victors with his computer troubles. Nick remembered seeing a search history filled with information on various toxic plants, including the Tears of Medusa. He hadn't thought much of it at the time, assuming it was research for a patient or perhaps a personal hobby of the doctors. But now, with the recent unexplained deep sleep of himself still fresh in his mind, Nick couldn't help but wonder if there was a connection between Rose and the doctor.

"Could it be...?" Nick whispered to himself, doubt creeping into his voice. He shook his head, attempting to dispel the growing feeling of unease. "No, it can't be. Rose wouldn't..." Yet, the spot-on description from Eunice matching his experience continued to haunt him.

Nick contemplated the next steps, feeling the familiar pang of grief as he thought of his late wife. He could almost hear her encouraging him to follow his instincts and pursue the truth, no matter where it led or who it implicated. He had trusted Rose and thought they were building a friendship and maybe a relationship. How could she? He chided himself. He was going to let her explain herself before jumping to conclusions.

"Fine," he sighed, giving in to his inner voice. "I'll look into it, but I won't jump to any conclusions." Nick decided to take a methodical approach. Perhaps someone else had noticed something suspicious or out of the ordinary in Rose's behavior.

As Nick closed the app, he stood up and stretched his tall, lean. But first, he felt like he needed a nap. It would be good to shake off the remaining effects of whatever he was drugged with.

CHAPTER TWENTY-
FOUR

T he coastal breeze sent the electronic repair shop's door chime into a frenzy as it swung open, ushering in two uniformed police officers. The sunlight glinted off their badges, momentarily blinding Nick as he stood behind the counter. He squinted, trying to discern their expressions beneath their stern brows and mirrored sunglasses.

"Mr. Cern," the taller deputy began, his voice deep and authoritative. "We've been informed that you've continued an interest in the recent death of Mrs. Brooks."

"Interest?" Nick parried, feigning casualness. Inwardly,

his heart pounded against his chest like a caged bird desperate for freedom. "I'm just a concerned citizen, deputy...?"

"Deputy Harris," the man replied, his tone unyielding. "And this is my partner, Deputy Jenkins." The other officer nodded curtly but remained silent.

"Ah, deputies. Well, I assure you, I'm not meddling in any ongoing investigation," Nick said, maintaining an air of nonchalance. His fingers fidgeted with a tattered bookmark, betraying his disquiet. "But if there's something I need to know..."

"Actually, Mr. Cern, we're here to tell you to let the professionals handle this case," Deputy Jenkins interrupted, her voice firm yet laced with annoyance. "We don't need a civilian complicating matters."

"Complicating matters?" Nick raised an eyebrow, feeling a surge of indignation. "Your sheriff declared it natural causes and the case was closed. So, what is left for your professional skills? All I've done is ask questions—something any concerned citizen should do."

"Your questions are making the townspeople uncomfortable," Deputy Harris warned, his eyes narrowing. "You need to back off, Mr. Cern. This isn't some mystery novel you can solve in your spare time."

The mention of novels stirred memories of his wife, who

had always been by his side during their amateur sleuthing. Her absence left a void Nick struggled to fill, and the sudden injustice of being told to step back ignited his stubborn streak.

"Enough is enough, Mr. Cern," Deputy Jenkins said, striding forward until he was inches from Nick. "We've received complaints about your continued questioning of the townspeople despite our warnings."

"Furthermore," Deputy Harris interjected, "we have reason to believe you've been tampering with evidence."

"Tampering with evidence?" Nick scoffed, incredulous. "I've been doing no such thing! What kind of evidence is there that I could access in a death by natural causes?"

"Regardless, your relentless digging is obstructing our investigation, Mr. Cern," Harris growled, his eyes narrowing to slits. "We've tried being patient with you, but it's clear that you won't stop unless we take action."

"Are you threatening me with arrest?" Nick demanded, clenching his fists.

"Obstruction of justice is a serious charge, Mr. Cern," Jenkins warned, his voice low and dangerous. "We don't want to resort to such measures, but if you force our hand..."

"Fine," Nick snapped, his chest heaving with indignation. "You do what you must, but I won't stand idly by while there's a chance the truth is being buried. Arrest me if you want and we will see the legal ramifications on you and your whole damn department."

"We are concerned about your safety if you are in the way."

"Deputy," he said, his voice steady despite his racing thoughts, "I have no intention of getting in your way. But it's my right as a resident of Sweet Sea to seek answers. I won't let fear or your intimidation stop me."

"Mr. Cern," Deputy Jenkins stepped forward, her voice like ice. "This is your last warning. Cease all inquiries immediately or face the consequences."

The deputies turned on their heels and exited with the same briskness they had entered, leaving Nick feeling both defiant and vulnerable. Their threats echoed in his mind, intertwining with his desire to do the right thing. He knew he couldn't back down, not when something felt amiss in their quaint coastal town.

◆ ◆ ◆

Nick made his way down the cobbled streets of Sweet Sea, casting long shadows that stretched like tendrils across the town's antique charm. He clutched a small notebook to his chest, filled with scribbled names and addresses of those close to the deceased. The scent of salt and seaweed hung in the air, teasing him with memories of simpler days spent strolling along the beach with Lucy, lost in conversation. The interaction with the deputies still fueled his anger.

"Excuse me, Mrs. Westerby?" Nick approached the older woman tending to her rose garden, the vibrant petals a stark contrast against her weathered hands.

"Ah, Mr. Cern," she said, wiping the sweat from her brow with the back of her glove. "What can I do for you today?"

"I was hoping to see if you have seen Rose come home yet," he said gently, his voice laced with concern.

"Sorry, I haven't," she sighed, adjusting her straw hat. "I've known her to spend all day at that church."

"She wasn't there. Did you notice anything unusual leading up to today? Anyone acting out of character or any unfamiliar faces around town?"

Mrs. Westerby paused, considering his question before shaking her head. "Not that I can recall, but my memory isn't what it used to be." She looked at Nick with a mix of curiosity and caution, her eyes lingering on his notebook. "Rose isn't in trouble, is she?"

"Nothing of the sort," he reassured her. "Just trying to catch up with her, is all."

"Ah, well, I wish you luck, Mr. Cern."

"Thank you, Mrs. Westerby," Nick said as he continued down the street.

He visited a handful of other locations, asking about Rose and any observations. Some were hesitant, their eyes darting nervously around, while others spoke with unbridled passion, eager for the truth to come to light.

"Mr. Cern," a voice called from behind him, causing Nick's heart to skip a beat. He was getting really tired of people scaring him. Did everyone in the damn town approach people from the rear. They were lucky he wasn't armed. He turned to see Deputy Harris approaching, his face twisted into a scowl.

"Deputy," Nick acknowledged, his grip tightening on his notebook. "Is there something you need?"

"Word's gotten back to us about you still continuing your little investigation," Harris said, his voice dripping with disdain. "We told you to leave it be."

"Am I not allowed to speak with my neighbors?" Nick challenged, his voice laced with indignation.

"Your persistence is bordering on harassment, Mr. Cern," Deputy Jenkins interjected, joining them. "You're upsetting the townspeople, and that won't be tolerated."

"Just trying to find a friend. If Lucy comes up in conversation...well, I can't help that," Nick said, his chest swelling with determination. "But if you want to control who I talk to and when, we can have that discussion."

"Let the police handle this," Harris growled, jabbing a finger at Nick's chest. "You're walking a thin line, Mr. Cern. Don't make me come back."

As the deputies departed, Nick watched them go, his thoughts racing like a turbulent sea. He would have to add being watched by the police to his list of things to consider.

Nick returned to his shop. Unlocking the door, he was hit with a depressing revelation. If he didn't stay open more, he wasn't going to have a successful business. Everything was pressuring him to just live his life and forget Lucy. The shop needed him, his daughters needed him, and friends and law enforcement kept warning him of the dangers. He just couldn't give it up.

Almost on cue, his phone rang. He looked down at the name and grunted. Taking a deep breath, he swallowed and answered, "Hello, Rose."

CHAPTER

TWENTY-FIVE

"**W**here are you?" Nick asked. He kept his voice low and calm while internally, he fought the urge to lash out at her. He had trusted her.

"Sorry, I missed your call. I was helping out at the church."

"I guess I shouldn't be surprised."

"You know I love the church."

"No, not that." Nick took a deep breath. "I shouldn't be surprised that you would lie."

"Lie?" Rose seemed surprised. "I swear I was..."

"I went by there looking for you, and you were not there." Nick interrupted, no longer able to control his tone.

"Are you tracking me?"

"You mean after you drugged me and took the book?" The line was silent. "Is that enough reason to look for you?"

"Nick," Rose said. Her tone was soft and apologetic. "It isn't what you think? Let me explain."

"Explain what? How you probably killed or helped kill Lucy. Maybe how you have been playing me."

"I would never do that?" Rose's voice raised. "If you would listen to me, I can explain."

"I want the damn book back."

"Of course. Can I bring it by now?"

"I can't look at you right now. Drop it by tomorrow and then leave? I have no desire to talk to you."

"But…"

Nick hung up the phone.

❖ ❖ ❖

The night was uneventful. Nick was able to get a decent night's sleep and found himself wondering if Lucy had really passed away naturally. He was beginning to think he just might be crazy for pursuing this. He made it out of bed and went to his shop before eight. Mentally, he was drained and unenthusiastic about starting his workday. He was more hurt than angry at Rose. He wanted to know why and decided to give her a chance to explain herself when she came by. There was no excuse for it, but he wanted to know her reasoning.

Unlocking the shop door, he could see someone standing outside. He figured it was Rose. However, to his surprise, it was a customer. He welcomed her in and sold her a new set of headphones. That was two hours ago, and still no Rose.

Nick wiped the sweat from his brow as he watched Mrs. Wenkins, a flustered Sweet Sea resident, pace back and forth in front of his workbench. Her phone lay disassembled on the wooden surface, its cracked screen and water-filled device serving as a testament to her frustration.

"Are you sure you can fix it?" she asked, wringing her hands together with a worried glance at the scattered pieces.

"Of course, Mrs. Wenkins," Nick replied confidently. His fingers danced deftly over the tiny screws and delicate circuits, securing them into place as he replaced the shattered screen with a new one. "She'll be as good as new in no time."

Mrs. Wenkins eyed him skeptically, but remained silent, allowing him to work his magic. "Even with all that water?"

"Luckily, on these new phones, you have layers within layers. That water came from the outside case. The electronics inside seem fine. I tested each of them. Now, we are down to the screen replacement."

Nick's mind wandered back to his days as a tech executive, where he honed his skills and knowledge. Those days were long gone, but the thrill of solving a problem still coursed through his veins, igniting his passion for the craft. He had transferred that passion to solving the murder of his friend, and this momentary distraction was just what he needed to find passion back in the technology.

"Voilà!" Nick announced triumphantly, snapping the back cover onto the now-repaired phone. He pressed the power button, and the device sprang to life, its familiar display glowing brightly in the dimly lit shop.

Mrs. Wenkins marveled at the resurrected gadget, her face lighting up in sheer amazement. "Oh, Mr. Cern, I don't know how to thank you enough!"

"Think nothing of it, ma'am," Nick said, smiling warmly. "It's what I'm here for." He handed her the phone, and she clutched it gratefully, the tension in her shoulders dissipating instantaneously.

"You already paid, so the only thing left is to have a pleasant day."

"Thank you," Nick called out as she left the shop, her radiant expression a stark contrast to the storm brewing outside.

"Thank you, Mr. Cern," she replied, stepping out into the rain, her gratitude lingering in the damp air.

With a heavy sigh, Nick turned to face the cluttered workshop. It was time to clean up. Methodically, he tidied up the tools that had accumulated throughout the repair. The door chime sounded, and he looked up. Rose was standing just inside, the wind whipping her hair as the door shut.

Although it seemed like an hour, a few seconds of silence stood between them. Nick extended his hand and was the first to speak. "Book, please."

She rushed up to him and handed it off. "Here you go. If you would let me explain, I think I can clear all of this up."

"Really? "Nick was incredulous, and his stare emphasized it. "By all means, tell me why it was a good idea to drug me and steal evidence."

Rose was visibly shaking. Her timid demeanor seemed more fear than sorrow. "You have been working this investigation very hard. You aren't sleeping, and if you are eating, it is very poor. Have you looked at yourself in the mirror?"

Nick looked down at the glass case. He was unusually pale, and the dark circles under his eyes were more profound than he had remembered. His eyes leveled on her. "So?"

"So, I added a harmless sleep tonic to your tea, hoping it would put you to sleep. I tried to convince you to sleep on your own, but you wouldn't."

"You drugged me!" he yelled. "I am a recovering addict. Do you know what that could have done to me? I could have relapsed or worse."

"I made sure that I took that into consideration. It was all plant-based and had no narcotics in it. I really tried to help you take care of yourself."

"Sounds like bullshit to me. Why did you take the book?"

"I was afraid you would wake up and go right back to it. So, I thought I would keep you from working."

"Why do you feel the need to lie again?"

"I'm not lying," she pleaded, tears starting down her cheek.

"Then why did you give the book to Martha?"

"Martha?" She was confused for a split second, but then the realization hit her. "Ohhh. No, I did not give it to her. I did show it to her, though."

"Why in the hell would you do that?"

"She is my friend and asked about it. I didn't see the harm."

"Another betrayal. We said we wouldn't bring other people into the investigation."

"I didn't. She asked about what you and I were doing, and I said it was sort of like a book club. I was showing her what I had with me. That's all."

"Really?" Nick was calming, but still thought she was holding something back. "Why in the hell would she care so much about what we were doing?"

Rose was silent. She looked down at her feet, and her body language shifted. Nick couldn't tell why, but it was suspicious.

"Why?" he asked again.

Rose took a breath and shouted, "Because she knows I have fallen in love with you. These last few weeks have been great, and I know you lost your wife, which is sad, but you are my soulmate. I can feel it. There, you happy now?"

The room began to spin, and he braced himself on the counter. That was different from the direction he expected. Before she walked in, he assumed she was part of the crime, but it was all because she cared for him. It was too much. "I need you to leave."

"Did you hear what I said? I am…"

Nick held up his hand. "Stop. I heard you. I need time to process this. Please just leave."

"But."

"Now."

Reluctantly, Rose turned and left the shop. Long after the door closed, Nick stared out the windows. The rain had stopped, but the storm was still out there. He had to push down his feelings for Rose and the situation. God help him. He believed her and why she did it. It wasn't any more acceptable, but at least he felt a little better.

Thunder clapped outside. He had been in the town long enough to know that that was the sign of a big storm coming in. With the book back, he flipped to the page he had dog-eared the night before. It outlined the plant that he believed was used to kill Lucy. It would be nice if he could find a specimen of it. He wasn't sure yet what he would do, but he knew he needed a sample. With no telling how long the storm would last, he decided now was the best time to get it. He grabbed his coat, locked up the shop, and headed outside.

As he locked the door, the wind picked up outside, casting the scent of salt and seaweed through the narrow streets of Sweet Sea. Nick's heart thudded in his chest as he stepped into the night, the shadows enveloping him like a cloak. His resolve burned brightly, illuminating the path before him as the storm threatened to engulf the quaint seaside town.

The wind howled around him like a chorus of vengeful spirits as Nick made his way toward the woods. The trees loomed ahead, their gnarled branches reaching out like skeletal hands. He entered the forest, darkness wrapped itself around him, and the scent of damp earth and decaying leaves filled his nostrils.

"Damn it," he muttered, stumbling over a fallen branch. The shadows danced in the faint moonlight that filtered through the dense canopy above. He steadied himself against a tree trunk, collected his thoughts, and forged onwards.

The search was not easy. The undergrowth grew thicker, tangling around Nick's legs and threatening to trip him at every step. Moisture clung to his skin, and the air felt heavy with the weight of some unseen presence. He was growing increasingly frustrated with the obstacles.

At the point he felt he had gone too deep into the forest, he stopped in his tracks. Before him lay a small clearing, bathed in an eerie glow from the cloud shrouded moonlight above. In the center stood a plant unlike any Nick had ever seen. Comparing the description in the book to what he was looking at, Nick knew it was the one he was looking for.

He stared at the plant, his heart heavy with the implications of the discovery. A new fire ignited within him, fueled by grief and determination. Nick took a cautious step forward, his eyes locked on the toxic plant before him. He couldn't help but wonder if this seemingly innocuous growth had somehow played a part in Lucy's tragic end. Swallowing the lump in his throat, he knelt down to examine the plant more closely.

The plant's white flowers, with their almost translucent petals, shimmered with an iridescent sheen around a gnarled mass of twisting vines and jagged leaves. As he studied the plant, he couldn't deny the eerie beauty it possessed. His fingers brushed against the delicate petals, feeling a cold shiver travel up his arm.

His mind was racing with questions and theories. With practiced precision, he pulled a pair of latex gloves from his pocket, snapping them onto his hands with a satisfying snap that echoed ominously through the otherwise silent woods. He carefully plucked a single leaf from the plant, placing it gingerly in a small plastic bag he had brought for this purpose. He knew further analysis would be needed, and he was determined to leave no stone unturned in his quest for answers.

Nick stood up and turned to leave, but he couldn't shake the feeling that he was being watched. A sense of foreboding hung heavy in the air as if the very trees themselves were whispering a warning. But despite the fear gnawing at the edges of his mind, he knew he couldn't turn back now.

He walked away from the sinister plant, his mind

swirling with questions and dark possibilities. The fern-like leaves seemed to reach out towards him, as if they were trying to ensnare him in a deadly embrace. He couldn't help but shudder at the thought of what this plant might have done to Lucy. She had been so vibrant, so full of life for someone her age – it was unfathomable to think that something as innocuous as a plant could have snuffed out her light so cruelly. But the evidence was right there, staring him in the face.

Walking towards the edge of the woods and back on the street, Nick had a sudden realization. Someone must have known about the plant, its potency, and perhaps even Lucy's susceptibility to it. But who? And why?

"Could it be one of her colleagues at the library?" he mused aloud, brushing aside a low-hanging branch as he trudged through the undergrowth. "Or perhaps someone from her past? Or maybe?"

He flipped to the front of the book. It was a library book. That means there was a history of who checked it out. It could be a long shot, but maybe one of his suspects would be on that list. The thought sent a chill down his spine as if an icy hand had gripped his heart. Whoever was responsible for Lucy's death had gone to great lengths to ensure her silence. And now that he was on the trail of the truth, could he find them because they had a library card? It put a smile on his face.

He paused for a moment, taking a deep breath as he tried to get his bearings. The woods around him seemed to close in as if sensing his resolve, but Nick refused to be deterred. Shadows clung to every corner of the trees, Nick was not one to falter in the face of danger, but he had the distinct feeling he was being watched. He held his breath, not wanting to inhale. Silence surrounded him. The implications of this self-revelation were as chilling as it was profound. If someone in Sweet Sea was willing to kill to protect their secrets, then no one was safe – least of all Nick himself. If someone was out there, they were absolutely still. He waited a few seconds, and with a slight disappointment in psyching himself out, he continued.

After about ten minutes, Nick found himself at the forest edge. The town and his shop were just a short distance away. With a grim nod, he turned back towards the town, his mind racing with the possibilities before him. He would need to find someone to examine the plant sample closely, consult with experts, and dig deep into the lives of those around him. It wouldn't be easy, but he was not a man to shy away from a challenge.

CHAPTER

TWENTY-SIX

Nick walked purposefully along the edge of the woods, his hair barely ruffled by the gentle breeze. This was the dangerous time of a storm. When everything settled down, the worst was gearing up. He scanned the ground as he walked. He was sure someone had been watching him earlier, and he was interested in finding footprints. It was on the way back to his shop, so he saw no harm.

Within the woods, the tree clusters were alive with the rustling of leaves and the chirping of birds, their melodies bittersweet in the face of the grim task Nick had set himself.

But beneath the symphony of nature, there was an underlying sense of danger and suspense, as though the very trees were holding their breath, waiting for something to happen.

Nick paused, his keen eyes catching sight of a scrap of fabric caught on a branch. He approached cautiously, pulling out his smartphone to document the find. As he snapped a photo, he reflected on how far technology had come since his days as a Vice President in corporate America. The time spent repairing computers had served him well, and now, it aided him in his quest for justice.

"Could this be from the person I thought was watching me?" he wondered aloud, his voice barely audible over the cacophony of the woods.

As he continued his search for signs, Nick was reminded of his own past addiction, a demon he'd fought and conquered. He knew that the road to recovery had made him resilient and persistent, traits that now served him well as he navigated the treacherous terrain of this investigation. It occurred to him that this desire to solve Lucy's death was an addiction in itself. One that he was dangerously close to consuming him. At least, Rose thought so and probably his girls as well.

He thought he saw movement a few feet into the woods. Without hesitation, he stepped in. As he pressed on, the forest seemed to close in around Nick, each rustle of leaves and birdcall echoing the danger lurking just out of sight.

The shadows lengthened, stretching their dark tendrils across the forest floor as Nick pressed deeper into the woods. The crisp air nipped at his exposed skin, but the unsettling quiet pricked at his senses. The chirping of birds had been replaced by an eerie silence, only broken by the occasional rustle of leaves above. He was more sure than ever that someone else was out there.

"Who's there?" Nick called out, his heart pounding in his chest. He scanned the area, searching for any sign of the source of his unease. He didn't expect an answer, but one could hope. Could it just be the wind playing tricks on him?

"Hello, Mr. Cern."

The voice came from the darkness, low and menacing. Nick spun around, his eyes locking onto the tall figure that had materialized seemingly out of nowhere. A jagged scar marred the man's left cheek, a sinister reminder of some past violence.

"Who are you?" Nick demanded, his voice steady despite the tremor of fear coiling inside him.

"Someone who doesn't want you poking your nose where it doesn't belong." The attacker lunged forward, driven by unknown motivations.

"Wait!" Nick cried out, but it was too late. The assailant's fist connected with his jaw, sending him reeling backward. The book and sample flew from his hands. Desperation fueled his movements as he threw a punch of his own, but the attacker easily dodged it and retaliated with a swift, brutal side kick to Nick's ribs.

Nick gasped, struggling to regain his footing. The pain radiating from his injuries made focusing difficult, but he knew he couldn't afford to back down now.

"I can inflict more pain than you will ever know," the attacker replied, a cruel smile twisting his lips. "If you know what's good for you, you'll drop this investigation."

"Never," Nick spat back, his defiance igniting a spark of anger in the other man's eyes. He attempted another punch, putting all his weight behind it, but the attacker parried effortlessly and sent him sprawling to the ground with a well-placed shove. Nick felt his ankle twist and give out.

Nick fought to keep the black spots at the edge of his vision from swallowing him whole. "Why did you kill her?"

"You're a fool," the attacker said, turning on his heel and disappearing into the shadows once more. "And fools don't live long, Mr. Cern."

As the sound of retreating footsteps faded into the distance, Nick lay on the forest floor, battered and bruised but determined to see his quest for justice through to the end. The pain was nothing compared to the anguish he felt knowing that Lucy's killer was still out there, taunting him from just out of reach. The attacker may not have known it, but by attacking him, he confirmed Nick was right, and that was all he needed to continue. But who the hell was the scar-faced man? This was something new.

Nick crawled to the nearest tree. With the help of its steady build, he managed to stand to his feet and start moving again. Blood was dripping from the deep gash on Nick's forehead, blurring his vision as he tried to focus on the path ahead. The pain in his twisted ankle was nearly unbearable, but he gritted his teeth and forced himself to keep moving. He couldn't afford to waste any more time here in the woods, not while Rose remained unaware of the danger, they were in. He retrieved his lost items and stumbled slowly forward.

"Damn it," Nick muttered under his breath, swiping at the blood with his sleeve before reaching for his phone. With shaky fingers, he pulled up the GPS app, praying it would lead him back to civilization – and safety. He had lost all sense of direction after the blows to the head.

As he limped through the thick underbrush, every step sent ribbons of agony shooting up his leg, a stark reminder of the consequences of his actions. A younger, healthier version of himself might have been able to fend off the attacker – or at least escape with fewer injuries. But those years of self-destructive behavior had left their mark, both mentally and physically.

Nick's breathing grew labored, each gasp punctuated by a sharp stab of pain in his ribs. Still, he pushed forward, driven by the knowledge that he had to protect his loved ones from the threat that now loomed over them all. "Almost there," he told himself, his voice barely audible. "Just a little further."

As the first hints of rain began to filter through the trees, Nick finally stumbled upon a familiar landmark: an old wooden bridge that led back to the heart of town. Relief washed over him, quickly followed by a wave of exhaustion that threatened to pull him under. The rain thickened.

His injuries weighed heavily on him as he forced himself to take one step after another, each movement bringing him closer to safety. But even as he hobbled toward home, Nick knew this was just the beginning of his journey. The attacker remained at large, and the truth behind Lucy's murder was still shrouded in darkness.

Nick's legs trembled as he pushed open the door to his shop, the hinges creaking in protest. His body ached from the ordeal in the woods, but the sight of his familiar surroundings brought a measure of solace. In spite of the pain, an overwhelming sense of relief washed over him as he took in the scent of oil and electronics as well as the comforting hum of the refrigerator.

Closing the door behind him, Nick stumbled up the stairs and into the living room of his above apartment, the weight of his twisted ankle threatening to buckle on the stairs. He collapsed onto the couch, the worn upholstery embracing him like a long-lost friend. Crimson droplets fell from his forehead and stained the fabric, a reminder of the danger he had faced and the impact. As he tried to catch his breath, his thoughts went to Rose, and a pang of guilt tightened in his chest.

The shrill ring of his phone pulled him out of his reverie. Grimacing, he fished the device out of his pocket, wincing at the jolt of pain that shot through his ribcage. The screen displayed Kaley's name and picture, a smile so like her mother's graced her young face. She was driven by her desire to make sure her father was safe and well, a constant source of worry for her.

"Hey, pumpkin," he answered, forcing a lightness into his tone that he didn't feel. He purposefully left his camera off in hopes that she would not see how injured he was.

"Hi, Dad!" Kaley's voice was like sunshine breaking through storm clouds. "How are you? I wanted to check in on you."

"Ah, you know me," Nick replied, trying to keep his voice

steady despite the throbbing pain in his head. "Just tinkering around and getting dirty."

"Really?" Kaley's tone was tinged with suspicion, her concern for her father evident. "You sound... I don't know, different? Why is your camera off?"

Nick's fingers trembled as he clutched the phone to his ear. The pain radiating from his twisted ankle and the throbbing cut on his forehead were nearly unbearable, but he couldn't afford to show any weakness. Not now, not when Kaley was on the line, her voice a beacon of warmth in the cold aftermath of the attack.

"Ah, it's just been a long day, sweetheart." He couldn't bear to tell her the truth of what he'd been through, not when she had already lost so much. "Plus, I think I am having Wi-Fi issues, so I have the camera off to help with the bandwidth."

"Are you sure, Dad? I can fly down and help you with your shop if you want."

Nick closed his eyes, imagining the bright curiosity that danced in her eyes, so reminiscent of her mother. He exhaled slowly, steeling himself against the urge to confess everything. "I'm fine, pumpkin. Just some work stuff is getting to me, that's all."

"Work stuff." The words tasted like ash in his mouth, an ignominious substitute for the truth. But how could he tell her about the danger stalking them all, about the shadowy figure whose motivations remained shrouded in mystery? To reveal such a truth would be to invite chaos into their already fragile world.

"All right," Kaley said, clearly unconvinced. "Just promise me you'll take care of yourself, okay? You've been through a lot, Dad. We both have."

Nick hesitated, torn between wanting Kaley's comforting presence and protecting her from the danger that lurked in the shadows. But as he glanced at the bloodstains on the couch and the way his ankle throbbed with each heartbeat, he knew he couldn't risk involving her any further.

"Thanks, pumpkin, but I've got this. You focus on your studies, all right?"

"All right, Dad. But call me if you need anything, okay?"

"Promise," he said, his heart swelling with love and gratitude for his daughter. "If it makes you feel better, I got lots of sleep the night before last. I think it was the most I have ever had."

"How did you manage that?"

"Just had some relaxing tea." He tried to smile at his inside joke, but his literal insides hurt to make that motion. "I think I may even go to sleep soon and get more rest."

"That's awesome. I'll let you get to that. Love you, Dad."

"Love you too, Kaley."

As the call ended, Nick allowed himself a moment of quiet reflection, staring at the ceiling with heavy-lidded eyes. He knew his investigation had put him and Rose in danger, and he resolved to be more careful and strategic in his next moves.

Nick's fingers traced the edges of the deep gash on his forehead – a painful reminder of what that lurked within the shadows. Heaving himself out of the couch, he hobbled to the window and stared out into the encroaching storm. The wind whispered through the trees, carrying the scent of damp earth and unspoken secrets. In the distance, a lone bird called out, its melody both haunting and beautiful.

CHAPTER TWENTY-
SEVEN

Nick Cern was awake and out the back door of his above-store apartment just as the first rays of morning light painted the quaint coastal town in soft pastel hues. The birds sang their early melodies overhead, and the sea breeze was light. He stepped outside, limped towards the beachfront, and smiled. The rain was gone. He took a deep breath, savoring the crisp air that reminded him of new beginnings. His late wife would have loved it here, he thought. The waves were crashing in a soothing, yet powerful rhythm. After another good night's sleep and the calming atmosphere, he was ready to take on the day. Sore from the beating, he was happy. Odd as it sounded, it gave him confirmation he wasn't crazy.

After about twenty minutes of taking it all in, he turned back to his store. As Nick approached the storefront, he suddenly froze in his tracks. Overnight, the once-pristine glass store window had been transformed into a jagged spiderweb of cracks, shards glistening like angry teeth under the sun's gentle touch. The door lock hung broken and useless, a mocking testament to his attempts at security.

"Dear God," Nick yelled, his heart pounding like a jackhammer. He cautiously stepped inside, aware of the sharp crunch of shattered glass beneath his shoes. Every nerve in his body screamed for him to run, but he couldn't leave the place that represented his hope for a fresh start in tatters.

The store's main room was in chaos – computers and electronic parts lay strewn about like the aftermath of a technological typhoon. But amidst the wreckage, something caught Nick's eye. A single monitor screen was awake, casting an eerie glow on the disarray. He hesitated for a moment before stepping toward it, the weight of dread settling heavily upon his shoulders.

'BACK OFF OR ELSE' – the words seared themselves across the screen in bold, red letters. A chill slithered down Nick's spine, his mind racing with questions and fears. Who could have done this? Was it just some bored teenager or someone with a darker motive?

"Damn it," he whispered, clenching his fists. Whoever was responsible, they had picked the wrong person to mess with. Nick had fought his demons in the corporate world and emerged victorious. He wasn't about to let some low life bully him out of his newfound sanctuary. His hand went to the bandage on his forehead. Was beating him up not enough?

"Think, Nick. Think," he urged himself, surveying the destruction with a calculating eye. He would need evidence, something to prove that this was more than just a random act of vandalism. His fingers tapped against his thigh, a habit he'd picked up during his days in corporate America – a time when challenges were met head-on, and failure wasn't an option. Nick's heart raced, the adrenaline pumping through his veins as he looked around his store. The shattered glass and broken door lock were enough to send shivers down his spine, but the message on his computer screen unsettled him even more. His once-peaceful store now felt tainted.

He glanced back at the threatening message, the crimson words burning into his memory. 'Back off or else' – this was no empty threat. The perpetrator had made it clear that they wanted him gone and would resort to violence if necessary. Hell, he had already been a victim of some violence.

What would they do next? Kill him? They made it clear: someone wanted him gone, and they would not hesitate to hurt him if he didn't comply. Despite his fear gnawing at the edges of his mind, Nick felt a surge of determination.

"Okay, Nick, stay calm," he said to himself, taking deep breaths to steady his nerves. He knew that panicking would only make matters worse. "Call the police. That's the first thing you need to do."

He pulled out his phone and dialed the emergency number, his fingers shaking as he pressed each digit. When the operator answered, he spoke quickly but clearly, conveying the urgency of the situation. "Hello, I need to report a break-in at my store. There's damage, and there's a threatening message on my computer screen. I'm really worried for my safety."

"Sir, can you please provide us with your name, location, and a brief description of the incident?" the operator asked, her voice steady and professional.

"Of course," he replied, regaining some composure. "My name is Nick Cern, and my store is located at 1214 Ocean Drive in Sweet Sea. I arrived this morning to find the front window smashed, the door lock broken, and the message on my computer screen. It says, 'Back off or else.' I believe someone is trying to intimidate me."

"Thank you, Mr. Cern. We're sending deputies to your

location right away. Please stay on the line with me until they arrive."

"Thank you," Nick said, feeling a small measure of relief at the prospect of help. Even as he waited for the police, his mind raced, trying to piece together who could be behind this attack. He refused to cower in fear – he would face this threat head-on, just as he had always done.

"Are you hurt at all?"

"Not from the break in."

Before the 911 operator could ask anything else, the faint sound of sirens gradually grew louder, eventually coming to a stop outside Nick's store. He glanced through the broken window, watching as two deputies stepped out of individual patrol cars, their faces set in bored expressions. They ambled toward him, hands resting on their hips. He recognized Sweet Sea's finest.

"They're here. Thank you." He hung up.

"Mr. Cern?" Deputy Jenkins said, stepping over the glass. "We're here about your call."

"Please, come inside and see for yourselves."

The officers entered the shop, their eyes scanning the shattered glass and damaged door. One of them let out a low whistle before turning back to Nick. "What a mess," he said, his tone casual, as if he were discussing a spilled cup of coffee rather than a blatant act of vandalism.

"Look, I'm not concerned about the mess right now," Nick interjected, his voice rising slightly in frustration. "Someone broke into my store and left a threatening message on my computer. That's what I need help with."

"Threatening message, you say?" The second deputy, Fred Harris, peered over Nick's shoulder at the computer screen. "Well, it doesn't look like anyone got hurt, and nothing seems to have been stolen. Our advice? Let it go, Mr. Cern. You can't undo what's been done, so just move on."

"Move on?" Nick stared at the deputy incredulously. "This wasn't just some random act of vandalism! Whoever did this had a clear motive – to intimidate me. And who knows what they might do next? It's proof that I'm right."

Deputy Jenkins stepped between them and faced Nick. "Hold on, boys. We will work the scene and see what kinds of details we can find. And Mr. Cern, the only thing this proves is that you pissed someone off, or some kids were having fun."

"I know. I pissed off the killer."

He was looking at his forehead. "What did you do to your head? And is that a black eye?"

"I got beat up. Someone attacked me in the woods and told me to stop investigating."

Deputy Harris fought back a smile. "The sheriff told you

that before, but with less pain."

"I appreciate the commentary. Can you please just do your job? Between last night's attack and this, I don't think I'm safe."

"Sir," Deputy Jenkins sighed. "We deal with cases like these all the time. Most of the time, it's just someone looking for attention or trying to scare you. There's no need to get worked up over it."

"Worked up?" Nick could feel his face reddening with anger. "My store has been broken into, and my safety is at risk! How can you expect me to just 'let it go'?"

"Was anything stolen?" Deputy Harris asked from the corner of the room.

"I just found it and called you. I have no idea. Looking around, though, I see several expensive things, so I don't think so. Maybe."

"Do you have any video surveillance?"

Nick drooped his head. "No. I didn't think I would need it in such a small town."

"Look," Deputy Jenkins intervened, raising a placating hand. "We understand your concern, but our resources are limited. We will look around, make a report, and see if anyone knows anything. Although not how I would put it, but I agree, you should clean up, fix the door, and figure out if anything was stolen. Chances are, nothing else will happen."

"Nothing else will happen?" Nick's voice trembled as he tried to control his emotions. He paced the small room, his heart thrumming in his chest with each step. "How can you be so certain? I need protection, not dismissal. Can't you see that I'm a target?"

"You're still kind of new to this town. Have you had any recent disputes with anyone in town? Any disgruntled customers, perhaps?"

"Of course not!" Nick protested, frustration flaring within him. "Everyone has been nothing but welcoming since I moved here. Well, everyone but the sheriff's department, that is."

"Are you sure about that?" Deputy Harris pressed, his gaze unrelenting. "You're new to Sweet Sea. There are bound to be people who feel threatened by your presence. It wouldn't be surprising if one of them decided to teach you a lesson."

"Teach me a lesson?" Nick retorted, indignant. "You're making it sound like I brought this upon myself!"

"Did I say that?" Deputy Harris asked, feigning innocence. "All I'm saying is that we must explore every possible angle, Mr. Cern."

As the interrogation continued, Nick felt a growing sense of unease. Instead of reassurance and protection, he was being made to feel like a suspect in his own break in. The room seemed colder, the air heavier with each passing moment.

"Is there anyone else you can think of who might have a reason to target you?" Deputy Jenkins questioned, examining Nick's face for any sign of deception.

"Nobody comes to mind," Nick whispered, his voice trembling. He had thought the police would be on his side, but now it appeared as though even they couldn't be trusted. "Whoever it is, I am in real danger here?"

"Mr. Cern, we really don't have the manpower to give you a personal bodyguard," the deputy replied, his voice taking on a patronizing tone. "We'll file a report, of course, but beyond that, there's not much we can do. Our advice still stands let it go. Once you know if something was stolen or something we can track, we can dig deeper."

Nick clenched his fists, struggling to contain the surge of frustration and fear that coursed through him. He had thought calling the police would provide some semblance of security, but their indifference only served to deepen his sense of vulnerability.

The deputies spent about an hour walking the room, looking at devices, and measuring damage to the walls. Once they felt they spent enough time, they turned to Nick. "We will be in touch."

"That's it? You come in, blame the victim, and leave?" Nick said.

"What would you have us do?"

"Dust for fingerprints or something."

"It's a store. Essentially, a public space. People will leave all kinds of prints. Shall we go around and accuse every customer you have had? It wouldn't be productive."

Nick hadn't thought of that. The deputies were right, but he would never tell them that.

As the officers turned to leave, he knew that he was ultimately alone in this fight, left to grapple with an unseen enemy and an uncertain future. The shattered glass crunched beneath Nick's feet, the sound as grating as the officers' dismissal. He watched them walk away without a backward glance, their indifference leaving him feeling more alone than ever. His heart raced, and he tried to steady his breath, the frustration bubbling inside him like a kettle left on the stove, forgotten until it whistled its fury.

Alone, Nick went into the back room to get a broom and dustpan. He heard the door chime at the front of the store. His first thought was that the vandal had come back, but his second thought was that maybe the deputies had returned to help. He ducked back into the main store. No one was there. He moved quickly to the door and looked outside. He didn't see anyone.

"Hey there, Mr. Cern?" The soft, feminine voice came from a corner, startling him.

Nick turned to face a stunningly beautiful middle-aged lady looking over some damage with a stern look, her tight ponytail matching the authority in her gaze. Although she was dressed in street clothes, he instantly recognized her as Sheriff Joan Kent.

" What is with this town? You scared the hell out of me," Nick replied hesitantly, biting back the acidic remark that threatened to escape. "Can I help you?"

"Actually, I came to see if I could be of any assistance." The sheriff's eyes swept over the broken window before meeting Nick's once again. "I received word about what happened here, and I thought I'd have a look for myself."

"Really?" Nick couldn't help but let some of his bitterness seep into his tone. "Because your officers just told me to 'let it go' and 'move on.'"

Sheriff Kent frowned, the lines on her face creasing further. "Well, I'm not one to let things go so easily, especially when there's a potential threat at hand. Mind if I take a look around?"

"Be my guest," Nick said, stepping aside to allow the sheriff space.

Sheriff Kent made meticulous observations as they walked through the store together, asking Nick specific questions about the break-in and threatening message. For the first time since discovering the damage, Nick felt a glimmer of hope - someone was finally taking him seriously.

"Mr. Cern," the sheriff began after completing her inspection, "I want you to know that I'm going to do everything in my power to find out who's behind this. You deserve better than what you've been given so far."

"Thank you, sheriff," Nick replied with a sigh of relief. "I just want to feel safe again."

"Understandable," the sheriff nodded, her steely gaze unwavering. "I'll make sure my team is on top of this case. In the meantime, I suggest you take precautions - change your locks and install a security system if you haven't already. It's better to be safe than sorry."

"Will do," Nick agreed, feeling a renewed sense of hope. "And if there's anything else I can do to help, just let me know."

"There is one thing?"

"Let me guess," Nick said. "Stop looking into Lucy's death."

"There's that. But, no, I was going to say avoid dark places and try not to go anywhere alone or at night until we know what's going on. I can tell by the bruises and cuts across your face that you might be in danger. I don't have an idea whether it is connected to your questions or not. I just want you to be careful."

"I can do that. I appreciate your help." Nick wanted to say something else, but he wasn't sure she would be willing to hear it. His old therapist in New York said to be more vulnerable with people. He decided to try it. "There's something else."

"Sure," the sheriff looked slightly apprehensive.

"I think you and I got off on the wrong foot. Please know that I don't think you are bad at your job. Far from it, I could never do what you do. I understand that you are following the evidence, and said evidence has led to your declaration of Lucy's death being natural. And I am fully aware that it may indeed be natural. However, I have to know for sure. I can't," he paused. "I'm not capable of letting it go."

The sheriff's features softened, and her tone was calm, "And why is that?"

Nick swallowed. "My wife died a little over two years ago, and I was in a really dark spot. I did everything wrong. I became addicted to prescription drugs, shut out my girls, and was just a wreck. It was hard to pull out of that. I eventually did, and when I got here, Lucy was the first friend I made. Even though it was only a friendship, she helped fill the void of my dead wife. When she passed, all those other feelings attached to my wife came back. I was holding on by a thread anyway, and now, this is helping me not go back to drug addiction because I have something to focus on. I know that is a lot, but does that make sense."

"More than you know," she said. "I lost my husband a few years back. He was the sheriff before me and died in a shootout."

"So, you do get it. I just wanted you to know the why and that I wasn't just an asshole. I won't keep you any longer, but I thought I should share."

"I appreciate it. Just be careful, please."

"Thank you. And please, let me know if you find anything."

"Of course. We'll be in touch," Sheriff Kent said before taking her leave.

As the door clicked shut behind her, Nick allowed himself to process the events that had unfolded. His emotions were a tangled mess of fear, frustration, and now, a cautious optimism.

◆ ◆ ◆

Nick had spent most of the day taking inventory and

cleaning up the mess. Nothing had been stolen, which unnerved him even more. At least a burglary would make him feel less threatened. It was going to be a long night and he knew it. The locksmith had shown up a few hours after he called them, and he had an extra deadbolt added to the door.

He stepped out of his shop to get a good look at the window. He was going to need three big pieces of plywood until he could get a replacement glass. It occurred to him that he had yet to learn where the closest hardware store even was. There had to be one around town somewhere.

He pulled his coat collar up around his neck to fight the chilly air and stared at the quiet streets of Sweet Sea, wondering where he could turn for help now. He knew people, but other than Rose, they were just acquaintances. And he was not going to call Rose. More alone than the first day he moved here, Nick started going through his phone to find a hardware shop.

"Hey there," a soft voice interrupted Nick's thought, causing him to look up. He turned to see a woman his age with long, curly brown hair and glasses, her hands clasped tightly around a worn notebook.

"Hello, Rose. Can I help you?" Nick asked warily, his nerves still frayed from the interrogation.

Rose studied his face. She reached up to touch his

forehead. As Nick pulled away, she said, "Oh my lord, what happened to you?"

"It's a long story."

"Are you okay?"

"What do you want, Rose?"

"I was walking over to the diner when I saw your window."

"Vandals got me."

"They beat you up, too?"

"No, that was someone in the woods last night."

"The woods? What were you doing in there at night?"

"It doesn't matter. Do you need something?" He let out a deep sigh of irritation to drive home his annoyance.

"Actually, I might be able to help you," she replied, a determined glint in her eyes. "I know you hate me, but you clearly need a friend."

He thought for a moment and said, "I'm fine. But thank you."

"There's nothing I can help with?"

Nick eyed her cautiously, weighing his options. But as he considered his current predicament, he realized he had little choice but to accept whatever assistance he could find. "All right," he agreed hesitantly. "Do you know where the closest hardware store is?"

"I do. What do you need?"

"Plywood. I have to cover up this window until I can get someone out to fix it."

"We have a few at the church. I will drive over and get what we have and bring them back."

"I can do it. Just need to know where."

"No, I want to help. I will go."

As they stood on the sidewalk, surrounded by quaint storefronts and the distant sound of waves crashing against the shore, Nick couldn't help but feel a little better. He knew he was taking a considerable risk by taking Rose's help, but with no one else to turn to, the prospect of facing his troubles alone seemed far more daunting.

"Fine. Just bring it back here," Nick agreed finally, turning back to the window. "Just know this doesn't mean things are good between us. You really betrayed my trust, and I am not sure we can come back from that."

"Understood. I just hope you can find it in your heart to forgive me some day." Rose walked down the cobblestone street towards the church. Nick wasn't sure, but he thought she was crying.

CHAPTER TWENTY-EIGHT

Nick stared at the wood covering his large window. He missed his ocean view, but knew it would only be two more days before the replacement arrived. It had been five days since he ran into Rose, got the wood, and completed the makeshift repairs. In that time, he had not said another word to her. He was still too angry.

The attack had deterred him, but didn't stop him completely. He became more subtle in his investigation and practiced restraint when he felt the need to challenge someone directly. The information flow was slowing down, and he wondered if he was ever going to solve the mystery.

The phone next to the register started ringing. He picked it up expecting a customer, but was pleasantly surprised to hear Susan Priser. "Good morning, Susan. What can I do for you?"

"Good morning," she replied. "I have that information you asked for on who has checked out *The Brown Grass* over the last year. It appears it was an extremely popular book."

"Great." The sarcasm from Nick was obvious, but if Susan noticed, she didn't respond. "How many?"

"It goes on for about two pages double spaced. Would you like me to email it to you?"

The last email from a librarian was from Lucy about twenty days ago before she was killed. It did seem appropriate that a list that might help him solve the mystery would also come through email. "Thanks. Do you have my email address?"

"It's attached to your library card. I will send it right over. Can I ask what you are hoping to find?"

"Just curious. I know Lucy loved the book and thought it would be fun to do some memorial for her around it. The sheriff is releasing the body to Michael any day now, and I want to get prepared." It was a lie, and he hated it. However, he was not taking any chances.

After exchanging pleasantries, they hung up. Nick

kept refreshing his phone until he saw the email. Quickly, he opened the attachment and started scanning the names. Susan had been right; this was a lot of people. He didn't mind. He knew which names to check for. Within thirty seconds, he found three names he recognized. One of those was Lucy, but the other two surprised him. Rose had checked the book out a month prior to the incident, and Eunice Edwards a month before that. The two people who helped him the most were the only names he recognized. He scanned the list two additional times looking for the doctor or even Michael's name, but came up empty. He would have settled to find Harold Finch, but as the library maintenance man, he could have read it without checking it out. What was he going to do now? This new information made him want to question Eunice and Rose again. But he really didn't want to talk to Rose.

He had to get a tighter grip on the clues. Assuming he was still correct, and Lucy had been poisoned, he focused on who did it. Pulling out a notebook from under the workbench, he tore a page out and randomly started a brain dump on the paper.

>Rose and Eunice checked out the book. – However, I was attacked by a man in the woods. Could they have hired him?
>
>The Historical Society needed money, and none of them,

except Eunice, would even give him a direct answer. Why?

My shop was vandalized, and a message was left. This means I got close to the killer and know who they are.

The killer had to know about poisons and what plants were nearby.

The doctor said it was natural causes which is clearly not the case. Which means he is either guilty, incompetent or in on it in some other way.

The sheriff and her deputies keep telling him to drop it and stop investigating. What do they have to hide? What is the harm in asking questions?

Rose poisoned me. She said it was to "help," but what if she was trying to kill me? She seems remorseful, but is it an act?

Eunice has been very helpful in trying to solve the mystery, but why?

The Doctor had a web page open on his laptop about deadly plants. It was after Lucy died. Is he messing with me? Did I get through to him and was he doing his own investigation?

Lucy left all her money to the Historical Society and cut her nephew out. He seems okay with it, but it could be an act.

Harold, the janitor, is grumpy and creepy. He helped find the body. Did he know it was there?

Susan got promoted at the library after Lucy died. Could that be a motive? Not sure if money was involved in the new role.

The nephew is a recovering drug addict who is set on trying to clear his name. He seems to be trying too hard.

Lucy felt nervous and possibly scared before her death. Something about giving the person time to do the right thing. What was that about?

Michael had financial trouble.

The doctor had a beard. The kids said they got money from a bearded man and the next day the doctor shaved.

During the initial investigation, Lucy had something under her nails. What was it? Why was it never mentioned again?

Nick stopped writing and looked at the disoriented information on the page in front of him. He checked it over and remembered one other thing.

Lucy left the Historical Society Benefit angry on the night of her death. Possibly arguing with the doctor.

He stopped writing again and read through the list one more time. It looked like he captured everything. Now, what?

A cell phone ringing interrupted his thoughts. It wasn't

his phone. He looked around the shop, searching for the source. His hearing led him from one wall to the other. The echo in the showroom with the wood on the window was real. Closing his eyes, he focused on the noise, and it led him back to his workbench. He opened the top drawer and saw it was Lucy's phone ringing. He had forgotten he put it in there. After initially getting the device, he searched it, found it had nothing helpful, and threw it in the drawer. But now it was alive. The screen read, 'Unknown Caller.'

Carefully picking it up, Nick put it to his ear and said, "Hello?"

His heart pounded in his chest like a jackhammer as he listened to the voice on the other end of the line. He could feel the cold sweat forming on his brow and trickling down his temples. The caller's deep, menacing voice was laced with a hint of a Southern accent that sent shivers down his spine. It was obvious they were using one of those voice-changer devices like in the movies.

"Little buddy," the killer taunted, "you're playing with fire. I thought you had stopped, but I can now see that you just can't stop digging."

Nick's grip tightened on the phone, knuckles turning white. This person had the audacity to call him directly, clearly unafraid of being caught. The anger in him wanted to reach through the phone and strangle the person, but he stayed calm, fearing for what the killer might do next.

"Listen, whoever you are," Nick said, his voice barely above a whisper but steady as steel. "I'm not going to stop until I find out who you are and bring you to justice. So, go ahead – taunt me, threaten me, call me a 'little buddy.' But know this, I won't back down."

"Brave words," the killer sneered. "But bravery alone won't save you from what's coming."

"Then I guess we'll see who has the last laugh," Nick replied, defiance ringing in his tone.

"Stop investigating the case," the killer warned, their voice cold and chilling. "You don't want to mess with me, jackass. You have no idea what I'm capable of."

"Please," Nick replied, trying to keep the tremor out of his voice. "Leave me alone. What are you doing?"

For a moment, there was nothing but silence on the other end, the empty void of sound echoing in Nick's ears. Then, the killer spoke again. "You'll find out soon enough, little buddy. And when you do, it'll be too late."

With those final words, the line went dead, leaving Nick in a state of panic and frustration. His hands shook as he placed the phone back on the table, cursing under his breath. He couldn't let this person continue terrorizing Sweet Sea, but every lead seemed to hit a dead end.

He couldn't shake the image of the killer's words winding around him, binding him tighter and tighter with each twisted syllable. It was as if the threat had taken on a life of its own, wrapping itself around his throat and threatening to choke out the last of his resolve.

"Playing with fire," Nick whispered, his voice shaking with anger and terror. He could feel it, a seething heat that coiled beneath his skin, the potential for destruction simmering just below the surface. "What kind of sick game is this?"

His mind raced, thoughts skittering like pebbles across the surface of a stormy sea. Images of Lucy, her smile as warm as sunlight, flickered through his mind – a beacon amidst the darkness that threatened to consume him. He would never forgive himself if anything were to happen to someone else because of his investigation.

"Think, Nick, think," he urged himself, pacing the length of the room, each step a sharp reminder of the weight that bore down upon him. "You've faced worse before. You can do this."

A memory surfaced then, dark and treacherous - his past addiction. The relentless grip it had held on to him, tightening like a vise. But he'd fought back, clawed his way out of that abyss. Wasn't this just another battle to be won?

As if on cue, a flurry of thoughts and images flooded his consciousness—every clue, every lead, every sleepless night spent pouring over case files until his vision blurred and his head ached. In those moments, it seemed as though the answer was just beyond his reach, taunting him from the shadows like a malevolent specter.

As he contemplated his next move in the investigation, Nick couldn't shake the feeling that he was dealing with a ruthless killer who wouldn't stop until he was caught. But Nick knew he couldn't give up either.

"Damn it," Nick muttered to himself, his eyes narrowing in determination. He would do whatever it took to unmask the killer. And no matter how many obstacles reminded him of his own past addiction, he wouldn't back down. "I'm tired of this intimidation."

He didn't want to leave his daughters without a father, but he couldn't just stand knowing there was a killer in their community. Everyone had secrets, but whoever this was, they could not be allowed to walk among others and smile like nothing happened. He knew what he needed to do. He had to confront this killer and soon. Justice had to be served.

Nick picked up the phone and called the library. Susan answered on the third ring.

"Hey, Susan. It's Nick again."

"Hey. Did you get the file?"

"I did. Thank you. I have a favor to ask. I am looking for a meeting spot for a few friends. Like the book club, I mentioned earlier. Any chance I can rent out the library tonight?"

"Hold on." The sound of flipping pages filled the receiver. After a few moments, Susan came back on. "It looks like there are no reservations tonight, so it's all yours."

"That's great. Thank you. Anything I should know?"

"I will leave the key under the orange rock by the door, and just clean up after yourselves. That's it."

"Wonderful. Thank you." Nick hung up.

Nick had the beginnings of a plan. He was going to lure the killer to the library and capture them. He had evidence, but it was all circumstantial at best and hard to prove. He would also have to get the killer to admit it on a recording. A smile spread across his face. He knew what to do and had a lot of work to prepare.

The first thing he did was print out a hundred flyers with a simple sentence. It read, "I know who killed Lucy." He didn't put his name on it or any other details. He figured if the killer saw it, he would get another phone call. He spent an hour going through town and hanging them up. Paying special attention to his suspects, he made sure he slipped one under the door to the doctor's office, Michaels House, the church, and hung two on a lamp post outside Eunice's Antique shop. He then went back to his shop, gathered the electronics and tools he would need, and put them in a bag for tonight.

With all that done, he sat behind his shop counter and waited. If he guessed correctly, he would get another call on Lucy's phone soon. He didn't have to wait long.

Lucy's cell phone buzzed on the table, the screen lighting up with an unknown number. He glanced around the room, his heart skipping a beat as he hesitated for just a moment before reaching out to answer the call.

"Hello?" he said cautiously, his voice betraying a hint of anxiety that he tried unsuccessfully to suppress.

"Little Buddy..." The voice on the other end was deep and menacing. It was a voice that seemed to ooze darkness, seeping into every corner of the room, and casting a shadow over his very soul. "I thought I made it clear for you to back off. Is killing you the only way to get you to stop?"

"Who is this?" Nick demanded, his grip tightening on the phone as he fought against the fear and anger coursing through him.

"Ah, now that would be tellin', wouldn't it?" the voice replied, its tone dripping with malice. "But I figure with you keeping this up, you'll find out soon enough."

"Is this some kind of sick joke to you?" Nick shot back, unable to quell the mixture of frustration and dread bubbling within him. "You took a life."

"Joke? Oh no, little buddy," the voice sneered. "This is far from a joke."

Nick's mind raced as he searched for any sign of weakness or vulnerability in the killer's words, anything that could give him a clue to their identity. But all he found was a void, bottomless and impenetrable. He had to play the long game here to suck in the killer.

"You are going down," he whispered, anger lacing his voice. "Turn yourself in, or I will tell the sheriff tonight who you are."

"Scary. How do you know that I'm not the sheriff?" The voice laughed, a chilling sound that echoed through the room like a cold wind. "You think you are so smart? You got it all figured out. For your sake, I hope not. You have no idea what I'm capable of."

"Then show me!" Nick shouted into the phone, his patience wearing thin. "Come and get me."

"Patience, Little Buddy," the voice replied, its tone icy and remote. "I'm enjoying this. You'll find out soon enough. And when you do, it'll be too late."

"You are working on my schedule now. I know who you

are, and if you don't want me to turn you in, meet me in the library at eight tonight. If not, I will go directly to the sheriff. I have all the evidence I need."

"How stupid do you think I am? If you had everything, you would have already told them. There is nothing in it for you to wait."

"Is that all you've got?" Nick retorted, though he could feel a cold sweat beading on his forehead. "Taunts and threats?"

"I think you saw in the woods the other night that there are no threats."

"I do think you are pretty stupid," Nick said with a smile. "But that has nothing to do with it. While doing this investigation, I have had to close my store a lot, and the damage you did is expensive. I just want some money, and I will keep it quiet."

The killer seemed to contemplate the ask. It was evident to Nick that the killer was getting desperate and instinctively knew that if someone else died, then the murder of Lucy would get a lot more eyes.

"How much?" the killer asked. The voice modulator they used hid the voice, but not the emotion in it.

"I'll tell you tonight. Eight at the library, or I spill it. Bye."

"Wait!" the killer yelled, but it was no use. The line went

dead, leaving only silence in its wake.

"Awesome!" Nick said, his heart pounding in his chest as he put the phone back in the drawer. The anger and fear that had been simmering earlier was now excitement and nervousness. He was in control now. Forcing himself to take a deep breath, he steadied his nerves.

He looked around the room, taking in the familiar surroundings that now seemed somehow tainted by the presence of this unknown menace. His thoughts swirled with questions, doubts, and fears, forming a vortex that threatened to consume him entirely. This had to work perfectly, or he could end up dead too. He would face the darkness head-on, unmask the killer, and bring justice to those who needed it most.

"Game on," he whispered, steeling himself for the battle ahead. And with that, he began to prepare. In the background, he could hear Lucy's phone ringing again. He didn't answer.

CHAPTER

TWENTY-NINE

The library was an architectural marvel, its mahogany shelves towering like ancient redwoods with a labyrinthine network of aisles stretching out in all directions on two floors. Rays of sunlight filtered through the stained-glass windows, casting colorful hues on the worn wooden floorboards. In the center of the second floor, stood an imposing mahogany desk - Lucy's old command post - now eerily vacant.

Nick paced restlessly around the central desk, his fingers drumming against the polished surface as he mentally reviewed the intricacies of his plan. He knew that the killer would come to this place, drawn by the same insatiable thirst for knowledge that had brought him and Lucy together in the first place. But Nick needed more than just intuition; he needed solid evidence - something he could use to finally put an end to this nightmare.

"All right, time to set the trap," he muttered under his breath.

In the back corner of the library, there was a small alcove lined with shelves of dusty old memoirs and biographies. It was here that Nick began building his snare. He carefully rigged a motion-activated camera to one of the shelves, positioning it so that it would capture the face of anyone approaching the alcove.

"Gotcha," Nick whispered as he tested the device, feeling a surge of satisfaction when the camera snapped a photo of his own grinning face.

One by one, Nick went through the library's second floor, placing high-definition video cameras at different angles. Lastly, he had set up the final camera concealed behind a decorative vent on a first floor wall, and it was pointed at the front door. With the camera linked to his laptop, he could monitor the killer's movements in real time, ensuring that he wouldn't lose sight of them for even a moment.

Nick's trap was simple yet effective, utilizing the

murderer's fear of being caught, they would come here, and the video and audio of the cameras would seal their fate. If something happened to him, when the hidden devices were ultimately found, the killer would be caught anyway. In addition, he had affixed a tiny pressure-sensitive pad beneath the carpet at the door leading to the basement, which would send an alert to his smartphone whenever someone touched it, just in case Harold came up.

Not wanting to be surprised again, he also took a non-technical approach. To ensure that he would be alerted when the trap was sprung, Nick had rigged a series of fishing lines, their ends tied to several small bells. These were strategically positioned around the library, hidden from view but designed to chime as soon as someone moved down a path without a camera.

He took one last look around the library before retreating to into his hiding place – a narrow alcove between two tall bookshelves. Crouching there, peering through a tiny slit, his heart began to race with anticipation.

As he waited in the shadows, the weight of his decision bearing down upon him, Nick couldn't help but think about how far he'd come from the man he used to be - a broken, desperate addict lost in the stormy seas of despair. But now, with the trap set and his heart pounding in anticipation, he felt a renewed sense of purpose surging through his veins.

He continued to wait, his body cramped and uncomfortable, but his mind alive with determination. He glanced at his phone every few moments, willing it to vibrate with the notification he longed for. As the minutes crawled by, Nick's senses sharpened. The library's musty scent clung to his nostrils; the ticking of a distant clock echoed in his ears like a heartbeat. Shadows stretched and shifted across the floor as clouds drifted outside the windows, casting an eerie pallor over the room. His eyes began to drift closed.

The library door creaked open, and a shadowed figure stepped inside, their eyes scanning the dimly lit room. Beneath a black trench coat, their hands were clad in tight gloves; a peaked cap obscured their face from the security cameras. Nick's eyes shot open ad hid heart pounded as he watched the figure move stealthily, seeming to float across the floor, their measured steps almost inaudible. They glanced around nervously, their gaze falling upon the small display set up near the entrance. With a satisfied nod, they moved up the stairs to the second floor.

Nick knew his plan would work, but he was still surprised it did. He could cut the anticipation with a knife. This was it.

The figure reached the top of the stairs, their fingers

brushed against the delicately rigged wires hidden at the top. Their right ankle triggered another wire and wrapped around their ankle. A soft click and two ringing bells echoed through the library, sending a shiver down Nick's spine. The figure froze, their eyes widening as they noticed their mistake. Panic seized them as they realized they were standing in the lion's den, the predator now the prey. Their breathing grew more frantic as they struggled to escape, desperation etched into every movement.

They glanced around the library, looking for any sign of their hunter, but Nick remained hidden. The figure's eyes darted from shelf to shelf, seeking a way out – but instead, they only found more shadows, more potential hiding places for the man they knew was watching.

"Smile, you're on camera," Nick called out from his hiding spot, unable to contain himself any longer. "You're caught! It's over!"

The figure's head snapped toward the sound of his voice, their eyes narrowing with determination. With one last desperate attempt, they yanked at the wires, hoping to break free. The figure contorted with frustration, veins bulging at their temples as they strained against the trap. The wires bit into their flesh, drawing droplets of blood that stained the polished library floor. Sweat trickled down their brows, stinging their eyes and blurring their vision. After a few tugs, the fishing line broke, and they walked toward Lucy's desk.

Nick continued to watch from the shadows, knowing he would need to act soon, but something held him back – a strange mix of fear and satisfaction. It had been a long time since he'd felt this alive, fueled by adrenaline.

"What the hell?"

Nick recognized the voice. He stepped out from behind the row of books, and his hands braced for action. His hair was plastered to his forehead with sweat, his blue eyes ablaze with determination. "You wanted to see me? Here I am."

Lifting his hat up, Michael stared back at him. Nick had hoped he wasn't the killer. Their similar paths of addiction had him rooting for the young man. But, unfortunately, here he was.

"What's with all the fishing wire?" Michael asked, clearing the last of the obstacle. "I came here like you asked."

"Why did you do it?" Nick asked.

"I needed the fix. I figured it wasn't a big deal. It wasn't like she ever went without any. I was weak."

Nick became instantly enraged. "Not a big deal. What the hell is wrong with you? That woman took you in and helped you through your addiction. Luckily, I had my daughters, but most people have no one."

"I figured no one would notice."

Nick dragged his hand down his face. "There's something really wrong with you."

Michael sat down in the chair by the table. He was wringing his hands and shifting in the chair.

"Are you high now?" Nick asked.

"No. I swear. I haven't had a fix since Aunt Lucy died. It just didn't seem right."

"At least you have moral's somewhere in there."

"Did you bring me here to berate me? What's done is done. If I could take it back, I would. Everything's done, so can't we move on?" Michael said.

"No." Nick grabbed a bookend from the table. It only now occurred to him that he should have brought a weapon. As it was, he was exposed. "I want you to turn around, put your hands behind your back, and let me zip tie you."

"Is that really necessary? I figured that as a fellow recovering addict, you would know what it was like and help me. Not turn me in."

"You have lost all sense of reality. Either you turn around voluntarily, or I will hit you until I can do it. Call it payback for that scar faced man you had attack me."

"Hold up. What scar faced man?"

"Don't play stupid with me. The guy told me to stop

investigating. Not to mention the vandals that tore up my shop. Was that you or him?"

"Your store was vandalized? That's horrible." Michael seemed genuinely shocked.

"Nice try. You can deny those things, but I know the crime you did do, and that will get you life."

"I don't think so. Maybe a few months and a program. I figured you wanted me here to help with the program."

Nick was confused. "Wait. What did you think I meant when I told you on the phone to be here? A party?"

"On the phone? Maybe you are high. It was in the note you sent me." Michael reached into his pocket and produced a piece of paper. "I'll read it to you. I know what you did, and I want to help you. Come to the library at eight tonight, or I will have to turn you in."

"Let me see that." Nick crossed the room, the book end at the ready in case Michael tried to attack him. He snatched the note from Michael's hand and read it. "I didn't send this."

"Are you playing games with me? Who else would have sent it? And you were here."

The two men stood in tense silence, their senses heightened as they strained to detect the slightest hint of movement or sound. A draft of cold air brushed against Nick's face, carrying with it the unmistakable scent of flowers.

"Michael, do you smell that?" Nick asked, his heart hammering in his chest as the cloying odor intensified.

"Yeah," Michael replied, his voice barely a whisper. "It's like something sweet."

"Something's not right," Nick said. "What did you think the note meant by, 'I know what you did'?"

"Thought you found out I was taking a pill or two here and there from Aunt Lucy's medication. She thought it was the doctor, but it was me."

"So, you didn't murder her?"

"No!" Michael yelled. "Is that why you wanted me here? You think I killed her? How many times do I have to say it?"

"I didn't want you here," Nick explained the conversation with the killer and the flyers. "The killer must have sent that to you to fake me out. But why?"

"That's a good question," a female voice said from the top of the stairs. "Maybe you need to stop playing games and come clean yourself."

Both men looked up. Rose stood at the top of the stairs, a look of disgust and guilt on her face. In her right hand was a small pink handgun. She slowly walked towards them. The gun was steady in her hand.

"Rose?" Nick asked.

She waved him towards the desk with the end of the

barrel. "Sit down. We need to talk."

CHAPTER THIRTY

"**P**ut the gun down, Rose," Nick spoke softly and in a calm tone. "We can work this out."

"Really?"

"Sure," Michael added. "There's no reason for anyone else to get hurt."

Rose paced back and forth, her eyes darting between the two. After a few moments, she stopped and made eye contact with Nick. The whites of her eyes were red, and mascara streaked down her face. "I really cared about you, Nick. I really thought that after such a short time, we had a bond that could last a lifetime. But I can't ignore this."

"I care about you, too," Nick responded. It wasn't a lie. Until she drugged him, he had really thought they could have something. "Just put the gun down and we can talk this out."

She lowered the weapon slightly, a compromise of sorts. She swallowed hard and said, "Just tell me, why?"

"Why what?"

"Why did you do it, Nick?"

"Do what?" Nick asked.

Rose looked at Michael, the confused look on his face unable to be hidden. "Did you help him, Michael?"

Michael's eyes narrowed. "With what?"

"Don't play stupid with me," Rose yelled, visibly crying now. "I can't believe this is happening. My heart is breaking, but I can't let you get away with this."

Nick put up his hands. "Hold on. Why are you here?"

"I got your note." She sighed. "But I just can't run away with you. It's not right. You know, 'Thou shalt not kill' and all."

Nick smiled. "What did the note say?"

"Is this where you pretend you have amnesia or something?"

"Seriously, Rose. What did the note say?"

"Fine. I'll play your game. It said that you killed Lucy, but it was an accident. You tried to cover it up with this investigation, but couldn't take it anymore and was going to run away. You asked me to meet you here tonight and go with you."

Michael stepped away from Nick.

"Does that sound like me?" Nick asked. "Whoever sent that note didn't know we weren't talking because you drugged me."

"You drugged him?" Michael asked.

"Not now." Nick said, turning to Rose. "I ask you again. Does that sound like me?"

"Not now," Rose admitted. "But here you are. Exactly where you said you would be."

"I didn't send it. It's obvious that whoever sent it didn't know I wasn't talking with you. That we had a falling out over the drugs."

"She drugged you?" Michael perked up. "Are you using again, Nick?"

"Yes, to the first one, and no to the second," he said, his tone dismissive. "Why would I distance myself from you and then ask you to run away with me? Does that make any sense?"

Michael stepped further away from Nick. Nick noticed and shook his head. Idiot, he thought.

"I mean, I guess. That does seem weird. Who would send it then?" Rose asked.

"The same person that sent me mine, I guess," Michael said.

"You got a letter, too?"

"I did. It was different. It claimed that Nick had proof that I was err... guilty... err... of a crime. I came to defend myself."

Rose lowered the gun. "Why would someone do this?"

"That's a good question. Someone wanted us all here." Nick looked around, wondering if this was all a distraction to keep him from noticing someone else coming into the library.

"What is going on?" Rose asked.

"Perhaps, I can answer that," Doctor Victors said, stepping up behind Rose. He grabbed her hand and took the gun before she could respond. "And thank you for bringing a weapon. It will be much easier to use yours than the one I brought."

"Did you get a letter, too?" Michael asked.

The doctor looked at Nick and smiled.

"He sent the letters," Nick responded. "He used you two as a distraction."

"Sort of. You three have been nosing around, and unfortunately, I am not going to get any peace until the three of you are gone." The killer's eyes widened in surprise as if they hadn't expected Nick to be so confident. Doctor Victors swallowed hard, his throat bobbing with fear. "How did you know?"

"Call it intuition," Nick said, his voice steely. He moved

closer to the nervous figure, sizing them up with a calculating gaze. The gun in the doctor's hand was shaking. "Or maybe it's because I've been watching you."

"Watching me?" the doctor repeated, alarm seeping into their tone. "For how long?"

"Long enough," Nick answered cryptically. Images of late nights spent poring over clues swam through his mind. All those sleepless hours spent obsessing over the case, searching for answers that would bring him closer to the truth and to get justice for Lucy. "I knew you'd slip up eventually. And I was ready for you."

"Clearly," the doctor muttered, their voice laced with bitterness. "But if you had proof, then the police would be here. So, it looks like you are caught in your own trap."

"I wouldn't exactly say that."

"Any last words?" the doctor asked, his gaze cold and unyielding.

Nick smiled. "Just tell me why you did it."

"You expect me to monolog and give you time to figure out how to escape. This isn't a book or a movie. You can't get away from a gun pointed at you."

"Humor me, please."

"Fine. She accused me of stealing her medicine. But it was that little shit over there." The doctor waved the gun toward Michael. "Lucy didn't believe me. She said she was going to change her will again and take all her money from the Historical Society. We would get nothing."

"So, you killed her over money?" Rose gently asked, held motionless by his grip on her neck. The gun alternated between her head and the others.

"Not just money, but yeah. The Historical Society was going to go broke, and it was all my fault. I made some bad decisions, and well, I didn't want it to crash on my watch. Especially since it's my legacy. I don't expect you to understand. It was the only option. My father and grandfather built that society."

"Or you could have just failed," Nick said. "People make mistakes and fail every day. It is part of life."

"Not for me," the doctor yelled. He was visibly shaking and seemed to become a little unhinged. "Enough, turn around."

Michael turned a hundred and eighty degrees immediately. Nick didn't move.

"Do it now," the doctor said.

"I don't think so," Nick said.

The doctor shook his head, a mixture of defiance and resignation playing across their features. "Your fate. I'll just get it over with."

"Fine by me," Nick replied, reaching out to point at the bookcase behind him. He felt a grim satisfaction as the killer flinched in recognition. "I have filled this library with cameras and audio devices. They have been recording the whole time."

"I'll just grab them after you're dead."

"That would be a good plan, except I am streaming it offsite. For the non-tech in you, Doctor, that means you can't get to the footage."

"You're bluffing," the doctor said.

"Nope. But hey, take a chance if you want."

For the first time, Nick could see the confidence drain from the doctor's fate. It seemed he was beginning to understand he had no way out.

"Wait!" the doctor cried out suddenly, their eyes pleading for mercy. "Can we make a deal? You wanted money, right?"

But it was too late for that. Rose took advantage of the doctor's confusion. She stomped on his right foot, causing the gun to go up. An elbow to the rib cage bent the doctor over, the gun randomly firing before dropping from his hand. She turned towards him and let out with a kick square between his legs. With a cry of pain, all the air in the doctor's lungs was expelled, and he dropped to the floor. Rose picked up the gun and stepped back. Nick didn't wait. He rushed towards the doctor and grabbed the fishing wire that had caught up

Michael earlier, and quickly bound the doctor's hands. He put up no resistance at all.

"Was it worth it?" Nick asked, his voice calm but firm, as he studied the killer's desperate face. The dim light from a single overhead lamp in the library cast eerie shadows on the tall bookshelves that surrounded them. The smell of aged leather and paper filled the air, a stark contrast to the fear and tension that permeated the room just a few minutes earlier.

"Is what worth it?" the doctor spat out, his breaths coming in shallow gasps as they struggled against the wires that held them captive.

"Taking innocent lives," Nick replied, his eyes never leaving the killers. "Causing so much pain and suffering. You took an oath."

"Like you care!" the doctor scoffed, bitterness dripping from every word. "You couldn't save Lucy, could you?"

Nick's jaw tightened at the mention of his late friend. He had to remind himself not to let the killer's taunts get under his skin. "I may not have been able to save her, but I will make sure no one else suffers because of you."

"Your self-righteousness is nauseating. I should have had that hired thug kill you. It would have saved me much trouble," the doctor sneered. "But it won't change anything. You think you've won, but you're just as trapped as I am. We all have our demons, don't we, Mr. Cern?"

"Maybe so," Nick conceded, his thoughts drifting to his past addiction that still haunted him. "But my demons don't lead me to murder."

"Enough!" the killer yelled; their face contorted with rage. "You think you're better than me? That you're some kind of hero?"

"Hardly," Nick said with a humorless smile. "But at least I'm trying to make things right."

"Good luck with that," the doctor snarled, making one last futile attempt to break free. "You better hope you got it all on camera. You're a druggy. No one will believe you over me."

With a sigh, Nick reached into his pocket and pulled out a cell phone. The glass screen glinted in the dim light as he moved towards the doctor with a determined stride. "The police can take it from here."

"Wait," the doctor said, their voice suddenly softer, almost pleading. "Please, just tell me one thing. Why... why did you do it? Set this trap for me? Why couldn't you just let it go?"

"Because Lucy deserved better," Nick replied without hesitation. "And because I couldn't let you destroy any more lives."

The doctor's eyes narrowed, but they said nothing more. As Nick called the sheriff and explained all the details and video proof, the room was filled with an eerie silence, broken only by the faint rustling of pages from the books that bore witness to the end of a deadly game.

"Hey, Nick," Michael said. "I think I might need some help."

Nick turned to see Michael on the floor, blood oozing from a bullet wound in his chest. Nick and Rose rushed to his side. The wound was bleeding slowly. Nick removed his jacket and pushed it against the wound. "Keep pressure here," he told Rose.

"I can help," the doctor said.

"I wouldn't trust you to handle a hang nail," Nick said, heading to the first aid station. He grabbed bandages and an assortment of antiseptic and went back to Michael.

"Does he have a fever?" the doctor asked.

"Would you shut up," Rose responded. "We don't need your help."

As Nick cleaned the wound, he noticed the bullet had exited out his back. He wrapped both sides and continued to put pressure on the wound until help arrived.

The subdued doctor sat on the floor, his hands bound behind them with the cold fishing wire. Nick stepped back to survey the scene, his heart still pounding in his chest from the adrenaline and triumph of having caught Lucy's murderer. He looked around the dimly lit library, the dark wooden shelves looming like ancient guardians as if they had silently watched over the deadly game that played out in their midst.

"Nick," the doctor whispered, his voice laden with defeat and regret. "I never meant for things to go this far."

"Neither did I," Nick replied quietly, feeling the weight of his own past mistakes bear down on him. He leaned heavily against a nearby bookshelf, the worn spines of countless novels pressing into his back as he tried to regain his composure.

"Lucy was... special." The doctor's voice cracked with regret and Nick could see the tears begin to pool in the corners of their eyes. "She didn't deserve any of this."

"No, she didn't," Nick agreed, his voice thick with emotion. His mind raced through memories of Lucy—her warm smile, her passion for literature, the friendship they'd forged in the short time they'd known each other.

The sound of sirens pierced the still night air, growing louder as the police vehicles approached the library. Nick stood tall, his gaze fixed firmly on the defeated killer before him, as the red and blue lights flickered through the windows, casting shadows that danced across the walls like ghosts.

"Your time is up," Nick told the doctor, his voice steady and resolute. "Your ride is here."

The sheriff and her deputies stormed into the building, their authoritative presence filling the room with a sense of finality. Nick couldn't help but feel a small measure of relief. He had done what he'd set out to do—he had caught Lucy's killer and, in doing so, had found some semblance of closure for her death and a chance at redemption for himself.

The two deputies first on the scene exchanged quick glances before approaching, their faces somber. They seemed to hesitate for a moment, but ultimately trusted Nick's instincts. They cuffed Doctor Victors with swift precision, who winced as the cold metal bit into his wrists.

"Doctor Victors, you're under arrest for suspicion of involvement in the murder of Lucy Brooks," one deputy recited, his voice firm yet tinged with disbelief. "You have the right to remain silent. Anything you say can and will be used against you in a court of law. You have the right to an attorney..."

As the officer continued reading the Miranda rights, Nick couldn't help but feel a grim satisfaction. Despite the years spent behind a desk in corporate America, his instincts hadn't dulled – at least not when it came to protecting the people he cared about. Grief still weighed heavily on him, but he had found a new purpose in Sweet Sea.

"Thank you," Nick said quietly to the officers as they led

the doctor toward the car. He knew this arrest was just the beginning of a long road for justice, but at least it was a step in the right direction.

The officers nodded solemnly, and the sounds of the seagulls overhead blended with the murmurs of the gathering crowd outside. As Doctor Victors was placed into the back of the police car, his once-confident demeanor now replaced by silence, Nick's thoughts turned to Lucy. She may not have been family, but she was a friend – and he would ensure that her memory lived on in the small coastal town that they both loved.

Nick had a lot of evidence and confessions to give the sheriff. It could wait. Paramedics came in and at once went to Michael's side. He stepped back and watched them work, hoping that in the end, the police would not find fault in his proof. With one last look at the rows of books that surrounded him, Nick allowed himself a small, sad smile. The mystery was solved, and though the scars of the past would never fully heal, perhaps now, there could be peace—for both the living and the dead.

The wind whispered through the branches of the ancient oak tree as if carrying away the town's sordid secrets with it. Doctor Victors stood motionless among the throng of townspeople; his once confident demeanor now crumbled to dust. His eyes, like two hollow pits, stared into the void, unable to meet the gazes of those who had trusted him for so long.

As the police officers prepared to leave the scene, Nick approached them and extended a hand. "Officers, I just wanted to thank you for your help today. It's been a harrowing experience, but I know we've all done our best to see justice served."

"Of course, Mr. Cern," the deputy replied, shaking Nick's hand firmly. "You've been instrumental in solving this case, and we're grateful for your assistance."

"Please let me know if there's anything I can do to help Michael," Nick added earnestly, concern for the young man's wellbeing etched across his face.

"We'll keep you informed, Mr. Cern," the deputy reassured him. "And we appreciate your commitment to the community."

The doctor remained silent. His posture stooped and defeated as the police drove him away. No words could account for the betrayal he had inflicted upon the community, nor could they absolve the life taken by his hands. The weight of his actions bore down upon him like an iron vise, crushing whatever hope he may have held onto.

As Nick watched the scene unfold, a curious mixture of emotions swirled within him. There was satisfaction, certainly, as the man responsible for Lucy's death would face the consequences of his deeds. Yet there was also a profound sadness, the realization that Sweet Sea, a place he had come to cherish, had been betrayed by someone so deeply ingrained in its fabric.

As the remaining police cars pulled away from the scene, their sirens silent now, Nick glanced back at the gathering of townspeople. They stood together in the fading light, their shared purpose and gratitude palpable in the air.

CHAPTER

THIRTY-ONE

Nick Cern stood by the window of his store, gazing out at the rain-slicked streets of Sweet Sea. His fingers tapped rhythmically on the windowsill, restless energy coursing through him as he mulled over the speech he was to make at the funeral.

The bell over the door rang, jolting him from his thoughts. Frowning, Nick glanced at the clock, it was time for them to go. He hesitated for a moment, then strode towards the front door, his nerves piqued.

"Michael," Nick said, surprise etching across his features as he took in the figure before him. Lucy's nephew stood on the doorstep, drenched from head to toe, clutching a manila envelope tightly against his chest. His eyes darted around nervously, and his shoulders were hunched as if under a great weight. "I thought Susan was picking me up.

"She went to the church early to help set up. I told her I would swing by and get you."

"I could've drove."

"I don't mind."

"How's the shoulder?"

"It's healing," Michael said. "Just can't lift anything. It's been a while since I felt this helpless. The pain is a little more bearable though."

"I hear you. I wouldn't take pain meds, either. Not worth the risk of relapsing."

"For sure, that part really sucks. But you got this. Remember, you are stronger than you know. You ready?"

The coastal rain long ceased to be a drizzle and had turned into a torrent, soaking both men as they rushed to the car. After ducking into the car, Nick stared at the darkened streets outside. The dreary weather mirrored his thoughts. As the moisture trickled down the glass panes, Nick's eyes caught sight of a figure standing in the shadows across the street. It was Eunice watching him intently. With a sudden jolt, the woman stepped out from her hiding spot and made her way toward the antique shop. There was something off about her, but that was a mystery for another day.

The news of Lucy Brooks' memorial swept through the small town like a storm, leaving shock and disbelief in its wake. Friends and family gathered in hushed clusters on the streets, voices trembling as they exchanged whispered condolences.

After the word spread of Doctor Victor's arrest and the allegations against him, the atmosphere in the town shifted from grief to outrage. The once-respected figure now faced the scrutiny of those who had trusted him implicitly.

The authorities delved deeper into the tangled web of Doctor Victor's actions and the people of Sweet Sea mourned the loss of their beloved librarian. No longer united by trust, but by a desire for truth and justice, they vowed to see Lucy's final wish fulfilled: to unmask the darkness that had stolen her away from them. And though the shadows of suspicion loomed heavy over the small town, one thing remained clear, no matter the outcome, the memory of Lucy Brooks would forever live on in the hearts of those who loved her.

As the car pulled away from the curb, the coastal breeze carrying the scent of salt and seaweed allowed him a moment of reflection. He thought of his late wife, her love of books, and their shared dreams of a peaceful life by the ocean. And he thought of the promises he had made to Lucy, to her nephew, and to himself.

"Justice will prevail," he whispered, the words lost on the wind as they drove towards the church.

◆ ◆ ◆

The rain had stopped. Nick stood by the police car, watching as a small crowd of townspeople gathered near the church. Their faces were a mix of curiosity and concern, eyes darting beneath their umbrellas between the sheriff, the approaching people, and Nick himself. He could hear their hushed whispers, questions hanging in the air like fog over the ocean.

"Can't believe it," murmured an elderly woman with a shock of white hair framing her face. She was walking by Nick with a younger man. "Doctor Victors, involved in the murder?"

"Lucy was such a sweet girl," a middle-aged man added, shaking his head slowly. "She didn't deserve this."

"Who's that fella?" a younger woman asked, her gaze fixed on Nick. "He looks familiar."

Nick felt the weight of their stares, but he knew he couldn't walk away now. He'd come too far and fought too hard to see justice done. He squared his shoulders, determined to face the scrutiny of the community he now called home. His eulogy reading would go fine.

"Excuse me!" a voice called out, silencing the murmurs. Nick looked to find a bespectacled man making his way through the crowd with a warm smile. "You're Nick Cern, right? You've been helping Lucy's nephew?"

"That's correct," Nick replied, returning the smile cautiously. "I couldn't just stand by and do nothing."

"Good for you," the man said, extending a hand. "I'm Tom. I own the local diner down the street. Lucy was a regular customer, always brightening up the place with her presence. What happened to her is a tragedy, but I wanted to thank you for stepping up when others might have looked the other way."

"Thank you, Tom," Nick said, shaking his hand firmly. "I only did what I thought was right."

"Still," Tom insisted, "it takes bravery to confront something so sinister in our small town. It's reassuring to know we have people like you among us. Stop by for a free meal anytime you want."

"I agree," chimed in the elderly woman who had spoken earlier, her expression softening. "Thank you, Mr. Cern, for helping Lucy and seeking justice for her."

"Much obliged," added the middle-aged man, nodding approvingly.

"Please," Nick said, touched by their words, "call me Nick. I'm just glad I could help in any way I can."

As more townspeople stepped forward to express their gratitude, Nick couldn't help but feel a glimmer of hope amid the chaos. He'd lost so much in his life, but perhaps Sweet Sea could be the place where he'd finally find meaning, solace, and – most importantly – a true sense of belonging.

"I guess that makes you one of us now," the sheriff said, coming up with the row of people. "And stop leaning on my car."

Nick stood up and turned. "Sorry, sheriff."

"I'm just busting your chops. How do you feel?"

"Honestly? Not really sure. I'm sad, happy, and satisfied all at the same time. I feel kind of guilty about those last two."

"I get it. The sense of accomplishment is overshadowed by the reality of the loss. It will get better."

"I hope so."

"I'm heading in. You coming?"

"Yeah, sure. Right behind you."

The warm glow of camaraderie washed over Nick like a sea breeze as he stood amidst the gathering crowd at the church entrance. The sun dipped below the horizon, casting long shadows across the pavement. He could hear the rhythmic crashing of the waves against the shore, punctuated by the murmurings of the townspeople around him.

"Nick," said a woman with a kind smile. He recognized her from his shop. "You've shown us all what it means to be a part of this community."

"Thank you so much, Mrs. Whitaker," Nick replied, his voice tinged with the relief and gratitude that swelled within him. "Your words mean more to me than I can express."

"Ahoy there, Nick!" called out a jolly, rotund man wearing a captain's hat. "I'm Captain Bill. I just wanted to say that you've done us all proud. This town could use more folks like you."

"Thank you, Captain Bill," Nick responded, feeling a surge of warmth towards these people who'd been strangers not so long ago. He kept questioning himself. Who were all these people? "I guess it is easier to hide in Sweet Sea than I thought."

"Nick," a gentle voice called, rousing him from his contemplation. It was Mrs. Thompson, the elderly woman who lived next door to Rose. Her eyes shone with unshed tears as she reached out to touch his arm. "You did right by Lucy, dear. She would be so proud of you."

"Thank you, Mrs. Westerby," Nick replied softly. "I just wish I could have done more."

"Sometimes, all we can do is shine a light on the

truth," she said wisely, her wrinkled hand squeezing his arm reassuringly.

Nick nodded, swallowing the lump that had formed in his throat. As he turned towards the church, the last rays of sunlight cast long shadows across the cobblestone streets as if bidding farewell to the darkness that had plagued Sweet Sea.

"Lucy," he whispered beneath his breath, a silent promise to honor her memory and continue the fight for justice. "Rest now."

As Nick looked around at the faces of the townspeople, he realized that they were no longer simply faces in a crowd. They were becoming friends, neighbors, and allies – the very foundation of the life he was building here in Sweet Sea.

In the midst of sorrow and chaos, Nick found solace in the knowledge that he was now part of something greater than himself – a community united by a common desire for justice, healing, and love.

With each step he took, Nick felt the weight of the past lifting from his shoulders. The road ahead was uncertain, but one thing was clear – no matter what challenges lay in wait, Nick Cern would face them head-on, armed with the knowledge that he had found a place to call home and a community that stood beside him.

"Sweet Sea," Nick thought with a sigh of contentment,

"I'm home."

He followed the line of visitors into the church. Patting his pants pocket, he verified he had enough tissues.

CHAPTER THIRTY-TWO

Nick stood at the entrance of the Sweet Sea Historical Society, inhaling the musty scent of old building materials and well-worn furniture. The heavy oak door creaked as he pushed it open, revealing a receptionist desk and shelves filled with historical artifacts and memorabilia. Sunlight filtered through the tall windows, casting eerie shadows on the worn floor.

"Ah, Mr. Cern," a voice called out from behind an imposing wooden desk. "You've arrived just in time for the meeting."

Nick offered a polite smile to Martha, the society's

administrator, as she led him through a set of double doors. He took a seat among the gathered members. He glanced around the room, taking note of the familiar faces and one that was noticeably absent.

"Where's Michael?" Nick asked, folding his arms across his chest.

"We have accepted Michael back as promised. However, he is making a coffee run for the group. He said he would get you something," replied Eunice, the newly voted chairperson with the Doctor's exit. "He has changed his attitude and has promised to behave himself."

"Uncooperative no more?" Nick said, his brows furrowed in concern. "He cares deeply about this town's history, and his aunt believed in second chances. So, thank you."

"Second chances are all well and good, but we will see," Eunice sniffed, adjusting her spectacles. "We cannot afford to be associated with a recovering drug addict who shows little interest in our cause."

"Michael may have made mistakes in the past, but he's trying to change," Nick argued, recalling their conversations about Lucy and her love for Sweet Sea. "I think he deserves the chance to prove himself."

"Mr. Cern. Nick. I understand your sympathy for Michael, which is why he is here. We will only hope for the best. He has been welcomed with open arms. And speaking of welcome, welcome to yourself. We are glad to have another member of our community on the team.," Eunice insisted, her voice firm. "I'm thankful that you joined the society and dedicated significant time and resources to ensure that Lucy's contributions are properly recognized. Welcome to our new treasurer."

The group of people applauded and stopped when Michael entered. They scampered from their chairs to recover their coffee orders. Once everything was distributed, including a hot tea for Nick, they sat down to get down to business. Hesitantly, he sipped the tea, praying he wouldn't fall asleep.

Nick clenched his jaw as the meeting continued, the feeling of being part of something bigger and excitement bubbling beneath the surface. He hoped Lucy could see his stepping up and Michael's involvement to find common ground in their shared love for history.

As the members filed out of the room two hours later, Nick approached Eunice once more, confusion etched on his face. "I want to ask you a question," he declared, locking eyes with the chairperson. "Why were you so helpful when no one else would barely talk to me?"

"Very well, Nick," she replied, her expression softening

ever so slightly. "I knew something was amiss with Lucy's death. The doctor had asked me to check out a book for him at the library. It was the first and only time he did that. When I returned the book, it occurred to me that it was about poison, which is what you were claiming. I knew I had to do something."

"*The Brown Grass*?"

"Yes, that's the one."

"Thank you," Nick nodded, a small smile tugging at the corner of his mouth. As he left the building, the weight of responsibility settled heavily upon his shoulders.

The following morning, Nick stood outside the local coffee shop, the warm scent of fresh pastries and brewing coffee wafting through the air. He had called Michael earlier, suggesting they meet here to discuss the future. Nick's heart ached for the young man, knowing all too well the struggles that come with addiction and the rebuilding of one's life while dealing with a death of a loved one.

"Nick?" a hesitant voice asked, pulling him from his thoughts. He turned to find Michael standing before him, with his hands shoved into the pockets of a worn jacket. The wind tousled his unkempt hair, emphasizing the dark shadows beneath his eyes and the hint of stubble on his chin.

"Hey, Michael," Nick greeted, extending his hand in a friendly gesture. "It's good to see you. Let's grab a table inside, shall we?"

"Sure," he replied, eyeing Nick warily as they entered the bustling coffee shop and found a quiet corner to sit down.

"I wanted to talk to you about the future," Nick began, folding his hands on the table. "I understand that you feel they're not doing enough to preserve your aunt Lucy's legacy."

"Yeah, that's right," Michael muttered, looking down at the table. "I just think I could do more, you know? She meant so much to this town, and I want to make sure I honor her memory."

As he listened, Nick felt a pang of empathy for the younger man. He knew that Michael was grappling with his own demons, and the desire to honor Lucy was likely born from a need to prove himself worthy of her memory.

"I want you to know that I understand where you're coming from," Nick said gently, reaching out to place a hand on Michael's shoulder. I think it's important that we work together to ensure that she is remembered and celebrated in the way she deserves."

"Really?" Michael asked, his eyes meeting Nick's for the

first time. "You'd do that? Help me make sure they don't forget her?"

"Absolutely," Nick assured him, a determined glint in his eyes. "Lucy was an incredible woman, and her contributions to this town should never be overlooked or forgotten. We will work together so that everyone can come together in honoring her memory."

"Thank you," Michael whispered, a hint of hope flickering across his face. "I appreciate your support, it means a lot."

Nick nodded, giving Michael's shoulder a reassuring squeeze. Together, they would find a way to reconcile the past and create a brighter future, all while ensuring that Lucy's memory lived on within the hearts of those who loved her.

"One other thing. I need your help."

"Of course," Michael leaned forward.

"You and I are both recovering addicts. We have both lost a loved one very close to us. We hang on the precipice between relapse and success. I want you to keep me straight, and I will keep you straight. Would that be okay?"

A silence hung in the air as Michael mulled over Nick's words. "That would be awesome."

"One of my daughters gave me the address of a grief counselling group outside of town. I looked them up. They also have a substance abuse from grief meeting. I think both of us could benefit from it. Will you go with me, so I don't feel so awkward."

"I don't do well with talking with strangers." Michael looked down and shifting in his seat.

"You don't have to talk until you want to. I just need a friend."

"I'll go for you." Michael paused and thought for a moment. "Do you think they will have snacks like the groups on tv?" They both laughed. "No seriously."

The aroma of freshly brewed coffee enveloped Nick and Michael as they sat at a corner table in the bustling local café. Outside, the sun cast an orange glow on the cobblestone streets and the tranquil waters of the Sweet Sea. "We got this," Nick said with a smile.

As Michael and Nick stepped out of the coffee shop, the cool ocean breeze tousled their hair, and the scent of salt mingled with the aroma of freshly brewed coffee. Seagulls cawed overhead, their cries harmonizing with the distant sound of waves crashing against the shore. It was a typical day in Sweet Sea, the kind of day Lucy would have loved. Michael glanced over at Nick, his eyes reflecting gratitude and newfound determination.

They strolled along the quaint streets of Sweet Sea; the

town's cozy charm enveloped them like a warm embrace. Couples walked hand-in-hand, children darted between shops with laughter bubbling from their lips, and the occasional dog barked a friendly greeting. Everything seemed brighter with the entire ordeal behind them.

"Feels good, doesn't it?" Nick asked, his hair ruffled by the wind. "Working together to preserve Lucy's memory."

Michael glanced over at Nick, his eyes reflecting gratitude and newfound determination. "Yes, it does," he replied, a small smile playing on his lips. "I never thought we'd get this far, but you made it happen, Nick."

"She brought us together for a reason," Nick mused, his gaze drifting toward the horizon where the ocean met the sky. "She knew we could accomplish great things if we just set aside our differences and focused on what truly matters."

"Are you going to stay involved with the historical society now that they have invited you back in?" Nick asked as they approached the old Victorian library that had once been Lucy's home away from home.

"I think so," Michael answered, his gaze lingering on the ivy-covered facade of the library. "It's what Aunt Lucy would have wanted, and I want to do right by her. Plus, I missed the work the society does."

"Good," Nick nodded approvingly, his heart swelling

with pride for the young man who had come so far in such a short time. "You have a lot to contribute. Don't ever forget that."

"Thank you," Michael murmured, his voice choked with emotion. "I won't."

As they stood outside the library, Nick couldn't help but feel a profound sense of satisfaction. He had played a part in reconciling Michaels and the historical society, ensuring they could work together to honor Lucy's memory. And while he knew challenges were still ahead, he was confident they would face them united, just as Lucy would have wanted.

"Come on," Nick said, clasping Michael's shoulder and steering him toward the library entrance. "Let's go tell Lucy all about it."

Michael nodded, his eyes shining with renewed hope, and together, they stepped through the heavy oak doors. Just inside the entrance was the newly finished bust of Lucy. A plaque rested just below the art. It read: "In honor of Lucy Brooks, thanks for the history!"

CHAPTER THIRTY-THREE

The rain clouds were gone, and the sun was out. Nick couldn't help but think that it mirrored his mood. It felt good to feel the warmth through the window of his cozy little shop. The store was filled with the soft hum of whirring fans and the gentle clatter of tools against metal. A faint scent of soldering wire lingered in the air, mingling with the aroma of freshly brewed coffee. The walls behind the counter were lined with shelves adorned with both new and old computer parts and various knick-knacks that Nick had collected over the years.

Hunched over the workbench, he carefully examined

the exposed innards of a laptop. His lean fingers danced with practiced agility as he turned a precision Phillips-head screwdriver, delicately prying free a stubborn component. As he worked, the ghost of a smile played on his lips—a testament to his newfound sense of purpose in this quiet coastal town. He could feel the weight of his past addiction and loss lifting ever so slightly as he lost himself in the intricate world of circuitry and code.

"Hey there," a hesitant voice interrupted Nick's reverie. He looked up from the disassembled computer to see Rose standing in the doorway, her face the very picture of trepidation. She wore a simple floral dress, its colors muted to match the softness of her gaze. She wrung her hands together nervously, her fingers twisting around each other like anxious vines.

"Rose," Nick greeted, setting down his screwdriver. "What brings you here?"

She took a tentative step into the shop, her eyes darting between Nick and the laptop as though unsure which demanded more attention. "I... I wanted to talk to you," she hesitated, biting her lip. "About... well, about what happened."

Nick studied her face for a moment, his own expression unreadable. He could see the weight of unspoken words hanging heavily on her shoulders, and despite his lingering unease about their previous encounter and what she did, he felt a pang of sympathy for the fragile figure before him. He sighed softly, gesturing towards a small seating area in the corner of the shop.

"Alright," he said, his voice even but tinged with caution. "Come have a seat, and let's talk."

Rose took a deep breath, her voice barely more than a whisper as she began. "Nick, I'm so sorry for drugging you." Her eyes glistened with unshed tears, and she lowered her gaze to the floor. She shifted in her seat, the soft rustle of her dress punctuating the silence that had settled between them.

"I never meant to hurt you," she continued, her voice cracking under the weight of her remorse. Her hands fumbled in her lap, twisting the fabric of her skirt as if wringing out her guilt. "I just... I didn't know what else to do."

Nick studied her intently, his eyes narrowing ever so slightly as he weighed her words. He could see the genuine regret etched into the lines of her face, and yet some part of him still clamored for caution, a lingering reminder of lessons learned through pain and deceit. "Rose, listen."

"Wait. Can I explain?" Rose asked tentatively, her voice tinged with desperation. "Please, Nick. I just want you to understand why I did it."

Nick regarded her for a moment, his expression

inscrutable. It was clear that she wanted, no needed, absolution, but was he willing to grant her that chance? To entertain the possibility of trust where it had been so callously betrayed before?

"Alright," he said finally, his tone measured but not unkind. "But it better be a damn good explanation."

Relief flooded Rose's features, though it did little to dispel the tension that hung in the air. "Thank you," she said, her voice trembling with gratitude. "I promise you won't regret it."

She hesitated, gathering her thoughts like scattered beads on a broken string. As she began to weave together the tale of her actions and their consequences, Nick found himself drawn into her world, a tangled web of secrets and shadows that both repelled and intrigued him.

And as Rose laid bare the darkest corners of her soul, Nick felt something akin to empathy begin to stir within him. For he too knew the taste of desperation, the corrosive power of fear and the crushing weight of guilt. And despite the lingering specter of doubt that haunted his thoughts, he found himself wanting to believe in the possibility of redemption, both for Rose and for himself.

"Please, Nick," Rose implored, her eyes beseeching him to understand. "Can you find it in your heart to forgive me?"

Nick looked at her for a long moment, his gaze searching hers as if seeking some hidden truth amidst the stormy sea of her emotions. And then, slowly, he nodded.

"Let me start with my father," Rose began, her voice soft and hesitant as she unfolded the story. Nick listened attentively, his eyes never leaving hers even as the shadows in the room seemed to grow deeper and more oppressive. "He was a district attorney, one of the best in his time. He dedicated his life to punishing the guilty and bringing justice to those who had been wronged."

Rose paused, her gaze drifting towards the window as if seeking solace in the beautiful day that streamed through the glass. "But the job took its toll on him. His health started to deteriorate - his heart, mostly. Sleeping a few hours, a night and obsessed with his cases. We lived in this town, but he worked in San Diego about four hours away. He was home on weekends, but still working. The stress was too much, and he had to retire early and became a lawyer in this town. I watched as the man who had once been a beacon of strength and courage became a frail shadow of his former self. Even after retirement, he couldn't sleep. I would hear him pacing the halls of the house. He couldn't stop thinking about the guilty that he was not able to prosecute." Her voice broke, a single tear slipping down her cheek.

Nick felt a pang of sympathy for Rose, understanding the pain of watching a loved one suffer. He remained silent, allowing her to continue at her own pace.

"His condition worsened, and we were desperate to find a way to help him," Rose confessed. "We tried every treatment available, but nothing seemed to make a difference. That's when I turned to... alternative methods. I came across the book." She hesitated, biting her lip as if steeling herself to reveal the darkest part of her tale.

"*The Brown Grass*," Nick interjected.

"Yes. I was just reading a mystery, but later found out the plants were real and nearby. Specifically, a rare herb that was said to have miraculous sleeping properties with no side effects. I believed it could save my father, so I acquired some and concocted an elixir for him to take. But," her voice trembled, "I needed someone to test it on first. To make sure it wouldn't cause any harm. I took it and the book was right. I got the best sleep ever, woke up rejuvenated, and tried it on my dad the next day. It had the same result."

A heavy silence settled over the room as Nick processed her words, his mind racing with questions and doubts. It was clear that Rose had acted out of love and desperation, but that didn't excuse her actions.

As they sat in the brightly sunlit shop, Rose's gaze

remained fixed on Nick. She seemed to be searching for some sign of understanding or acceptance in his face. But all she saw were the dark circles he previously had under his eyes and the lines that creased his brow. She knew them as clear signs of exhaustion.

"Nick," she said softly, her voice filled with concern. "You looked so tired. I can't imagine how hard it must be for you to hear all this."

Nick couldn't deny that her words struck a chord within him, but he was determined to see this conversation through to its conclusion. He gave her a weary smile and nodded for her to continue.

"I kept telling you to get some rest," Rose pleaded, her hand reaching out to touch his arm. "I was afraid it couldn't wait. You need to take care of yourself, too."

As much as he wanted to resist, Nick knew that she was right. His body had craved sleep, and his mind had started to feel muddled. She really did think she was doing the right thing. But he wasn't sure that was enough. Was he ego getting in the way? Was doing the wrong thing for the right reason okay? In the end, he decided it was. He cared about this woman.

"Rose," he said. "I... I want you to know that I forgive you. We all make mistakes, and sometimes those mistakes hurt the ones we care about. But your intentions were pure, even if your methods were misguided."

His words hung in the air like a delicate thread, connecting them through shared pain and understanding. Rose's eyes glistened with unshed tears, her lips trembling as she tried to form a response.

"Thank you," she whispered, her voice choked with emotion. "That means more to me than I can express."

Nick offered her a small, reassuring smile, his eyes crinkling at the corners as he did so. He could see the relief washing over her features, releasing the tension she had been carrying since stepping foot in the shop. And with that simple act of forgiveness, a weight lifted from his own shoulders as well. The burden of resentment and suspicion dissipating like a morning mist.

As the silence stretched comfortably between them, Nick ventured further, his fingers tapping out a nervous rhythm on his knee. "You know, despite our somewhat rocky beginning," he began, a playful glint sparking in his eyes, "I find myself quite fond of you as well."

The unexpected confession brought a blush to her cheeks, and she ducked her head momentarily, flustered by the compliment. "You remember that, huh," she admitted softly, stealing a glance back at him.

He nodded with a smile. "You're very special even though I don't think I will ever drink tea again."

She let out a nervous laugh and a tear ran down her check.

"Would you..." Nick hesitated, the vulnerability in his eyes betraying the significance of his next words. "Would you like to go out with me sometime? On a proper date, I mean? No mysteries or hidden elixirs, just us. We can start fresh."

Rose's breath caught in her throat as she processed his question, the impact of his request making her heart race with anticipation. She looked at him, taking in the hopeful expression on his face, and felt a sense of certainty wash over her.

"I would love that," she said, the corners of her mouth quirking into a smile that reached her eyes. "I think we both deserve a chance to get to know each other without any complications. And I promise, no more elixirs."

"Agreed," Nick responded, his own grin widening at her acceptance. He leaned back, feeling an unfamiliar sense of contentment blossom within him. He had hope for a brighter future, free from the shadows of his past, and the promise of companionship from someone who had already shown him so much kindness. "But, I have one more question for you."

She wiped her damp cheeks. "Anything."

"Where did you get such a tiny pink gun and do you know how to shoot?"

She laughed causing more tears to fall. "Yeah, sorry about that."

"No seriously," Nick said. "I didn't know they made them that small and cute. I may get one for each of my daughters."

"That's a long story, but one I would be happy to share." She left the offer floating between them.

"First topic for our date, then. Here's to new beginnings," he proposed, raising an imaginary glass in toast.

"New beginnings," Rose echoed, her eyes shining with shared optimism as they sealed their fledgling bond with a mutual understanding that transcended the spoken word.

"Let's do something simple for our first date," Nick suggested, as he fiddled with a small screwdriver in his hand. "How about a picnic at the park near the beach this Saturday around noon? We could enjoy the fresh air and some good food."

Rose contemplated the idea, her head tilted to one side as she considered their options. "I like that," she agreed, her voice soft and thoughtful. "We can each bring some dishes to share. I make a mean quiche, if I do say so myself."

Nick's eyes sparkled with amusement, a playful grin tugging at the corner of his mouth. "Uh. For now, let me make all the food."

Rose looked at him, her eyes serious. She couldn't tell if he was kidding until he smiled.

"I'll bring something sweet, then. It's my mom's famous chocolate cake recipe. She always said it was the key to happiness. "

"Sounds perfect," Nick replied, his own smile reflecting the warmth in Rose's expression. The thought of sharing such an intimate part of her past touched him deeply, and he felt a newfound sense of connection with her.

"Alright, it's settled then," Nick confirmed, rubbing his hands together in anticipation. "A picnic by the sea it is."

They talked for a bit more until they both had to get back to their respective jobs.

"Thank you, Nick," she murmured, sincerity lacing her words. "For everything."

"Thank you, too, Rose," Nick responded, his hair catching the light as he nodded in appreciation. "I'll see you on Saturday."

"See you then," she echoed, pausing for a moment to take in the sight of him and the kind smile that graced his lips.

With a final wave, Rose turned and walked towards the door, her footsteps light against the shop's wooden floors. Nick watched her go, his heart swelling with the promise of new beginnings.

As the door swung shut behind her, he was left standing amid the scattered tools and computer parts that surrounded him, the lingering warmth of their conversation wrapping around him like a comforting embrace. The anticipation of their first date stirred within him, filling him with a sense of wonder and hope that had long been absent from his life.

"New beginnings indeed," Nick said to himself, his thoughts drifting towards the future as he returned to his work, the rhythmic hum of the shop's machinery providing a soothing soundtrack to the unfolding story of his newfound companionship.

CHAPTER THIRTY-FOUR

Nick Cern stood behind the counter of his renewed repair shop, running a cotton cloth over the smooth glass displays. The scent of cleaner filled the air as he glanced around at rows upon rows of electronics, an affectionate smile gracing his face. It had been months since he moved to Sweet Sea, and opening up this store felt like the first step towards finally healing from the loss of his wife. Lucy had helped him through the last bit. But that was two months ago. Since then, he had kept to himself and was excited to start anew with Rose. He cared for her, but couldn't trust her. Not yet. She had only left his shop an hour ago and he already missed her. That had to mean something.

The door chimed, and Nick looked up, his salt-and-pepper hair shimmering in the warm afternoon light streaming through the windows. Sheriff Kent walked into the shop, her tan uniform neatly pressed, the badge on her chest gleaming. Her hair was down and she wore more makeup on than he had ever seen on her before.

"Nick," the sheriff began, her voice apologetic and sincere, "I'm sorry to bother you, especially after the challenges we've had. I hope there are no hard feelings."

"Same back at you."

The sheriff looked down for a moment before meeting his eyes. "I probably shouldn't share this, but what the hell. With all your evidence, Doctor Victors confessed. He even gave up the guy he hired to beat you up. We are told that they picked him up in San Francisco. Just thought you should know."

"Thank you. I really appreciate that."

"Also, the second autopsy was done before the funeral. It appears she was indeed poisoned by that plant you found. I guess Lucy had read that book enough or knew it well enough to know the symptoms and that there wasn't a cure. She just didn't know who. They tell me she only had enough time to send that email after ingestion, which probably means it was given to her at the event that night. At least, that is what the facts say. Anyway, I just wanted to share and say thank you again. You have pretty good instincts."

Nick's eyebrows furrowed as he took in the sheriff's somber expression. "What's going on, sheriff? Is everything all right?"

"Not really. I know I don't really have a right to ask, but I need your help."

"I don't hold a grudge. What do you need?

"We've found three dead girls," Sheriff Kent said, the weight of the news settling heavily in the quiet store. "We're having trouble accessing their phone, and we could really use your help."

The gravity of the situation hit Nick like a wave, overpowering the serenity of his surroundings. He remained silent for a moment, his mind racing. The sherriff had never called him by his first name. This was now twice in a row. Was this a sign she was warming up to him? Despite the tragedy, it wasn't his place to intervene in a police investigation. But then again, if he could offer any assistance, wouldn't it be the right thing to do?

"Of course, sheriff," Nick finally replied, setting the cloth down. "I'll do whatever I can to help."

"Thank you." The relief in the sheriff's voice was palpable, as if a significant burden had been lifted from her shoulders.

As Sheriff Kent started to explain the situation in more detail, Nick's mind wandered to his own past, to the years spent climbing the corporate ladder and the technological expertise he'd acquired along the way. He'd left that life behind to escape the memories of his wife, but now, it seemed that his skills might be of use once again. Was this why he was here?

"Nick? Are you with me?" The sheriff's voice drew him back to the present.

"Yes, sheriff. I understand the urgency of the situation," Nick replied, trying to push away the unsettling thoughts. "Let's get to work."

"All right, here it is," the sheriff said, pulling a sleek, black smartphone from her pocket and handing it over to Nick. It was in a plastic bag, but he could still touch the keys. "Just leave it in the evidence bad, please."

"Thank you," Nick replied, taking it with a solemn nod. As he cradled the device in his hands, he couldn't help but imagine the lives of which ever of the three girls who once owned it, now cruelly cut short. He shook off the morbid thought, focusing instead on the task at hand.

"Let's see what we can find," he said, his fingers dancing over the screen as he attempted to unlock the phone. The store was silent except for the soft clicking of keys being pressed.

Nick's brow furrowed as he navigated through layers of encryption and security measures, his mind working furiously to decipher the barriers keeping him from the information that could potentially solve this heinous crime.

Minutes slipped by, the sheriff observed Nick's progress with a mix of admiration and impatience. "I can't thank you enough for doing this. We've been at our wit's end trying to break into this thing."

"Always happy to help, sheriff," Nick replied without looking up, completely absorbed in his work. The digital walls that protected the phone's secrets proved to be more complex and intricate than he had anticipated. Despite his grief and the weight of the situation, Nick felt an old spark ignite within him, the thrill of unraveling a puzzle that had confounded others.

Finally, after what felt like an eternity, Nick let out a victorious sigh as the phone's home screen appeared before him. "Got it," he announced, his heart pounding with a mixture of relief and excitement.

"Fantastic work!" the sheriff exclaimed, clapping him on the back. "I knew we made the right choice coming to you." Her eyes sparkled with gratitude as she regarded Nick and a new bond was forged between the two at that moment.

"Glad to help. Good luck."

"You know," the sheriff said. "We have a budget for contractors. I can get you a little money if you want to help us out in the future. Nothing dangerous, but we really don't have an electronics expert and like I said, you've got good instincts."

"That would be great."

"Consider yourself deputized, my friend," Sheriff Kent said with an air of camaraderie. "Also, you can call me Joan. Maybe we can catch dinner, and I will talk to you more about helping us out."

Nick was in shock. He couldn't be sure, but it felt like the sheriff was hitting on him. She was pretty and seemed nice. He was pretty sure she could physically hurt him, though. However, what could one dinner hurt? He smiled, feeling a renewed sense of purpose as he stood alongside the sheriff, prepared to confront the darkness lurking within their peaceful town.

He smiled. "Two dates in one day. I can't wait to tell the girls."

ABOUT THE AUTHOR

Brian Daffern

Brian Daffern is a native of California and was born in San Diego. He currently resides in Georgia with his wife and four daughters. In addition to being an author, he is a well-educated Marine, a senior leader at a well-known technology company, a paranormal investigator, and a member of the Scientific Coalition of UAP Studies.

www.ingramcontent.com/pod-product-compliance
Lightning Source LLC
Chambersburg PA
CBHW060345260626
47160CB00006B/2205

BOOKS BY THIS AUTHOR

Prince Albert In A Can

Prince Albert, Book 2: The Beast School

Prince Albert, Book 3: The Realm Pirates

The Ambient Knight

The Gossamer Gambit

Lethe

Alien-Ated: Astonishing Interviews Of Alien Encounters